Downfall

The Creativity Stone Series—Book 1

ENDORSEMENTS

Rolling on at a quick pace and set on an distant world, *Downfall* resembles an old *Star Trek* episode. Like all fantasy, it takes real-world issues, in this case religious legalism and moralism, and explores the underlying ideas in a new setting while cutting out some of the intellectual baggage from our own world. Caleb is clearly well versed in the Bible and uses familiar verbiage to explore theological questions in this bizarre religious community.
—John Nobel

Downfall takes you on an unforgettable journey navigating through faith and bitter betrayal.

Chalk full of heart-wrenching emotions and trials, this wholesome story reflects the fragility in ourselves and the grace of savior.
—Rebecca Monroe

If you have ever struggled like Gideon and Saul with leadership issues and the standards required for the task, this book is for you. You'll find yourself being challenged by the main characters as they go through the journey in this fantasy world.
—Devorah Brock

DOWNFALL

The Creativity Stone Series—Book 1

Caleb Ward

ELK LAKE PUBLISHING INC

PUBLISHING THE POSITIVE
Plymouth, Massachusetts

COPYRIGHT NOTICE

Library Cataloging Data

Names: Ward, Caleb (Caleb Ward)

Downfall: The Creativity Stone Series Book 1 / Caleb Ward

332 p. 23cm × 15cm (9in × 6 in.)

ISBN-13: 978-1-64949-479-5 (paperback) | 978-1-64949-480-1 (trade paperback) | 978-1-64949-481-8 (e-book)

Key Words: Christian fantasy books for adults; Christian fantasy new worlds; Christian fiction for men; Christian fiction fantasy books; Inspirational Christian fiction; Discovering real Christianity; Christian romance

Library of Congress Control Number: 2021953498 Fiction

DEDICATION

This book is dedicated to Jesus, who came to earth, died for our sins, rose from the grave, and is coming back again. May everyone who picks up this book grow in knowing his love.

ACKNOWLEDGMENTS

I'd like to thank my mom, Britt Ward, who encouraged my love of reading since childhood. I'd like to thank my dad, Sam Ward, for believing in me and providing me with the resources that made this book possible. And I'd like to thank my grandfather, Linton Ward, for seeing my passion for storytelling and encouraging me to pursue it.

Most of all, I'd like to thank Jesus. Without him, nothing would be possible.

PROLOGUE

NOVITAS, YEAR UNKNOWN

Tradus stumbled forward into the darkened chamber. The cavern surrounding him was empty, the walls and ground smoothed by years of rushing water. But now, only the occasional watery plink acted as a reminder of the underground river. Blood dripped from the stab wound in his chest, a gift from the people trying to wipe out the last of his race.

He could easily use the red glowing crystal in his hand to heal himself, but the stone always had a price. Ever since he'd taken it out of his chest, he'd refused to use the crystal to help himself. He wouldn't change that now because doing so would defeat his purpose.

Tradus held the wound and tried to keep his blood inside his body as he leaned over.

He prayed that no one inhabited this planet. He couldn't risk someone finding his crystal and using it.

He picked up a sharp rock and began to write on the ground.

This is a warning: The stone you see before you is called the—

He didn't know what to call the small crystal that endowed its wielder with incredible power limited only by their creativity and imagination. They had a word for his crystal back on his planet, but he could hardly take the time to explain the complexities and history of his world in one short note.

The gash in his chest throbbed, and he squeezed the rock in his hand tightly. He would never see his world again. Even if he did make it back alive, his family was long gone.

He had been sleeping peacefully on his mat when the attack had come, silent and swift. His wife and children hadn't even woken up. Now, they never would.

A noise had awakened him before the knife pierced his chest right below the rib cage.

Since his crystal had been taken out of his chest, the soul tie was broken, and the crystal wouldn't darken when he died. Unbound crystals were much more powerful. Their only limitation was the creation of other crystals like themselves. He couldn't let them get a hold of his. So as the knife dug in, he grabbed the crystal next to his mat and disappeared into another world.

He stared at the stone in his hand. All his problems could be traced back to it and its false promises. People were corrupt, shortsighted, and not meant to have their own creativity as their only limitation. That's what he would call it, the Creativity Stone.

He went back to writing on the cave floor.

This is a warning: The stone you see before you is called the Creativity Stone. It has the power to create and destroy—the power of God. While it can create beauty and life, it can also inflict untold destruction and evil. Under no circumstances should you use this stone. Its power is meant only for God.

Once finished, Tradus placed the stone on the ground. He let out a sigh of relief as its mind-numbing influence left him.

DOWNFALL

The Creativity Stone, seeming to sense it would be there for a while, let out a flash of red light. Dust solidified below it, formed a pedestal, and raised the stone off the ground. The light pierced the walls and ceiling of the cave, forming gems and crystals that sparkled with the Creativity Stone's red light.

Tradus stumbled to the side of the now-beautiful cave and sank down into a sitting position on the dusty floor.

"Please don't let anyone find this place."

Tradus's hand fell from where it had covered his wound. He closed his eyes and breathed his last.

CHAPTER 1

FIDES VILLAGE, NOVITAS—DAY 1, YEAR 371

Joshua hid behind the rich tapestry, trying to still his trembling body. Dedecus was infamous for his rash ideas, but Joshua, usually the more level-headed of the two, should have known better than to go along with his plan to sneak into the house of two Judges of Justice. As much as he loved spending time with their daughter, Namid, being caught in her bedroom would create a spiral of suffering for both him and the girl.

The room was spacious. Its stone walls surrounded them, creating an echo effect that magnified Namid's mother's ranting as well as any sound.

Joshua looked up at where Dedecus was hidden in the rafters and tried to hold in the scream that pressed against his throat. When they had snuck in through the window, Dedecus had climbed up there to hide as they waited for Namid's mother, Freda, to leave so they could rescue Namid from her daily religious instruction. But now, a small corner of his tattered brown tunic was visible. Joshua was sure Freda would look up and spot him.

He watched in horror as Freda, his only childhood fear, walked closer to the tapestry he cowered behind. He unsuccessfully tried to still his quivering body as he backed further into the white stone wall, praying as fast as he could that he remained undiscovered. Marvin and Freda had always terrified him, and while their daughter was one of his best friends, if it weren't for Dedecus's boldness, he probably would never see her because he was too afraid to go near her house.

He'd never witnessed the ill-treatment himself, but he knew from the bruises always appearing on Namid's face and hands that being caught in the fury of the Judge of Justices' wrath was like being at Sodom and Gomorrah.

"How do you expect to get to Heaven with that mouth of yours, missy!" Freda yelled at her daughter, who was hunched down at her desk, as she waited expectantly for a response.

"I'm sorry, Mother, all I asked was why God is so harsh and cruel to us when he was forgave the woman in John 8:1-11 who was a sinner and was about to be stoned, but Jesus stopped them."

Freda walked closer to Namid and glared down at her as Namid cowered under her harsh gaze.

"Exactly, not only did you question my authority, but you questioned God's ways. You're starting to sound like that child, Joshua, you've been hanging out with. Why you would ever waste your time with the son of the Judges of Mercy and his orphan-trash friend, Dedecus, is beyond me."

Joshua wished he dared to defend himself to Freda, but all he could do was stand there like the coward he knew he was behind the red and purple embroidered tapestry which held a stitched Bible verse of Job 20:23, *God shall cast the fury of his wrath upon them.*

"No, Mother, I just posed a quest—"

"Silence! I won't have you spending any more time with those people. They're filling your head with lies, and I don't want my only daughter to face God's wrath. You're eighteen now, nearly an adult—it's time to start acting like it. And so, as punishment for your sedition, tomorrow morning, you will get up at three a.m. and recite to your father and me the entire Old Testament!"

From his vantage point, he could see Namid open her mouth to say something, but she must have quickly realized how pointless and suicidal that would be and snapped her mouth shut.

Freda walked closer to Namid's desk and let out a sigh. "I'm only trying to help you, my daughter. I want you up in Heaven with your father and me, and that will never happen unless you get rid of these dangerous ideas and start being the perfect lady I know you can be. Now, repeat to me the seven remembrances."

Back at the beginning of Fides, when the New Day Separatists came from Earth to the world they named Novitas, the Judges of Justice had written seven things all good Christians must remember and follow. These, of course, were only some of the hundreds of laws the original judges and their successors had created to achieve perfection.

Namid quickly began to recite them. "Remember the consequences of your failure. Remember to remain pure in all thoughts and actions. Remember that God is found only through the law."

The seven remembrances were written in beautiful calligraphy across the walls in various places throughout Namid's room, but she didn't need to look to recite them. Joshua knew that ever since she was an infant, her parents had beaten them into her. By now, they were stitched in bright red letters across her soul.

"Remember to stay modest to keep others from sin. Remember to cast out the defiled. Remember to enact what others deserve. Remember, you're never good enough."

Joshua saw on her face each remembrance crushing a part of her spirit, one after the other. Every time he heard them, he wanted to run to Namid and hold her in his arms. He wanted to tell her how much God loved her and how she didn't have to be perfect. But he remained behind the tapestry, a coward.

Namid said each one perfectly, and he breathed a sigh of relief as the girl's mother nodded, marched off without saying a word, and slammed the door shut. He never realized how angry steps could sound until listening to Freda's fury-filled stomps heading down the hallway and finally fading away.

His relief was short-lived, however, when he saw the tears in Namid's hazel brown eyes. He wished he could do something. He wished he could take her up in his arms and tell her she was beautiful, and she was perfect the way she was. That she didn't have to be the person her parents expected her to be.

Dedecus jumped down from the rafters onto the floor in front of Namid.

Namid let out a startled gasp and stood up from her wooden chair.

The impact of the jump sent an echo through the room, and Joshua held his breath in hopes Namid's parents hadn't heard.

Dedecus's mischievous blue eyes twinkled as he grinned at her.

"What are you doing here?" Her eyes darted between glaring at Dedecus and staring at the door. "If my parents see you, we both would be in so much trouble," Namid whispered.

"You'll never guess what I did." Dedecus grinned. "Come on out, Joshie, there's no reason to be hunched over like a scared little baby. She's gone."

He once more glanced at the brown door. Tiny cracks traversed the wood from being slammed so many times.

He hesitated but then stepped out from behind the tapestry. "How many times do I have to tell you? My name is Joshua. How would you like it if I started calling you Dedie or something stupid like that?"

"Sounds perfect. You may call me Dedie the Great." Dedecus took a slight bow.

Joshua rolled his eyes.

Namid stared in surprise at Joshua, "How in the world did Dedecus convince you to come?" She laughed as she tried to wipe away and hide the tears from her cheeks.

"I have no idea, but it's definitely not happening again," Joshua said as he glared at Dedecus.

Dedecus laughed, although Joshua knew better. He was still trying to get past Namid's mother calling him orphan trash.

"All right, you two," Dedecus said, "I was thinking today we could get your royal clothes all dirty to match mine by going on an expedition behind the Emerald Waterfall. I heard there's a mysterious system of caves back there, and I want to check 'em out."

"But isn't there that huge, dangerous jump across the waterfall to get into the caves?" Joshua bit his lip and looked up at Dedecus, who stood over Joshua at six feet, four inches tall compared to his five feet four.

"Don't be a big baby, Joshie. You'll be fine," Dedecus said.

Namid glanced down at the Bible and countless study materials and books that covered her desk. "You heard my mother. I have so much studying to do if I'm going to be able to recite the entire Old Testament from memory tomorrow morning, plus if my parents catch me leaving or hanging out with you two, then I'm going to get a major beating."

"We'll have you back in time to finish memorizing, and your parents will never know you're gone. Besides, I dragged Josh all the way up here through the Earth tree outside your window. Do you really think we're leaving without you?"

Joshua looked at the two of them arguing, knowing Namid would cave in because she wanted nothing more than to escape and go exploring with them. Although, for his sake, he hoped the impossibility would come true, and Namid would be able to convince Dedecus that she couldn't go so they wouldn't have to go up the dangerous path, make that big jump through the waterfall, and go through those caves that, for all they knew, could collapse in on them.

"Fine, just let me change into more suitable clothing than this ridiculously frilly dress I'm wearing," she said, pointing down to the blue and gold dress her parents had bought her that dragged on the floor as she walked. Underneath that dress were two more layers of clothing to make sure only her head and hands were ever exposed.

Glancing at the door once more, she pulled up one of the floorboards to reveal a simple tan tunic and pants she'd hidden from her parents to wear when getting dirty on adventures with Dedecus and Joshua.

Joshua and Dedecus climbed down the tall tree outside her window to wait for Namid three stories down. Unlike most trees on Novitas, this one had grown from seeds brought from Earth and had rough bark and leafy branches jutting out from the trunk. All trees native to Novitas were like long smooth poles covered in tiny hair-like bristles.

A few moments later, Namid climbed down in mud-covered pants and a loose-fitting tunic. She'd let her brown hair out of the tight bun her parents insisted on, and the curls hung low on her chest. The only proof of her life as the problem child of the Judges of Justice was the ornate cross necklace her parents demanded she never take off and the bruises that ran up her arm.

Laughing, Namid removed her shoes and twirled around in the grass, her hair flying behind her as she danced. "I'm ready for an adventure!" she said, almost sing-songy.

DOWNFALL

"We should probably get going," Joshua said, glancing at the judges' large, white house that reached into the light green sky.

They took off on a path around the outside of the village to avoid anyone who would report Namid's whereabouts to her parents, trampling grass under their feet. Dedecus was in front, with Namid not far behind him and Joshua trailing in the back, wishing he had more boring friends. But he wouldn't trade his friendships with Dedecus and Namid for anything.

Joshua took one last look at the looming house behind them, praying that the Judges of Justice wouldn't check on Namid before the three of them returned.

CHAPTER 2

Namid raced after Dedecus, excited to have shed the tight, restrictive layers of clothing and the clutches of her parents—even though she knew she never could escape their judgments, expectations, and fierce disappointment in her.

She'd had specific instructions drilled into her all her life on how to live, behave, what she could enjoy, who she could be friends with, how to dress, and even how to speak. The seven remembrances played on a constant repeat in her head, haunting her every move, shaming her for every bit of laugher, fun, and dance that tempted her soul.

> You must fight to be noticed by God.

> There are billions of humans; if you expect to get to Heaven, then you better be perfect for God to notice you and save you from an eternity of torture.

Those words of her parents would forever be a part of her. Because if God were anything like what her parents taught, she would be in an eternity of torture no matter what.

One other memory played in her mind that competed with those her parents had implanted, and it made her smile. There was one night on Peaceful Plateau that made her think her parents had to be wrong.

Voices came within earshot down the path toward them. Namid always had to be on alert for those in the village who followed her parents like loyal dogs lapping up whatever morsel they would give, never once questioning whether it was poisoned.

The panic of being spotted in normal clothes with Joshua and Dedecus quickly turned into action as she abandoned her place with her friends and ran ahead of them and into the forest of palms that enveloped the village.

Joshua and Dedecus stood on the path, having planned many times what to do whenever someone could catch Namid with them, and so they simply stood there waiting for them to pass.

"Oh, great," Dedecus muttered as Ronald and Regina came into view.

Joshua breathed out a quick prayer, hoping they'd keep walking past and leave Dedecus alone. But he knew, like all followers of the Judges of Justice, the ever-holy Ronald and Regina wouldn't be able to resist some scorning of the black sheep of the village.

The sound of laughter reached Joshua's ears as the two approached them on the white gravel path.

Ronald wore the traditional long pants, long-sleeved wool tunic with a long neck, while Regina wore her dress that dragged across the ground, also with a long neck, as all good Christian men and women did.

Both made identical expressions when they saw Dedecus standing there, scrunching up their noses as if they smelled the most horrendous odor while holding their heads high.

"Well, look who we have here," Regina said, glaring at them, "the little child who has delusions of adequacy."

"I feel lucky for all the people who never had the pleasure to meet him," Ronald said.

They looked at each other and laughed.

Dedecus's face grew red, his freckles seeming to glow in contrast to his dark brown hair. He clenched his fists.

Joshua hoped he was trying hard not to punch out their perfect white teeth. If he weren't such a coward, he might consider doing it for him.

"So, tell me," Ronald said to Dedecus, "as an outsider, what do you think of the human race? Actually, don't bother answering—all that thinking might sprain your brain."

Joshua knew he should say something to stop Ronald and Regina. He wanted to say something, so he squeezed his eyes shut and tried to force words out of his throat. He tried to be the friend Dedecus deserved. But nothing came out.

"Listen, boy, I don't know why the Judges of Mercy would choose to save you, but you're a screw up just like your parents. Just do us a favor and show us your true colors now so God can dispose of you like he did them."

When Dedecus raised his fist, Joshua grabbed his arm and pulled him past Ronald and Regina down the path.

"And the little mercy mouse runs away once again," Regina taunted.

"Someday, I'm going to wipe those smiles off their faces," Dedecus said, his face still redder than the blood pumping through his veins. They both knew, however, that Dedecus was powerless to say or do anything against them. The Judges of Justice had tried countless times to get Dedecus thrown out of the village but had been unsuccessful thanks to Joshua's parents. If Dedecus started attacking people in the village, he'd be thrown out before his fist finished the punch.

They walked away, knowing Namid would catch up when she could.

"I can't wait for the day we're in Heaven and don't have to see those two anymore," Ronald said loudly to their backs.

After several minutes of walking, Namid caught up to them along the path beside the Fides Village, and then the three came upon the Pearl Cliffs that rose over the village to meet the Peaceful Plateau.

In front of them rose the Emerald Waterfall. Water drops fell individually like tiny emeralds, catching the sunlight and casting millions of tiny sparkles as they tumbled down, shattering on the rocks below to rejoin the group and lazily travel around the village. From the glittery white rocks to the lush green grass, the entire area sparkled as the sun's warm rays reflected off the water droplets.

Making their way up the side path, Namid and Joshua climbed the path carefully. Dedecus would often lean dangerously over the side or pretend to trip and fall off just to mess with them. While Namid would nervously laugh it off, Joshua would speak up and tell him to be more careful or the next time, he would fall. Dedecus would respond laughingly, "Relax, Joshie, I'm fine," and then pretend to fall off again.

Once they reached where the path met the waterfall, Dedecus jumped quickly through the water and landed safely on the other side. His body made an outline in the green water for a second before disappearing.

"Will Dedecus ever see nature as anything but a challenge?" Namid asked, laughing as they both stopped to catch their breath from the hike.

Joshua looked at the drop-off ahead of him—a massive expanse he could never make. He'd fall and die on the rocks far below.

Faintly on the other side of the five-foot distance through the deafening waterfall, they heard Dedecus yell, "Come on, Joshie, you baby turtle!"

"It's Joshua," he said in pretend frustration. Then he backed up, took a deep breath, closed his eyes, and took a running leap through the waterfall. His feet landed on solid rock, and he released his breath. He smiled as he opened his eyes.

"You were literally only in the air for two seconds," Dedecus said.

Namid laughed at their antics and then quickly followed them while trying not to think about the five-foot distance she had to clear and the many broken bones, or much worse, she'd get if she fell.

Once she joined them, they did their best to dry off. Joshua shook his light blond hair like a dog, sending droplets all over Namid and Dedecus.

Dedecus responded by getting a handful of water from the waterfall and pouring the green liquid down Joshua's back.

"Okay, you two, are we going to have a water fight or go exploring?"

"I've got the lanterns," Joshua said, pulling supplies out of his backpack and handed them out.

They threw palm hairs into the lanterns and ignited them with silica stones. Fire erupted in the lamps, and the cavern filled with light.

The path in front of them was barely high enough to walk through standing up. The sides were smooth, and water droplets fell from the ceiling every few seconds from the underground river above them. The walls and floor were white and wet, causing the light from their lanterns to bounce in every direction.

"Be careful, guys. All these rocks are wet and slippery," Joshua called out as Dedecus raced forward.

Namid followed quickly behind.

"Hurry up, you worrying snail," Dedecus called out. "We'll have this entire place already explored by the time you even step in." His voice echoed off the walls.

"One day, someone is going to get hurt, and they'll wish they'd listened to me," Joshua muttered as he zipped up his backpack and hurried after his friends.

As the trio surveyed further into the cave, the waterfall sounds were slowly replaced with the trickle of water rivulets. While they were usually talkative, today, they were quiet, each lost in their thoughts and surroundings, careful not to trip on any protruding rocks.

After several minutes, Namid stopped. "Um, guys, have either of you noticed that it hasn't really gotten any darker in here? This is an underground cavern—without our lanterns, it should be pitch black."

Surprised, Joshua looked around and realized she was right—it was way too light in there to be an underground cavern.

"The light's coming from up ahead. Let's check it out." Dedecus continued forward.

"It's probably just a hole or something where light is filtering in," Joshua said.

"No, that can't be it," Namid said. "The Peaceful Plateau should be above us, and there's no cracks or anything in the ground."

"Well, whatever the reason is, we won't know unless we keep going," Dedecus said.

Namid and Joshua followed after Dedecus—on their hands and knees when the ceiling was too low for them to stand. They slowly got closer to the mysterious light source.

At several points, the path split into several they could choose from. Each time, Dedecus chose the one that seemed to take them closer to the strange glow.

"We have to be past Peaceful Plateau by now and in the Northern Forests," Namid said. "I wouldn't be surprised if we're the first people to come down this path."

About a hundred feet further, they had to crouch low to fit through a small hole. The light had grown very bright and seemed to be directly ahead.

"It looks like this opens up into some kind of room," Dedecus called out while shielding his eyes.

Namid went next, following closely behind him. "Is there anything in there?" she asked.

"It's hard to tell. But, either way, there's a lot of light coming from it," he said, still crawling.

"Well, what's in there?" Joshua called out.

"Wow, umm … you're going to want to see this," Namid called back to him.

Something deep inside him warned him not to keep going, but they were too far in now, and his curiosity was getting the best of him, so he crawled the rest of the way through.

CHAPTER 3

MANNED SPACECRAFT CENTER, HOUSTON TEXAS, EARTH—OCTOBER 20, 1969

A herd of scientists rushed past Jefferson Gent in the long, white hallway, jabbering excitedly about some nonsense involving their Apollo spacecraft and the upcoming moon landing.

Jefferson rolled his eyes and scoffed.

The moon. Why waste all that time and danger when there was so much more in the universe?

He had much bigger goals in mind than something as simple as going to the moon.

His footsteps echoed down one of many hallways of Complex 69 of the Manned Spacecraft Center. The overhead hallway lighting flickered as he approached his office.

The smell of smoke reached his nose, and he grimaced. The scientist in the next office was a smoker. He'd sent several long letters of complaint about the stench, but the man insisted he never smoked. Jefferson covered his nose. How anyone could believe that fraud was beyond him.

He opened his office door, and the smell of paper and ink filled his nostrils. He quickly closed the door and smiled while scanning the messy piles strewn across his desk, various tables, and the floor. Maps and diagrams of the stars and his gadgets covered every inch of wall space. He walked toward his desk, careful to avoid disturbing anything. While some people, like the janitor, who now refused to enter, would say his office looked like the scene of a tornado, he knew exactly where every paper was. He didn't have a large office, so he had to make the most out of what he had.

He sat down, moving the stack of papers off his chair and into his lap.

"Simply, one planet will suffice." He scanned through the documents, searching for a single planet that could support life. Each sheet held long paragraphs of data on every planet scanned. While most puny government telescopes couldn't provide enough information, his own high-powered telescope worked well enough to gather the data he needed.

All he had to do was determine the right oxygen, hydrogen, and carbon dioxide balance combined with the distance to the nearest star and the presence of liquid water. Once he got done with a page, he'd throw the sheet over his left shoulder—if there was no useful information, and over his right shoulder—if more research was needed.

He was about to toss one of the last pages over his left shoulder when he froze. He leaned forward and reread the lines of data about a small planet, billions of light-years away. His heart beat faster, and he smiled.

Have I actually done it? Did I seriously discover our new home?

He stood and ran to the door, sending documents flying everywhere. He clutched the paper that could be the salvation of the New Day Separatists in his hand.

He burst out of his office, eager to contact the others.

"Whatcha got there, Gent?" a passing scientist asked.

Jefferson frowned. "Nothing, simply more data sheets to process."

The scientist shook his head. "You know you're welcome to join us on the Apollo research team. Of course, a man with your brain would be welcomed. Even with your ..." the man shifted awkwardly, "... personal convictions."

Jefferson gave him a fake smile, wanting to get rid of this dullard. "Thank you for the offer, but I shall pass. My research satisfies me immensely."

The man shrugged and kept walking.

Nullifidian.

He looked down at the paper again. Step one: Complete. Now, he only had to get them there.

CHAPTER 4

WHITE MOUNTAIN RANGE, NOVITAS—DAY 1, YEAR 371

Lincoln set up the last of the decorations and stepped back to ensure that everything was perfect. He beamed, proud of his work. His tired bones and muscles groaned, but he ignored them. The many hours he'd spent in the past week on this would be well worth it when he saw the sadness flee in terror and a bright and powerful smile grow on Adia's beautiful face.

Tomorrow was his fifteenth wedding anniversary, and he'd sneaked away to finish the rest of the preparations for his wife's surprise.

He knew his wife with every cell of his body as if God had created him for the sole purpose of loving and cherishing Adia, a fact he grew more certain of every day. In fact, he knew her better than she knew herself. He could tell that over the past few months, she'd started to slip back into her depression and into the lies that had been branded into her brain and soul her entire life. The lies her own parents and teachers had put there.

He had prayed for weeks about what he could do to cheer her up—to remind her that she was loved. That's when this idea had popped into his head, an idea he was certain was written by God himself and delivered directly to his mind.

He walked to the small, rocky entrance of the cave and covered up the opening with branches so it would be more of a surprise. The cave wasn't huge, but it was the perfect size for his idea. He couldn't wait for his beloved Adia to be surprised—he only prayed it would help.

He stepped into the bright glow of the morning sun and felt the warm rays rejuvenate his tired body as he began to make his way back to the village and to his Adia.

CHAPTER 5

EMERALD WATERFALL, NOVITAS—DAY 1, YEAR 371

Joshua crawled the rest of the way through the tunnel. His knees and hands hurt from the rocky ground, but he ignored them as he pushed across the rough crevice that led into the room. Finally, he reached the other side and pulled himself up. He stared, stunned, as he took in the surroundings, unlike anything he'd ever seen or imagined.

In the middle of the room stood a large pedestal about half their height with a red gem on top glowing so brightly his eyes hurt to stare at it. The gem was ragged and rough, with edges jutting out at awkward angles that could slice into a person's flesh if picked up.

Joshua, Namid, and even Dedecus stood by the entrance, enraptured by the stunning magnificence of the strange room and the red gem.

Surrounding them on all sides were polished diamonds, crystals, and rubies. They were all embedded in the smooth walls and ceiling, the light from the gem in the center hitting them and making them sparkle and glow. As a result, the entire room blazed with the splendor of the red gem, a stark contrast to the dark and rocky surroundings they had come from.

The rough rock behind them had given way to smooth stones there in the cave. Where the white rocks had been prevalent, this cavern contained a type of rock he'd never seen before with a much darker texture.

"What is this place?" Joshua asked barely above a whisper. All he got in response was the echo of his own voice.

In one corner of the room, a dusty skeleton sat leaning against the stone wall. Joshua froze. It must have been rotting there for hundreds, maybe thousands, of years. It looked as if it were about to crumble to dust with just a puff of air.

Dedecus walked toward the stone on the pedestal with his hand stretched out as if in a trance.

Joshua couldn't say why, but seeing his best friend going to grab the stone filled him with two very different, yet equally strong, emotions that ripped at his soul. The first was something he could only describe as a deep longing to take the stone for himself, to hold it in his own hands. The other was a strong sense of danger—not the normal sense of fear he frequently got—but a gentle nudging in his spirit warning him they must not touch it. Maybe he was unnerved by the skeleton's empty eye sockets staring right at him, but he was fairly sure there's more to it than that. Joshua's parents always said the spirit was moving and leading them. Joshua hadn't felt the spirit before, but what else could this feeling be?

Dedecus was close to the stone now—only a few feet away from being able to grab hold of it.

Joshua glanced back and forth between his friend and the gem. Then, both emotions collided with each other and bubbled up within him, combining into one force. "Stop!"

Namid jumped at his shout.

"What is it?" Dedecus jerked his hand back and looked back at his friend, frowning.

Joshua struggled to put his thoughts into words, "I ... I don't think we should touch it."

"What do you mean? I was just going to go and check it out."

"What's wrong, Joshua?" Namid asked, frowning. "You look panicked."

Joshua couldn't understand what was wrong either. He was always the cautious one of the group, but he'd never reacted so strongly to something before. He couldn't understand it. The warning was real—as if all of Heaven were screaming at him not to go anywhere near it. But it was such a beautiful stone that it made the whole room glow and sparkle.

"I don't know ... I just don't think it's a good idea to touch a strange stone ..." Hearing himself say it aloud sounded ridiculous, but with every fiber of his being, he couldn't let his friend touch that stone.

"Umm, guys," Namid said quietly, "look down."

Glancing at the ground, Joshua saw what she meant. Some sort of message had been carved into the floor by the pedestal.

> *This is a warning: The stone you see before you is called the Creativity Stone. It has the power to create and destroy—the power of God. While it can create beauty and life, it can also inflict untold destruction and evil. Under no circumstances should you use this stone. Its power is meant only for God.*

They stood quiet, Joshua thinking about the possibility and ramifications of the red gem being that powerful.

"This is a joke, right?" Dedecus said, breaking the silence.

"If it's a joke, it's an awfully strange one." Namid stared at the skeleton.

"Either way," Joshua said with all seriousness, "we should get out of here."

"So you believe it?" Dedecus took a step closer to the pedestal.

Joshua flinched. "I don't know. Let's just go."

"You're kidding me, right?" Dedecus said, "Can you imagine if this wasn't written by some crazy dude. What if this actually was an all-powerful stone that could be used to do anything we wanted? That would be so awesome!"

"I'm not sure if that's such a good idea, Dedecus," Namid said. "We can't just play around with something like that."

"So, you think it's actually some sort of *Creativity Stone* that can do anything?" Joshua asked.

"I don't know either," Namid said. "But you're definitely right; we shouldn't be messing around with something like that."

"I'll talk to my parents about it and show it to them. They'll know what to do with it." Joshua gestured at the skeleton. "It didn't do this guy any good."

"Oh, come on. Really, you two?" Dedecus groaned and gestured to the stone as it beckoned for them to use it. "The power to literally do whatever we want is at our fingertips, and you want to run away and call Mommy? I could use this to bring back my parents. I could have my family back, and we could live in a giant mansion and be happy for the rest of our lives. Namid, you could use it to make your parents kinder and more loving. You could wear and say whatever you want, and you could throw away the seven remembrances forever. We could literally make the planet whatever we want it to be and erase all the scars the world and God have left on us. But instead, you want to run to your parents and let them hide it somewhere, never to be seen again?"

"I'm saying that we can't go messing around with God's domain. He has a plan, and we can't go change that. We have no right to play God."

"Easy for you to say!" Dedecus shouted. "*You* have parents who love you. *You* have a whole village supporting you. *You* haven't been labeled an outcast your entire life because of your parents' mistakes. *You* get to do whatever you want. *You* live in a nice, cushy house and will one day be one of the leaders of our village."

Dedecus's face turned red, his thousands of freckles looking like spots on a ripe, red tomato.

Despite their differences and backgrounds, Joshua and Dedecus almost never fought, yet now every wound inflicted on Dedecus by the whip of the world grew red, and his anger poured out of him. Dedecus towered over Joshua, taking full advantage of all his extra eleven inches.

Joshua instinctively shrank back some but held his ground.

"Meanwhile, I live in a rundown shack, clinging to the few threads of memories I have of my parents while the whole village shuns me because they see me as a mistake—the black mark of the village. Your life might be perfect, but Namid's isn't, and mine certainly isn't! So where's this God of yours's amazing plan for my life? It became my right to use that stone as soon as God failed me by sending a thousand pounds of rocks on my parent's heads in an avalanche!"

"Well, I'm sorry I have parents who love me, and I'm sorry my life seems so perfect," Joshua said, barely above a whisper. He knew his friend enough to realize he was lost in the possibility that his life could be more than being an outcast until he died. And he couldn't blame him for it. But Dedecus wasn't thinking straight. "And whether or not you believe it, God does love you, and he does have a plan. He's here for you. Just because you can't see that plan doesn't mean we can just play with forces we don't understand."

"What if this is your God's plan?" Dedecus crossed his arms. "Your parents always talk about God's amazing plan and how we are a part of it, taking control of the destiny he's placed over our lives. Well, that's what I'm doing. Your parents say the Judges of Justice desecrate the name of God. Maybe he's given me this to stop those self-righteous monsters."

"This isn't how God works, though. He doesn't send people out to kill others." Joshua turned. "Back me up on this, Namid."

Namid flinched, "Well, that does happen in the Old Testament a lot."

"See?" Dedecus grinned triumphantly.

"What about the warning?" Namid asked quietly.

Dedecus let out an exasperated sigh and glared at Namid. "Fine, maybe God doesn't want me to use it. He really is a tyrant crushing anyone who tries to escape his rule."

Namid bit her lip. "God's not—"

"I get why 'mister perfect life' doesn't want to use the stone, but you, of all people, should agree with me, Namid. If God is as cruel as your parents teach, then he doesn't deserve to be God. Aren't you tired of sitting around and memorizing the thousands of rules your parents have? With this Creativity Stone, we could create our own world and be our own gods. We could have everything we've ever wanted, and neither of us would have to keep trying to climb out of the pit of imperfection God and this world has shoved us into."

They all remained silent for a moment, and Joshua prayed fervently that Namid wouldn't agree. He knew in his heart they shouldn't mess with that stone, but he had no way to stop both of them.

"How about this," Namid said. "We don't tell anyone about this place. My parents have a giant library I can use. If someone wrote this warning, and the only people to live on this planet have been the New Day Separatists, then that means at some point someone used it and hid it here. Maybe I can research more about this Creativity Stone. Then we'll decide together what the best course of action is—whether we test out using the stone or tell someone about it."

"Fine." Dedecus backed away from the Creativity Stone. The pedestal, even though it held what was possibly the most powerful object in the world, was ironically the only thing in the whole room that wasn't flawlessly smooth.

I must tell my parents. Joshua felt as if some looming tragedy would befall them if he didn't stop his friends. And yet, this seemed the only way to get Dedecus to not use it immediately. Maybe if they waited, they could either find some way to convince him it would be a bad idea, or Namid would search and not find anything, and they would eventually forget about the stone.

The trio made their way out of the cavern, none of them speaking to each other except when Namid tripped over a rock and fell to the ground, and Joshua asked if she was okay. What was meant to be a fun and exciting day of exploration had turned into a day where their differences and anger had torn them apart.

Thoughts of the glowing red Creativity Stone and of the possibility it could do all the note said it could—that it could actually give the user the power to create and destroy—beckoned Joshua. But touching that stone would mean death. He was certain of it.

CHAPTER 6

FIDES VILLAGE, NOVITAS—DAY 1, YEAR 371

Namid dropped into her room from her window and quickly changed into the many layers of clothing her parents insisted would keep her safe from impurity. She was careful to make sure to wipe off any dirt or mud that got onto her skin, erasing all evidence that she had fled her room, parents, and responsibilities. Then, she hid her raggedy clothes back in their hiding spot.

After checking in the mirror and straightening her hair to make sure everything was in order, she sat down at her desk to finish memorizing the entire Old Testament. She rubbed her hand against her throbbing head as she thought of all she had to get done. She had already memorized most of it, but she still had some of Lamentations and Leviticus left to memorize.

As she started to read, she tried to focus on the list of laws for cleanliness, but her mind and soul had turned into a battlefield, with two warring factions fighting for control.

On one side, Dedecus's promise of building a better world—a world of perfection—a world where she wouldn't have to spend hours memorizing Scripture each day and wouldn't have to hide her friends and who she was. She could finally live a life free of fear, the life that God and her parents were keeping from her.

On the other side, the warning from the cave echoed through her memory.

Create untold destruction and evil.

Under no circumstances should you use the power only meant for God.

Each side fought valiantly, destroying each other's points and arguments until she couldn't take it anymore and wanted to let out a scream to silence her thoughts. They would've been better off if they'd never seen the room. The stone had unlocked a powerful desire within her for all the things she'd believed could never happen—a life where her parents were proud of her and loved her for who she was instead of seeing her as a failure who would never reach Heaven.

Focus. If she couldn't achieve perfection for her parents by tomorrow ... she refused to let her mind wander there.

She reached for her cross necklace to rub her fingers along the ornate gold as she always did when she was in turmoil. Although she had to be careful—the edges were sharp, and she had cut her hand on it many times. However, when her hand touched her neck where the cross should have been, all she felt was her clothing.

Panic shot through every nerve in her body, and she went stiff. All thoughts of the stone, her friends, and studying were completely wiped from her mind as a bright neon sign flashed within her brain, screaming she needed to find that necklace.

She jumped into action, tearing apart her desk and then racing around the room, trying desperately to find the cross her parents had said she must never take off—it was to remind her Jesus had died on the cross because of her failures and mistakes, a reminder of her imperfection.

The necklace had been specially made, and if her parents discovered that she'd lost it, she would be in worse trouble than she could imagine. She could think of many examples of pretty terrible things her parents could and had done to her ... everything from starving her for two weeks to stoning her. Every cell within her body cowered at the thought of what was sure to happen once her parents saw the empty space on her chest.

And yet, her desperation yielded no golden cross necklace. No matter how hard she willed it to be, she couldn't find it anywhere in her room.

She thought back over her day to when she could have lost it, yelling at her brain to come up with a magical solution.

It must have dropped or broken off when she'd tripped and fallen when they were back in the caverns.

Her house was right by the waterfall, but Dedecus's was much further, so he would probably still be walking home. She looked down at the floorboard where she had her dirty clothes hidden, but she had no time to change into them.

At precisely six o'clock that evening, her parents would be home from the trial they were presiding over—some ridiculous reason about the number six and how the number of evil could cause her to sin. She'd never understood their reasoning, but it didn't matter now. All that mattered was that it was now 5:37, and she didn't have time to change, make it all the way to the waterfall, go up the path, through the falls, find and retrieve the necklace, and make it all the way back to her room without the risk of her parents beating her home.

Her only hope—a very slim hope—was to have Joshua or Dedecus retrieve it. All she could do was try to hide its disappearance until then.

She ran over to the window and threw it open. The chirping of a bird reached her ears, but she couldn't take time to enjoy nature. She jumped out and climbed down the

Earth Tree, hearing a rip as she shimmied down the bark, but at this point, it didn't matter. Not caring who saw her, Namid raced down the path to find Joshua and Dedecus.

With her long, curly, brown hair whipping in the wind, she raced down the path as fast as possible, praying she could catch up to the boys in time and make it back to her room before six, praying God would understand her mistake and not bring wrath upon her for another failure.

Trying to drown out her fearful thoughts, she focused on the thudding of her feet on the pathway, each step carrying her closer to Joshua and Dedecus, her only saviors in a world determined to crush her.

CHAPTER 7

FIDES VILLAGE, NOVITAS—DAY 1, YEAR 371

Joshua shut the wooden door behind him and leaned up against it. He placed his hand against the small, rectangular table in the hallway, cluttered with papers and random junk.

His father walked out of the living room and grinned. His six-foot-tall stature dwarfed Joshua's small frame.

"Did you have fun exploring? You know, one day I'm going to come join you if I don't die of boredom first in all these meetings they're making me attend."

"Yeah, it was fine." Why was he asking? Did he know about the Creativity Stone?

His dad stared at him then turned his head back toward the living room. "Honey, can you come here?"

His mom joined them in the hallway.

"Can you tell me, does this look like a boy who had a good day?"

His mom tilted her head. "Well, he's leaning against the wall with his shoulders slouched and a frown on his face."

Joshua shifted awkwardly, uncomfortable with how his parents were dissecting his body language.

"What's going on, Joshua?" His mom took a step closer.

"I'm fine." Joshua sighed. "I got into an argument with Dedecus, though."

"I'm sorry to hear that," his mom said. "Do you want to talk about it?" She leaned up against the light blue wall.

Joshua opened his mouth to speak, then shut it. "I promised Dedecus I wouldn't tell anyone."

My parents would know what to do, but I can't risk losing Dedecus as a friend.

Joshua leaned against the door, relying on it to hold him up.

His dad put his warm and slightly sweaty hand on his shoulder.

"I'm fine, it's just that ..." Joshua tried to search for the right words. "How do you know that God is who you say he is? I mean, Namid's parents say he hates everyone because of his holy perfection and our wicked sin. Yet, you say now that we have Jesus there's only mercy and no judgment. But how do you explain Dedecus's hard life? Are the Judges of Justice right?"

"Dedecus has lived a hard life." His dad sighed. "But it's because of the cruel people who've turned God into a list of rules. The Bible says that all things are permissible and that Jesus came to do away with the Ten Commandments. All suffering and death in the world today is because of the law. If everyone would just turn from those remembrances, the world would be much better."

Joshua nodded at the familiar words. He'd mostly stopped asking his dad questions on theology. His dad was incredibly wise, but most of his answers were variations of "Jesus said the law is bad now." He found it best to simply trust that his dad knew what he was talking about.

But now he found himself unable to escape his questions. Ever since his argument with Dedecus, something didn't seem right.

Joshua stared at his dad. "But how did the law make Dedecus's parents die?" and should Dedecus be allowed to bring them back with the stone?

"I don't know. But it did. And if we reject the law, God will bless us."

"But that's easy enough for us to say. Our life is great."

"God has blessed us because we live in the freedom of his love, as he does with all who step out of the law."

"But how do you know all of this?" Joshua asked.

His dad smiled. "You'll learn all about this once you start your judge training when you're twenty. I'll give you the history of how we left Earth to settle this place and about the great man, Steven Waters, who began a journey to discover who God really was. Then by the time your appointment ceremony comes when you're thirty, you'll be all set to be an incredible leader until your firstborn takes the mantle."

Joshua sighed. He knew his father meant well, but he didn't need a reminder of his impending leadership. He had too many doubts, too many fears to ever be the incredible leader his father was. Why couldn't they just skip a generation?

A pounding sounded on the door Joshua was leaning on, and he jumped.

Joshua opened the door. "Dedecus?"

Dedecus stood on his doorstep, sweating and breathing heavily.

"I promise I haven't—"

"Namid needs us." Dedecus interrupted him.

"What's wrong?" Joshua stepped outside.

"No time. I'll tell you on the way." He took off running down the gravel path.

Joshua turned to his parents. "I'll be back later."

His mom smiled. "Okay, sweetie, just be back for dinner."

"We'll be praying for you, Son," his dad said.

"Thanks." Joshua turned and chased after Dedecus.

God, please let Namid be all right.

CHAPTER 8

EMERALD WATERFALL, NOVITAS—DAY 1, YEAR 371

Dedecus and Joshua ran back up the cliff to the jumping point, through the waterfall, and into the caves.

Dedecus's feet were getting blisters from his worn-down shoes and all the running he was doing. He looked down at Joshua's comfy-looking shoes.

His perfect friend's perfect life continued to haunt him. He gritted his teeth and frowned. When Namid had run up to him, he hadn't wanted to go get Josh's help. *Just leave him in his picture-perfect house where he lives a fairytale life.* But he couldn't leave Namid to be led to the slaughterhouse if her parents discovered the necklace gone. The search for the necklace would go faster with two sets of eyes instead of one.

At least Josh isn't giving me one of his annoyingly rational explanations.

Once they got up to the jumping point into the caves, Dedecus took a running leap and made it through the waterfall and to the other side of the five-foot gap the second time that day.

He started to dry off and groaned as Joshua tried to work up the courage to make the jump.

After a few seconds, Joshua took a few steps back and ran forward to jump through the waterfall. This time, though his timing was a little off, and his foot slipped as he pushed off. He made it through the waterfall but came up several inches short and banged, waist-high, into the ledge on the other side. He let out a loud yell and tried to grab onto something.

Adrenaline shot through Dedecus's veins, and he ran to the edge to peer down.

Joshua was grasping a protruding rock several feet below the lip of the cliff. His eyes were clenched shut and his body dangled over the drop.

Dedecus dropped to the ground and reached as far as he could to grab onto Joshua's hand. He prayed to a God he didn't believe in to save Joshua.

I can't lose one of the only people who actually care about me.

"I'm not sure I can hold on any longer," Joshua shouted. "My hand is slipping."

Blood seeped from a cut on his hand, making his grip slippery.

Dedecus came within a few inches of Joshua's hand but couldn't reach him.

Joshua's hand slowly slipped.

"No!" Dedecus shouted until his lungs emptied of all air.

Joshua seemed to fall down slowly, at first, then faster until his body smacked into the rocks over two hundred feet below.

Dedecus leaped up and tried to see through his tears as he jumped back over the gap and raced down the path, his heart nearly beating out of his chest. He prayed his best friend had survived by some miracle performed by the God Joshua always insisted was real.

He reached the bottom in record time and jumped across the rocks where the waterfall turned into a gentle stream.

Joshua's body lay unmoving. The rocks surrounding him were stained with blood—a stark contrast between pearly white and cherry red.

At the very least, Joshua had broken a bunch of his bones. He was lying on his side, his limbs flung to the side and his light blond hair covered in dirt and blood.

Dedecus fell to his knees over the body and felt for a pulse. Nothing. Only his friend's dead body. He sobbed uncontrollably, inconsolably, as God once again ripped those he loved away from him. He hadn't cried since the news that his parents would never hold him again. But in the face of another death, his tear ducts were reopened.

He grappled with the fact that in a single moment, a single misstep had changed everything ... His fault. He'd been the one who first found those stupid caves. He'd been the one who suggested for them to explore them. He'd been the one who had pushed Joshua to jump when he clearly wasn't ready.

All he could do was stare at his best friend's battered and bloody body. So much blood surrounding him. Staining the rocks red. It kept flowing out of Joshua, more and more blood turning the green waters around them into a murky yellow.

Dedecus stopped crying and clenched his jaw shut. "Fine, God, I'll do it myself."

He stood, ignoring the blood covering his pants. He raced back up the cliff, jumped through to the other side of the waterfall, ran past the ornate, golden cross lying forgotten on the ground, crawled through the tunnel, and finally crawled into the beautiful room with the Creativity Stone.

He gasped for air, trying to fill his lungs from the run. Every nerve in his brain was focused on what he was about to do.

Unlike last time, he marched up to the glowing red stone of infinite power. Ignoring the skeleton in the corner and voices of warning from Joshua, he let his soul and mind be consumed by the thirst for the power of the stone. He would be the creator and controller of his destiny.

This is only to save Joshua.

"This is what you get, God." He reached toward the stone. "If you didn't want me messing with this, then you shouldn't have let the one person who has shown me kindness and love die such a pointless death. Now, it's my turn to be God."

And with those words, he surrendered to the craving for the stone's power.

He touched it. Sharp jolts of electricity shot through his body. Goosebumps went up along his arms and legs.

He smiled and grabbed the Creativity Stone with his right hand, and when he touched it, a deep warmth filled his whole body. His mind exploded with knowledge and possibilities. Then, a blast of powerful, red energy shot out from all sides of the stone, sending waves of power through his cells and shattering all the gems in the wall and ceiling in the room. Broken shards of crystal rained down from above his head.

The small pebble in his hand enraptured all thoughts in Dedecus's mind. Its glow shone so brightly he could hardly look at it. It fed off his strength as much as he was feeding off it.

He allowed the power-fueled adrenaline coursing through his hand and into his body to hypnotize him. The stone was his, and he was the stone's.

"Make me a part of you," the stone spoke to his soul. "You have the power of God, but you're not God—yet."

An image of Joshua's lifeless body reminded Dedecus of why he'd grabbed the rock.

A bright flash shot out from the Creativity Stone, and a wind rushed around him. Suddenly, he was back outside the cave next to Joshua.

Dedecus grinned, feeling like a little kid getting to be in charge.

He gazed at his friend, no longer remorseful or sad. He had the authority to create anything, including life.

The stone flashed a deep red, and surges of fire shot out from it, swirling around and engulfing Joshua's limp body, lifting it off the rocks and into the air. Joshua's arms and legs shot straight out. His eyes shot open, and he arched his back, letting out a blood-curdling scream that echoed off the Pearl Cliffs. The cuts and wounds rapidly healed and disappeared—becoming clear skin again. Life shot through every cell, restoring color to his pale and clammy skin. He stopped screaming and went limp.

Joshua's tattered and bloody clothes were the only remnants of what had happened.

The light and mind-bending energy waves disappeared back into the Creativity Stone and dropped Joshua to the ground. This time as he landed on the rocks, a breath flowed through his lungs, and blood pumped through his veins once again.

Dedecus's body tingled with the dominance he had over life and death. He smirked and rubbed his hands against the Creativity Stone's rough surface.

So, this is what it means to be a god.

CHAPTER 9

EMERALD WATERFALL, NOVITAS—DAY 1, YEAR 371

Joshua took a deep breath, and a blend of sweet and earthy scents flooded his senses. It smelled like a rich garden. A warmth filled his entire body, and he sighed in contentment.

Joshua opened his eyes and squinted at the bright world around him. Directly above him was a gentle lake of blue water.

Water?

Joshua stared. Above him was some kind of clear ceiling with water above it.

Where am I?

He sat up and looked around. He was lying on grass softer than his own bed in a massive field that seemed to extend forever.

Something was off. He'd woken up in a strange place, and his memory of what had happened was foggy, but for some reason, he felt no fear.

"Hello, Joshua."

He jumped and whipped his head around to see a man in a white robe standing nearby.

The man laughed. "Sorry to startle you."

"Where ... where am I? And what's with the water above us?"

The man grinned. "Pretty cool, right?" He sat down next to Joshua in the grass. "What's the last thing you remember?"

Joshua searched his memory. "Dedecus and I were going to the tunnels because Namid had dropped her necklace. We were crossing the waterfall, and I ..." Joshua's eyes grew wide. "I fell."

The man placed a hand on Joshua's knee.

"Does that mean I died?" Joshua looked closer at the man. "Are you Jesus?"

The man laughed. "You honor me too highly. I'm only an angel—sent to deliver you a message."

"But aren't angels supposed to have wings and halos?"

The angel's eyes twinkled. "I can appear in different forms."

Joshua scanned the horizon. "Am I in Heaven?"

"Sort of, although if you saw everything, you'd never want to leave. Which is why you were brought to this field."

"You're saying I have to leave?" Joshua bit his lip.

"Dedecus is taking the Creativity Stone to revive you as we speak."

"So it was God's will that he take it?" Joshua plucked a blade of grass out.

"No. But God's plan can sustain broken and angry people adding a few curves in the road."

"What if I want to stay here? I've never felt this way before. Everything down there is so confusing and chaotic. But here, it's like all my fears and worries feel tiny. I don't want this to end."

The angel smiled sadly. "But God is not done with you yet."

"I need to know—who's right? Is God a free and loving Daddy who came to make us happy? Or is he a wrathful and judgmental God who will smite us?"

"Grace vs. judgment, who's right? Everyone tries to interpret God by taking some of his actions as the way he is totally—understandable considering humanity's short-term view. But what if you tried to look at God's actions through the lens of his personality. What if it's neither of the extremes?"

Joshua stared at the angel in confusion. "But—"

"That must be all for now. Dedecus is about to awaken you, and I still have a message for you to deliver."

Joshua sighed. Questions swirled around his brain, but they'd have to wait. "Okay. What do I need to know?"

Joshua inhaled long and deeply and then opened his eyes. Above him was the cliff he'd fallen from, and underneath him, the rocks he had fallen onto.

Dedecus stood beside him, grinning. He held the Creativity Stone. It glowed so brightly it hurt Joshua's eyes to look at it and blanketed Dedecus with a swirling red mist.

What just happened?

Then he remembered the angel's warning.

"What have you done?" Joshua stood and turned toward Dedecus.

"What are you talking about? I just saved your life. In fact, I actually brought you back to life. So, you should be thanking me."

"But you didn't need to save me."

"What are you—"

"I was in Heaven."

Dedecus shifted uncomfortably and arched his eyebrow. "Heaven. As in floating on fluffy clouds while playing a harp?"

"No. It was so much more incredible than that." Joshua searched for a word to explain what he'd felt, but nothing seemed to fit. "It was like everything was complete and fulfilling."

Dedecus rubbed his finger along the rough stone in his hand and rolled his eyes. "Sounds nice. But how do you know that wasn't just a dream? I saved your life. Maybe I shouldn't have if you're just gonna whine about it."

"The angel who greeted me also warned me that, among other things, I had to go back to my body and stop you at all costs from using that stone or something bad would happen."

"What are you talking about?" Dedecus clenched his jaw and laughed. "All I did with the stone was save your life."

"And what do you plan on doing with that thing now?" Joshua moved toward him with slow, deliberate steps.

Something changed on Dedecus's face—a shift of his mouth and eyebrows, a coldness that wasn't there before. His hand squeezed around the Creativity Stone.

"You cannot have this power—the Creativity Stone is mine! All my life, your God has failed me, so now I will become my own god. I will erase all the scars he's given me."

The stone flashed brighter with each word Dedecus spoke.

"You can't just erase scars or change history. They're a part of you. They are what God has used to make you into who you are today, and they will be used to—"

"Silence!" Dedecus shouted. His yell sent a blast of power through the air. Rocks and water were flung into the air as the red energy slammed into them. Joshua braced himself for the impact, but it rushed past him with no effect.

The waterfall still thundered on behind them, soaking their already-dripping-wet clothes. Dedecus continued his rant.

"I will be god. I will make my own world, and it will be everything this world is not. So, you can either join me as a true friend—or not."

Dedecus ripped off his bloodstained shirt and threw it to the ground. Before today, he never would've done that. He didn't have many clothes, to begin with, and couldn't spare any.

He's losing himself.

Dedecus held the stone against his chest, and fog swirled around him. The stone burned bright red against him. The energy ripped into him, creating a gaping hole where his heart should have been.

Joshua gasped.

Dedecus kept smiling. He shoved the stone into the hole where his heart used to be and became one with it. The hole healed itself and left a red glow coming from his chest.

The red mist became a whirlwind, whipping around his friend's body, lifting him off the ground.

Dedecus began to transform as the Creativity Stone claimed his soul. He let out a deep, guttural laugh. His muscles bulged, and every vein in his body glowed a purplish red.

"Dedecus?" Joshua shivered. His friend looked like a monster from one of those Earth stories Namid told them about.

"I am no longer *just* Dedecus. He was weak, pathetic, powerless. Now I am a *god*." His voice was deeper and sounded like it came from the depths of hell.

The red color of the stone swirled around the steely blue of his eyes, gradually replacing all color with a bright red. The eyes glaring at Joshua were no longer those of his friend.

Every part of him shined with dark radiance.

Joshua blinked rapidly, his eyes full of tears.

"You've always had the perfect life," Dedecus roared at him.

Joshua flinched.

"You and your perfect village are finally going to feel what I experienced my entire life. Either you can bow down to me as a god, or I'll show you who you should have been praying to all this time."

Dedecus slammed his hand against the ground. The dirt under him flew in all directions as light exploded out of his body, blinding Joshua. A tunnel of wind encircled him.

He was gone.

Joshua squeezed his eyes shut. He knew what was about to happen. But he was too late to stop it.

CHAPTER 10

HOUSTON, TEXAS, EARTH—JULY 14, 1971

Steven Waters shuffled his feet down the dark alleyway. Lampposts hadn't been installed in this area of town, so everything was shrouded in black. He glanced back and forth to make sure he hadn't been followed. Buildings seemed to rise up around him and melt into the smog of the Houston, Texas, skyline.

He came to the door with the bloodstain on it and knocked seven times.

An older woman with gray hair and wearing a long, white dress opened the door. She squinted her eyes at him. "Who are you?"

"I'm Steven, ma'am, Steven ... Smith."

"Leave." She started to shut the door, but he stopped it with his hand.

"Please, ma'am. After all this stuff with Lemon Vs. Kurtzman and the Pentagon Papers, I'm disgusted by what this world is turning into. I want to join you guys."

Somehow, the old lady's frown deepened. "How did you hear about us?"

Steven shifted uncomfortably. As much as he hated lying, he couldn't tell them the truth. If they knew his last name, they'd never let him in.

"I ... um ... heard about you guys through the lawsuit."

The woman let out a tense sigh and flicked a piece of lint off her dress. She stepped aside and opened the door wider. "You may come in. I'm Esther Kenmore."

He walked, with Esther behind him, down a hallway into a sparse living room lined with couches that looked like they should have been thrown away twenty years ago. Ten people, both men and women—and all much older—sat listening to a man Steven immediately recognized. He was standing in the middle of the room enthusiastically explaining something, waving his hands around like a madman.

"The genetic coding is imprinted into the device and then deconstructs to the smallest atom. Quantum information cannot be destroyed, and so by maintaining the genetic coding, nothing but the energy required to use the device will be lost. Then, utilizing a quantum theory I've developed, my device will connect those atoms with ones in a separate location, and the reconstruction process will occur. However, the subjects will merely feel as if they are stepping through a door."

The man was Dr. Jefferson Gent. Steven tried not to react when he saw the man Steven's father had tried to put into an insane asylum. He'd known they'd eventually cross paths, but the organization was relatively big, and he'd hoped he could slip in undetected. He tried to turn around, but Esther stood behind him, blocking his path.

Jefferson turned around and saw him. His eyes grew wide, and he clutched his fists. "Waters? What are you doing here?"

"I'm not—"

"Waters? You mean this is that no good heathen who tried to stop us?" Esther grabbed Steven's ear and yanked down.

"It's him all right," Jefferson said. "He looks younger than the last time I saw him, but he's got that same blond hair, slim build, and green eyes."

"Ahh ... no ... please, let me explain. Harold Waters is my father."

"Even worse, now he's sending his kids to spy on us?" a middle-aged woman in the room said.

"What'll happen now that he's seen our faces?" another asked.

Steven pulled away from Esther and pressed his back against the wall. He looked around as all eyes glared at him.

"No. My father disowned me when I became a Christian." That gave everyone pause. "I've seen what it's like out there: secularization, evolution, corruption, sexualization. It's horrible, and my father actively encourages it. I'm sick of all this twisting of the truth, and when I saw Jefferson on trial, passionately defending his beliefs and rights, it inspired me. I want to join the New Day Separatists ... to get rid of this sin that runs rampant and return to the laws God gave us."

"How can we trust you?" Esther glared at him.

Steven sighed. "Because my father is rich. He had just given me ten thousand dollars to start my own business before I told him I had become a Christian. If you let me join, I'll give you every penny of it as an offering."

The room was silent for a moment.

A man Steven didn't recognize started laughing. "What did I tell you guys? The Lord provides for the righteous. We separated from sin, so now the harvest is coming."

Esther grabbed Steven's hand and held it palm up. Her gray eyes stared into his, and he blinked.

"Are you serious about joining the remnant of the righteous in a world of corruption?" She maintained a death grip on his hand.

"Yes."

Before he had a chance to respond, she grabbed a knife and made a small slice on his palm.

"Then we shall perform the ceremony now and repeat it later when the whole congregation gathers." She released his hand. "Hold up your hand and repeat after us."

"I promise to remember," they all spoke as one voice.

"I promise to remember," he echoed.

"The consequences of my failure."

"The consequences of my failure." He was a failure. But he would be better now.

"To be pure in all thoughts and actions."

"To be pure in all thoughts and actions." This was something the world needed to learn—the iniquity sickened him.

"To remember that God is found only through the law."

He repeated it after her. Turning from the law of God was what had destroyed his father. He wouldn't let it destroy him too.

"To stay modest to keep others from sin."

As he stated this, his thoughts swirled inside his head. People really were disgusting, flaunting their sexuality like peacocks.

"To cast out the defiled."

He paused for a second. Did this mean he'd never see Lisa again?

If I stay with them, I will become them.

"To cast out the defiled," he repeated firmly.

"To enact what others deserve."

He restated the clause. No more handouts. He would work to earn God's good treatment. And anyone who didn't—didn't deserve his time.

"Remember, you're never good enough."

"Remember, you're never good enough."

Steven smiled. He was now a New Day Separatist.

CHAPTER 11

FIDES VILLAGE, NOVITAS—DAY 1, YEAR 371

"You knew exactly what you were doing when you stole those bush berries from farmer Tar, you despicable man. You have no right to call yourself a citizen of Fides," Freda said, shaking her thick Bible at the man on trial.

"I'm sorry, ma'am," the gray-haired man, Grover, cried. "My family and I haven't eaten in two days, and we were starving. Please forgive me."

"Why should we forgive you when God himself will never forgive you?"

Marvin's gut twisted as his wife's words sliced into the man hunched in front of them.

Marvin and Freda were at their ordained spots at the front of the room in the council hall. As the Judges of Justice, their jobs were to pass down God's judgment for the sins of the community.

Freda stood, towering over Grover and his family.

Marvin sat. He'd been groomed by his parents to become the Judge of Justice, like his ancestor, the great Esther Kenmore herself. His entire life was about the seven remembrances and the rules that accompanied them. But no matter how many times he prayed for God to give him the righteous anger his parents had always had—the anger his wife was experiencing now—all he could feel was pity for the man who had become a puddle on the floor in front of them.

Marvin had always been taught that God had given him the greatest honor by giving him the assignment of holding the community up to God's standard. But as he watched Grover shaking and sobbing, it didn't feel like an honor.

He loved the theological part of his job. He could go on for hours in eloquent terms about the wrath of God and the elect. But he'd never enjoyed this part of the job. In fact, it always filled him with shame.

Conversely, it came easily to his wife. She had grown up an ordinary citizen and had to work hard to get God to notice her for her constant holiness. And God had noticed her by having his parents choose her as his wife.

Marvin sighed and brought his mind back into focus, realigning himself with God's pure law. He stood, picked up his own Bible, and pointed it at Grover.

"The law is very clear." Marvin prepared himself to crush this family's life. "Starving or not is inconsequential, for sin is sin regardless of the circumstances. Therefore, you are to receive—"

The platform he stood on shook, the wooden beams cracking.

Marvin fell to his knees and thrashed his head around.

It wasn't just the platform. The entire room was trembling violently—dust fell from the ceiling as the foundations shifted.

"What's going on?" Grover's wife cried.

Glass shattered and rained down on Marvin's head as a chandelier crashed down from the ceiling. He frantically brushed the glass out of his hair and jumped off the platform, Freda followed close behind him.

The ground thrashed back and forth, making it difficult to stand.

DOWNFALL

One of the main pillars holding up the building cracked.

It must be an earthquake. Marvin knew the word from his Earth history studies, but it had never happened on Novitas.

"Everyone, get out before the building collapses!" Marvin shouted. He charged toward the door, followed by his wife and others in the room.

Water gushed out from the floor, spewing out and drenching them with the green liquid. The water pipe must have burst.

Whipping the doors open, they stumbled out of the council chambers. The ground continued to quake beneath them.

Villagers poured out of their houses and buildings, unsure of what to do as pillars and walls cracked and broke apart. Sounds of buildings crashing against the rumbling ground and screams of people flailing about filled his ears.

"Everyone, get to the church!" Marvin screamed, doing his best to quell the panic in his voice while also doing his best to hold on to some of his decorum.

Once everyone was outside, Marvin turned to look back and saw a plume of dust rising from the rubble and dispersing over the village, burning his eyes and making everyone cough. A layer of dust coated his tongue, and he spat.

Taking the lead, he stumbled past collapsing houses that had been there since their forefathers first settled this land led by his ancestor, Esther. Houses could be rebuilt— what mattered was getting everyone to safety.

"This must be punishment for the sins of the Judges of Mercy. Hopefully, this takes care of them," Freda panted out as they ran. Her voice was barely audible over the screams of the villagers.

Marvin didn't say anything. The Judges of Mercy were his enemies, but they were good people.

"Wait," Freda said, stopping her race to the church. "Where's Namid?"

Marvin froze. They turned to face the direction where their house stood. But all he saw was a pile of rubble.

"Namid!" he screamed, his voice cracking, his heart nearly beating out of his chest. He took off toward the house, ripping open the leather belt and flinging off the long robe that marked him as a judge so he could run faster. "God, please don't punish her. I know she hasn't been perfect, but I promise we'll work harder—she'll get there."

A large crack sounded, and water rocketed into the sky, mixing with the cloud of dust.

He saw Namid running toward them from his left, and his heart started beating again.

"Father, what's going on?" she yelled. The shaking ground caused her to trip over her dress.

"I ... I don't know," he said as they reached her.

Freda helped her up. "Wait a minute!" She grabbed the top layer of Namid's clothing by the neck. "Where is your cross necklace?"

"Not the time, Freda," Marvin said. "We have to make it to the church."

Another building—this time the library—came crashing down. Books and debris flew past them. Marvin clenched his fists. Their history and knowledge. He could only pray they'd be able to recover most of the books.

They ran toward the church, catching up with the throng of people racing up the steps.

Someone threw open the large wooden doors, and everyone streamed in, coughing and covered in grime.

Marvin slammed the doors behind them and marched to the front of the swaying building. The lights flickered overhead as the solar generator outside was jostled.

He made his way onto the stage. Before he reached the lectern, a blinding light flashed in front of them, and the earthquake stopped.

Dedecus suddenly appeared on the podium in front of them. He was shirtless, his pants soaking wet and covered in blood, and he looked much more muscular and taller as he towered over everyone. His whole body glowed red.

"Hello, Fides Village!" His voice boomed across the landscape of frightened people and bounced off the walls with more power than Marvin had ever spoken during a sermon. "You might know me as the orphan trash—the black mark on your otherwise perfect little village."

He slowly marched across the stage where an ornate, golden cross towered over them at about twelve feet tall. The sun hit it through the now-shattered windows and reflected off it, sending beams of bright light over them.

"I've come here today to change that—for no longer will I be your orphan trash, but instead, I will be your god."

Bolts of energy shot out of his hands and shattered the cross into billions of tiny fragments. Golden flakes from the cross scattered in every direction, and the whole area sparkled like glitter.

Marvin cleared his throat to speak, but Dedecus towered over him.

"I'm sick of your judgment, old man. At my parent's funeral, you said they deserved what they got. I was a grieving little kid who'd just lost his parents, and what did you do? You told me they were going to hell and deserved it, all because they had me before they got married."

The memory of his own words twisted in Marvin's gut. Such speeches left a bitter taste in his mouth, but he was only doing what God commanded.

Dedecus's red eyes glared at him.

"He actually did it," Namid muttered. She trembled. "He took the Creativity Stone."

"That's right!" he shouted, grinning, "I have the power to create and the power to destroy. And my first act as god is to do something that your God was very good at in the Old Testament—expressing wrath!"

A blast of power shot out from his chest and crashed through the holy sanctuary of the church, the energy exploding through the thick, white stone walls like they were paper. The ceiling was ripped from the metal beams and sent flying into the air.

People dove under pews and screamed as debris and large stones were hurled down onto their heads.

Marvin noticed a piece of stone flying toward Namid's head and dove into her to protect her from it—covering her with his own body, protecting her from the destruction.

The glorious temple that had been dedicated to the worship of the almighty God had shattered as if it were made of nothing but glass—reducing in moments the work and dedication of years to nothing. It was as though the years spent worshipping God and his almighty power meant nothing.

Marvin looked around at the chaos surrounding him.

Most cowered against the floor and under pews. Some ran about frantically while others ran to protect their families.

Dedecus, a curse from the devil himself, stood in the center of where the church used to be. He grinned and held his shoulders high.

"Where is your God now?"

CHAPTER 12

FIDES VILLAGE, NOVITAS—DAY 1, YEAR 371

Joshua's feet throbbed, and his lungs burned as he raced down the well-worn path that led to his house. He shoved his blond hair out of his eyes.

Everything was happening exactly as the angel had warned him.

Just run.

The sound of screaming filtered into his brain as he rushed past people running aimlessly.

One large house in front of him crashed into rubble, crushing the garden in the front yard. A massive haze of dust hit him in the face, stinging his eyes and burning his throat. He covered his nose and mouth with his tunic and kept running.

So many life-altering things had happened in the past hour, it would take him years to sort through and process. But now wasn't the time as he drowned it all out and focused on running.

He'd always seen his home as a kind of sanctuary—a safe place of comfort where he could be himself. No matter what happened around him in the world, he always had a home. He always had a safe space with parents to love and guide him.

When he reached his home, he stopped and squeezed his eyes shut as tears seeped out the sides.

The only thing standing before him was part of the wall where the living room had been and a mound of rubble.

"Mom? Dad?"

Joshua began to cry as he panted for breath from running so hard, the two sounds blending together to form an awkward gasping noise.

There was no way his parents had survived unless they'd gotten out in time.

He climbed into the rubble and dug where the living room used to be—where his father would sit and pray with him each night—where they would all sit around the fireplace and make s'mores in the winter—where they would sing and have little dance parties on Sunday nights.

"I still need them, God," he cried out.

He threw debris out of the way.

"Please don't take them home yet. I still need them!"

If they were dead, it would all be his fault. He'd had a chance to tell them about the stone. But he hadn't. He'd had a chance to stop Dedecus. But he hadn't.

With all his might, he heaved a large section of floorboards out of his way, throwing them off to the side in his frantic search.

Dust rose into the air, and he coughed.

He reached the floor of the house and still located no sign of them.

He found the stuffed animal his mom had stitched for him, a little panda that his brilliant three-year-old self had named Panda. His parents had given it to him, and he still slept with it even though he knew he was too old. The toy was torn and covered with dust, but he clung to it anyway.

Maybe the angel was wrong. Maybe they don't die.

He stood, realizing the rubble was too much to sift through.

"I ... I have to believe they're alive." He ran his hand through his hair. *Where could they be?*

A large explosion coming from the direction of the church shook the ground.

He ran with every bit of energy left in his body, praying the angel that had talked to him outside Heaven was wrong.

God, please let my parents be alive.

CHAPTER 13

FIDES VILLAGE, NOVITAS—DAY 1, YEAR 371

Joshua ran toward the church, and a cloud of dust smacked him in the face, stinging his eyes and making his throat burn.

The church had become a pile of rubble, along with the rest of the town.

People huddled in small groups on the grimy ground while a few darted about tending to the wounded.

Dedecus glowed with a red brilliance in the middle of where the church had stood. The red light emanating from his muscular body filtered through the dusty air.

His parents were nowhere to be seen, but Namid and her parents stood near Dedecus.

Dedecus grinned and spread his arms out wide.

He would kill them.

He had never imagined this horror would be possible from one of his best friends. But, if they didn't do something to stop him, everyone would die.

"How could you do this? I thought we were friends!" Namid shouted at Dedecus.

"So, did I," he said, "and yet I could never escape the fact that I was the black sheep. Being around you two made that fact all too obvious."

"We are your friends, Dedecus, but you're letting the power of that stone control you and cloud your judgment."

Joshua could barely recognize him anymore. His red eyes glowed as he glared down at Namid. He'd been completely consumed by the power and his anger.

"I begged for mercy, and yet all I received was judgment. Why do these people deserve any different?" he said through gritted teeth.

Joshua ran up beside Namid. He realized he was still clinging to his tattered, stuffed panda bear, but he didn't care at this point.

"Have you seen my parents?" Joshua gasped for breath.

"Of course, that's all you care about," Dedecus said. "All the suffering in the world and little Joshie has to run to his mommy and daddy." Dedecus marched up to Joshua and ripped the panda bear out of his arms. He held it up in the air for all to see. "This is your future leader Fides, a pathetic child." He spat on Joshua's shoes. "And it's what you people deserve."

"Hey! Leave my son alone!" Aaron ran up. Joshua nearly collapsed with relief.

"I don't know how you're doing this but stop it! You're hurting innocent people." Aaron marched over to Dedecus.

"Innocent?" Dedecus laughed. "Everyone here has either treated me horribly or stood by and watched it happen. All in the name of your manipulative God. Besides, I thought everything was okay with your God."

"What God commands is love, and this is not love."

"When did anyone ever show me love?" Dedecus's voice cracked.

"We tried but—"

"I don't want your excuses. I want this world to suffer for what it did to me."

Dedecus held out his hand, and red energy radiated from his body and lifted Aaron off the ground. He closed his fist halfway. The energy surrounded Aaron and pressed against him, crushing him. He screamed.

Joshua stood frozen, immobilized by fear.

"Stop this, Dedecus! You're hurting him," Namid said.

"Dedecus," Aaron choked out. "I'm sorry. Maybe we should have stood up to the Judges of Justice more and defended you more strongly. We could have even adopted you. But I was scared ... I didn't want to start a war."

Dedecus blinked, and his eyes widened. Suddenly, he was the little lost boy Joshua had met seven years ago, broken after his parent's death and in need of love.

Then his face hardened, and he let out a guttural roar. "Coward! Hypocrite!" He closed his hand tighter, and the energy squeezed Aaron in its grip. "That is what you are. And I am done with you." He shut his hand completely, and Aaron's body collapsed in on itself, crushing him completely and causing his bones to snap. Finally, he let him go.

Aaron's body fell to the ground. The man who always made him laugh, the man who pushed Joshua to be more than he thought he could, the man who inspired Joshua with his energy and love was dead.

"Nooo!" Trudy ran from behind them, holding a metal pipe, and charged at Dedecus.

Dedecus pushed out his hand, palms outward into the air. Power surged out and rammed Trudy. Trudy flew backward and landed twenty feet away.

Joshua clenched his fists and began breathing fast and couldn't get enough breath in his lungs. He was hyperventilating. His vision grew hazy, and he trembled violently.

Conflicting thoughts thrashed wildly in his head as the rest of the world faded.

Mom?

This is all my fault.

Dad?

I'm having a panic attack. I need to breathe.

The angel was right.

Dedecus, his best friend since childhood, had murdered his parents in cold blood out of spite and anger at what they represented—the perfect life he'd never had.

"Joshua." Namid shook his shoulders, and he snapped back into reality.

He ran to where his mom had landed, her body crumpled and broken.

"Joshua?" a faint voice called out to him.

She was alive. His mother had opened her eyes. Her breaths were slow and short.

"I'm here, Mother." He reached over to her and watched his tears fall onto her dying body. "I'll get you to a hospital; everything will be all right."

She looked at him and swallowed once. "God is calling me home."

"No!" he shouted, "I still need you!"

"I love you, Joshua. I am so proud of you, and I know you will make a great leader for our people."

"You don't understand. I'm no leader. I couldn't even stop Dedecus."

His mother, who had always been there to pick him up when he fell and encourage him to press on, closed her eyes for the last time.

They're with God—the place he'd just been, a place of perfection and joy and love.

But he still needed them. He wasn't ready to be a leader or carry on without them. He was only seventeen, not even an adult until twenty when he would start his training. He was a little kid, too scared to even stand up to Namid's parents. Too foolish to stop Dedecus when he'd had a chance.

His parents were dead because of him—it was his fault that Dedecus had taken the stone.

He should've immediately told his parents about it when they'd first seen it. He should've made the jump and not fallen. He should've been able to convince Dedecus to put the stone back.

Now he was expected to pick up the pieces of the village and lead them. But he wasn't even sure if he could manage to pick up the pieces of himself.

Joshua did what he'd done when he was seven, and several kids at school had been bullying and teasing him—he clung to his mother and wept.

CHAPTER 14

FIDES VILLAGE, NOVITAS—DAY 1, YEAR 371

Namid gasped. She wrapped her arms around herself. The Judges of Mercy were dead, which technically meant Joshua was now co-ruler of the village, along with her parents.

"That's right!" Dedecus shouted. "I've destroyed your little symbol of a perfect life. How does it feel to have everything ripped away from you so suddenly? The feeling you're experiencing right now doesn't even compare to what I have to live with every single day!" His face turned even redder to match his glowing red eyes.

"How could you do this, Dedecus?" Namid cried out. "We're the ones who loved you and were your friends."

"That's what I thought, but then you two tried to stop me from fulfilling my destiny, not the destiny your cruel God had given me, but my true one, the destiny I shall create!" Dedecus screamed at them. "All my life, you've been holding me back from it! But not anymore!"

Several of the villagers used his distracted ranting to charge at him from the side with swords to prevent him from bringing more death and destruction upon Fides.

One man swung his sword, sending it straight into Dedecus's chest.

Dedecus doubled over and grasped at the hilt. Blood gushed from the wound.

He stood up straight and laughed. He rolled his piercing red eyes and ripped the piece of metal out, flinging it off to the side where it clanged against the ground. The wound healed instantly. He brushed the blood off his chest.

"Really?" Dedecus laughed, "Did you really think a little weapon could stop a god?" He held out his hand and grinned. "But if it's a sword fight, you want."

Dedecus held out his right hand, and a black hilt entwined with red spirals appeared in it. Shiny metal grew out of the hilt, glowing red.

Once the tip had formed, Dedecus tossed the sword into the air. It spun and landed back in his hand, and he sliced through the man who'd stabbed him. The man collapsed. Dead.

Another two charged at him. He dodged their blades by launching himself in between them and twisting his body. Once he'd passed the blades, he spun in the air and landed on his feet facing their backs.

He quickly cut the first man to pieces before he had a chance to turn around.

Dedecus swung at the second, and the man held up his sword to deflect the blow. When the two swords met, a loud clashing sound echoed in the air. The momentum and power of Dedecus were too great. His sword shattered through the other one like it was glass. Dedecus completed his swing, slamming through the man's neck.

One other with a sword dropped it and ran away. Dedecus flung his sword at him, and it spun like a cyclone in the air, slamming into the man's back and sending him crashing to the ground with a thud.

"This is all the Judges of Mercy's fault," Freda shouted, "I knew they were wrong in letting that trash survive in the first place." She grabbed at Namid and tried to pull her away.

Namid pulled her hand from her mother's grip and pushed her to the side. "Dedecus, this won't change or fix anything!"

"I've spent way too long trying to climb a mountain with no peak. With my sweat and blood, I'd climb up to prove I was worthy, to prove I wasn't my parents. But I'm done climbing that mountain of perfection to your little God. The law is dead. Grace is dead. Only I remain."

Namid swallowed hard, searching for any sign of their best friend. But, unfortunately, the glowing creature before her was not Dedecus.

No! Her heart cried out. *He has to be in there somewhere*

The one who'd always protected her from any of the villagers who tried to tell on her to her parents couldn't be gone forever.

Then she ran over to where Joshua lay over his mom's body, weeping. "Joshua, I'm sorry, but right now, I need your help." She shook his shoulders. "We need to remind Dedecus of who he is. We should sing that song we wrote together—the one we wrote about our friendship."

Joshua lifted his head and faced her. His eyes were red and puffy. Snot leaked from his nostrils, and he made no effort to wipe it. "I can't."

"More people will get hurt if we don't do something."

"No. Don't you see? This is all my fault, my judgment. There's no hope, no plan, no way out of this."

"Joshua, we have to try."

"You try. Dedecus was right. I'm a coward," Joshua said, dropping his head again.

Namid shook him, but he refused to move. Instead, she pressed her hands against her temple and looked around frantically.

She turned around, and Dedecus was standing behind her. She jumped.

"Please, Dedecus, I know you're in there somewhere. Please don't hurt us."

He stared down at Joshua. "Vulnerability is weakness. You're pathetic, Joshie."

Joshua didn't move.

"But fine. If you guys insist on staying in a world where you will never be good enough to appease your cruel God, then I'll spare the two of your lives. After everything we've been through, I will allow the two of you to live as long as you leave me alone. I will leave your pathetic village to pick up the pieces and shall create my own world—a better world—a world not confined by the crushing weight of your wrathful God. A world I shall call Transcendence!"

He struck the ground with his hand, sending a massive bolt of lightning through the air, shattering through hundreds of the villagers gathered around and sending them flying backward onto the ground.

A swirling wind enveloped Dedecus. His dark brown hair and bloodstained pants whipped in the gust.

With a flash, he was gone.

Everything was still. All of nature was trying to figure out what had happened, leaving the survivors to try to pick up the tiny, shattered fragments of their lives and somehow put them back together.

CHAPTER 15

MANNED SPACECRAFT CENTER, HOUSTON, TEXAS, EARTH—NOVEMBER 2, 1971

Jefferson leaned against the back wall of the conference room and yawned at the boring speech being given.

"The Apollo 15 mission was widely successful, bringing us back invaluable data," the general said in his briefing. "But now the time has come to get to work on Apollo 16, where our astronauts will continue to make use of the lunar roving vehicle. Each team will be given new projects for the launch date, April 16th. You are dismissed."

Jefferson rolled his eyes as all the scientists jabbered excitedly about the next project.

If only they knew what I'm about to do.

"Gent, a word."

Jefferson took his eyes off the small-brained scientists to the even-smaller-brained general who had come down to give everyone orders.

The man marched toward him, scowling.

"Sir?"

"What exactly is it that you do here? Because based on our funding, you seem to suck up a lot of money but don't contribute at all to the Apollo missions." General whatever-his-name-was glared at him, but all he could focus on was the man's big, fluffy black toupee.

"I oversee a project to explore beyond the solar system. I've constructed a telescope I designed to—"

"Spare the speech. Rumors around the base say you're not interested in just staring at stars. Rumors say you're building a teleportation device to actually travel to one."

It's not a teleportation device, you imbecile, and I'd like to send you to a star and watch you and your obvious toupee burn at one million degrees Fahrenheit.

"You must be mistaken," Jefferson said calmly. "Teleportation is science fiction."

The general narrowed his eyes. "I've heard a lot about you. You might be some super genius and have won that lawsuit, but it's my job to make sure we're not wasting our money. Now we're giving you a lot of money, so I will ask you again, what are you working on?"

"A telescope."

"We'll see." The general grabbed Jefferson's arm with a vise grip. "Take my officers and me to your office, and we'll see what our money is going to. And I promise you that if we see we've been funding some crazy teleportation device or any other insane projects, your smarts won't be able to get you out of trouble."

Jefferson's mind raced. As small-brained as this general was, one look in Jefferson's office would reveal a lot more than data from a telescope. He was so close to achieving his dream, but they would take all his data and revoke his access.

Jefferson grabbed the general's toupee and flung it into the crowd. It smacked a short, fat guy in the face, and everyone turned. The general went bug-eyed, and he instinctively let go of Jefferson's arm to cover his shiny, bald head with the overhead lights reflecting brightly on it.

People started laughing, and Jefferson took several steps backward.

"It was a fake. I win the bet," someone said.

"I order you to stop laughing." The general ran to get his toupee back. Jefferson seized on the opportunity and took off out the open door.

He was already halfway down the empty hallway when he heard, "Hey, stop that man!"

Jefferson's shoes slapped against the tile as he took several turns down the complex's labyrinth of hallways.

If he went for the door, he'd be free. But he'd left his research and documents in his office. He needed one particular string of numbers, and he couldn't let those heathens get all his research, not when he was so close to finally being free of their ignorance and corruption.

His office door came in sight, and he pushed his nonathletic body harder. He listened for the pounding of feet, but all he heard were his own.

The smell of smoke from the office next to his came to his nose. The first time he'd ever been glad to smell it.

He reached his office and flung open the door. The wind caused his priceless papers to fly everywhere, but that didn't matter since he'd be destroying his research anyway.

He glanced at the overstuffed shredder. *No time.*

Smoke seeped through the open door, and he ran into the hallway.

What the heathens meant for evil, God will use for the righteous.

He shoved the door open to the neighboring office, and a wall of smoke assaulted him. He immediately found his prize sitting on the desk—a small lighter.

"His office is down this way," someone shouted from the hallway.

Jefferson went back to his office, slammed his door shut, and locked it.

He needed one sheet of data that contained the celestial coordinates of the planet they were going to. A world he'd named Novitas, Latin for newness, which is what this world would be for them, a new chance to start over and make the world perfect and sinless like it was before the fall.

He grabbed the sheet off his desk and stuffed it into his pocket.

"I'm sorry, my wonderful research," he said as he gathered up all the papers in his office into a pile on the ground. Jefferson had copies of the important stuff back at the New Day Separatist meeting house, but his stomach hurt with all the priceless information he was about to destroy.

He flicked the lighter. It sparked, but a flame didn't appear.

Someone pounded on the door. "Open up, Gent!"

"Oh, come on," he coaxed the lighter. "Work." He tried it again. It caught on fire but burned his finger and quickly went out again. He winced.

"Even if I were drunk, I could come up with a better design." Not that he'd ever be caught drinking.

"Open this door, Gent!"

He flipped the starter again, and a flame appeared. He dropped the lighter into the pile, and the papers became engulfed in yellow and blue flames.

A slam shook the door. They were trying to knock it down.

He ran to the window and threw it open. His stomach lurched as he stared at the grass down below. "Why did they have to put me on the second story?" he muttered. Even if he made it to the ground safely, there's no way he would make it out. The guards would surround him instantly.

Another pounding came at the door.

He needed a distraction and scanned the room for a solution. If he moved the desk in front of the door, would it only slow them down? *What else?* The fire had become a blaze. Smoke rose lazily to the ceiling right by the smoke detector. *The smoke detector!*

He threw open the filing cabinets and flung more paper onto the fire. Then he threw his chair in.

Beep, beep, beep. The alarm blared, rattling his eardrums.

"The complex is on fire!" someone shouted. The pounding of footsteps ran away from his door.

When they'd installed the smoke detectors, he thought they were incredibly dumb. One goes off, and it connects to the entire complex, making all the alarms go off. There had to be a more efficient system of tracking the fire. But once again, the stupidity of others was his blessing.

He pulled himself out onto the narrow window ledge and sharply inhaled.

About eight feet, so time in the air will be 0.705 seconds at a velocity of 22.69 feet per second, so that's an acceleration of 32.18 feet per second squared.

He shut his eyes and jumped, hitting the ground feet first and quickly crumpling into a rolling ball to spread the impact across his body.

He groaned. His feet and sides would have a serious bruise, but he'd live.

People streamed out of the complex doors, and he quickly merged with the crowd, making sure to avoid the general or his men.

He limped to his black Chrysler and sped off, the celestial coordinates to Novitas tucked safely in his pocket.

CHAPTER 16

FIDES VILLAGE, NOVITAS—DAY 2, YEAR 371

Adia sat in the middle of the rubble of the life she'd carefully built around her for fifteen years of marriage. The only person in her life who'd ever given her a reason to fight against the storm—the only person who ever told her she was worth something—was now buried beneath a pile of debris.

She grunted as she tried to get her shaking muscles to exert strength they didn't possess. The large, wooden beam wouldn't budge. Lincoln was somewhere underneath this rubble, and she would find him.

For the hundredth time in the past day since the attack from Dedecus that left her a homeless widow, she looked back at everything she'd lost. Lincoln had been a great man, an elder in the church, and the only one who'd seen her as something other than the stupid little girl her father had told her she was.

She spotted their calendar in the middle of the rubble. Today had been marked off as their fifteenth wedding anniversary. The day was supposed to be the glorious reminder of their deep love for each other. Now, the day would always be a reminder of her grief. Lincoln had been planning a surprise for her. He'd been excited about it all week. She'd never know what the gift was.

She tossed the calendar aside and continued digging and tried to lift up one of the large pieces of wall that had fallen over by pushing her shoulder up against it.

"Here, let me help you with that," someone said, running over to rescue her.

She could almost hear the man's thoughts. Oh, look at that pathetic Adia, always needing someone to save her.

"I've almost got it," she grunted.

"Sure, you do," the guy said.

Her neighbor, Trevor, pushed hard and quickly knocked the wall out of the way.

How pathetic. You can't even push over a wall.

"Can I help you with this, Ms. Rese?"

Now that Lincoln was gone, would she have to start going by her given last name? She hated the last name Gent and the expectations that came with it. Being a descendant of Jefferson Gent meant you were a genius, something she was not.

For a moment, she thought of going to her parents.

Adia's father, Jerold Gent, was a brilliant man. He'd designed the solar-powered generators that ran every house and building and created many inventions that helped with irrigation and food production. He was a man who was so smart no one could ever understand or relate to him as he rattled on about scientific principles. But, unfortunately, he was a man who could never quite understand what was wrong with his only child. Her emotions never fit into his perfectly constructed world of logic. She'd grown up never being able to live up to his expectations, never being able to understand what he was talking about.

She'd heard from some of the others that had survived the attack. She hadn't spoken to them in years and couldn't bear to hear mother's long sigh and see her father's perpetual frown. She was thirty-seven, but whenever she saw her parents, she became a five-year-old girl again who could never live up to her father's brilliance.

"No, I'm good. Thanks," she muttered.

"No problem," Trevor said. "I can't believe Dedecus would do this." He gestured to the destruction before them. "I always went to the Judge of Mercy's church, but now they're gone, the village has been destroyed, and a little boy who was best friends with the attacker is now the Judge of Mercy. Maybe Marvin and Freda were right. Look at what showing mercy got us?"

Adia ignored him and went back to digging.

"Do you need some help?" he asked again.

"Please, just go away."

After several long moments, she heard Trevor walk away. He seemed nice, but she had to do something for herself—for once.

Lincoln was the only one who'd ever told her she was smart, the only one who thought she was beautiful, the only one who could be her life preserver and rescue her from drowning in the depths of her depression. Her life preserver had been ripped away. She had nothing.

Adia picked up a framed picture of the two of them that had been taken in the weeks after they got married. The glass was shattered. She carefully removed the picture from the frame.

They were standing on a mountain south of the village. He'd taken her hiking that day. He'd always encouraged her to take risks and to make the most out of life by doing things she never thought she would or could do. They'd made it to the top of the mountain as the sun was setting, and that's where they'd taken the picture.

They stood hugging each other with the glory of the mountains and forest behind them. Everything was bathed in the golden and pink light of the sun, taking a bow for another hard day's work.

Even after a long day of hiking, Lincoln was glowing. Every pixel in the image of him shone with his thoughts of unconditional love toward her.

Looking at her own face in the picture—into her own eyes, she could see love for Lincoln, but something else swirled within her too—a familiar bully of a character trait that had stuck with and within her ever since she was only four years old, and her father first frowned at her after she'd been unable to solve a math problem he'd given her. It had been the first time he called her stupid.

She placed the picture on her chest and squeezed it.

"Happy anniversary, Lincoln," she whispered. "I'll be joining you soon."

CHAPTER 17

PEACEFUL PLATEAU, NOVITAS—DAY 4, YEAR 371

Joshua and Namid sat on the edge of the cliff of Peaceful Plateau, overlooking what was left of the village.

Up here, everything was perfect, a stark contrast to the broken chaos below. The white cliffs and Emerald Waterfall acted as a drop-off from the lush grass and golden Decus flowers. The flowers had a bright green stem with baby blue pedals and a golden trim around the leaves. They seemed to glow as they slowly waved in the wind. Golden-tipped butterflies lazily flew from flower to flower, collecting nectar.

Up here, Joshua could almost forget the events of the past four days. "573 …"

Namid sat in silence.

"How could our best friend kill 573 people?"

They stared ahead at what only four days ago was Fides Village. Now all they saw was rubble.

"How could the little boy we met eight years ago now be a murderer? And how am I supposed to be the Judge of Mercy now? I'm not an amazing leader like my parents. I'm just the scared child who couldn't stop even his best friend." Joshua's shoulders sagged lower. He shut his eyes and ran his hand through his hair. "We should've stopped him—that makes it our fault too. And does this mean my parents were wrong? We showed him mercy from the very beginning, and now look what happened."

Namid took his hand. In normal times, she would've never been allowed to make skin contact with a guy. In normal times, she wouldn't have been allowed to be sitting there with him. But these were no longer normal times.

Holding her hand, Joshua let his breathing slow.

"I better get back," he said to Namid. "The council has called an emergency meeting to discuss what to do next."

Normally, new judges would be trained to take on the role starting on their twentieth birthday—the day they officially become adults—until their thirtieth birthday when their parents would retire from being the judge. Then they'd throw an elaborate appointment ceremony for the new judge and their spouse, followed by a lavish celebration.

At only seventeen, Joshua had not yet begun his training. And while they would have the appointment ceremony in two days, no one felt like celebrating. He didn't want to give a big speech, and without his parents there, the appointment ceremony would feel hollow.

"Don't let my parents get to you, okay?" Namid looked away from the village and turned her tear-filled eyes toward him.

They stood and headed down the well-worn path to the village. He didn't let go of her hand until they reached the first decimated home.

Joshua walked up to the building where the council was meeting and let out a long sigh.

While the two leaders were the Judge of Mercy and the Judge of Justice, a council of seven others had been elected by the community to help the judges make decisions.

His parents had never enjoyed the council meetings. Eleven people in a room, including the judges, argued and rarely agreed on anything—twelve when the lead scientist Jerold Gent joined them. Now that his parents and four of the council members were dead, that left six, including him. The decrease in people didn't mean decision-making would be easier.

Joshua stepped into the stuffy meeting hall and braced himself for the hours of arguing and accusing that was to come.

"Ah, so good of you to make it, boy." Rupert, one of the council members, had disliked his parents and hadn't been shy in his criticism of Joshua either. He was a warrior and led the village's small army—a fact he greatly prided himself on. Although, the worst thing they'd ever fought had been tree bears that wandered into the village looking for food during the winter.

Namid's parents glared at him as he quickly made his way to the front of the room and to the empty seat.

"Now, before we begin, I urge the council to agree this child should not be a part of our leadership," Marvin, Namid's father, said as he stood before the council. "He is inexperienced and too young to help lead. He has yet to even begin his judge training."

"Now, wait a minute, Marvin," Don Davis, one of his parents' closest friends and Joshua's only true ally in the room, stood up for him. "The law is that once either the new judge turns thirty or both the current judges die, the title is passed down to the next generation. So it doesn't matter how old Joshua is, and just because his parents didn't agree with your harsh views doesn't change the fact that he has every right to be here."

Don was a great guy, but he had little respect from the other council members because he didn't have much money. Something Marvin, Freda, and Rupert never let him forget.

"Fine," Marvin said and sat down.

Sharon was the third and last surviving council member—and the current head member—a title that rotated each meeting. Sharon was a difficult person to read and was a woman of few words. Joshua's parents had told him that no one could ever tell what she was thinking or what she'd vote for or against until she did.

He gave a silent prayer of thanks to God that it wasn't Rupert's turn to be the head member.

Jerold Gent sat in the back, scanning some papers and mumbling incoherently.

Sharon made her way to the front of the room.

"Before we begin, we need to take a moment to honor the leaders we lost, regardless of your views. We lost our Judges of Mercy and four council members. Let's have a moment of silence for them."

For the first time ever, the council was quiet.

"Today, we've come together to discuss the recent attack on our community, how to facilitate clean up and rebuilding, and ways to prevent another attack from occurring."

Joshua shifted uncomfortably in his father's seat. He was sweating in the suit he had to wear.

Followers of the Judges of Mercy wore light and loose clothing, but his parents had always worn suits for the formal meetings.

The tie around his neck felt like a noose.

"As we all know," Sharon continued, "the horrible attacks that took place three days ago were perpetrated by Dedecus, a friend of our newest member, Joshua. Joshua, would you care to elaborate on how this happened?"

All eyes turned to Joshua.

"Sure ... so um, a few days ago, he and I found a stone in the caves behind the waterfall along with a note that said it held the power to create and be like God—"

"And why didn't you come to us immediately, boy?" Marvin stood to face the council and pointed at Joshua.

"This just proves my point. Joshua is nothing but a child. We need experienced and wise people leading, not a foolish child who is partly responsible for this whole mess."

"Sit down, Marvin, and let him continue," Sharon said, rolling her eyes.

Attention turned back to Joshua.

He tried to hide the tears threatening to escape his eyes. This whole incident was his fault. Marvin was right—he wasn't worthy of being a leader. He wasn't worthy of his parent's legacy.

"Dedecus wanted to use it, but I stopped him, and we left. Later, he realized we'd forgotten something in the caverns, so we went back." He had to be careful not to reveal that Namid had been with them. "Then ... um ... I ... uh ... kinda fell off the cliff and ... died."

Everyone stared at him in shock. Even Jerold looked up from his research.

"Dedecus used the Creativity Stone to bring me back to life, but then something else happened—"

"Get on with it, child," Rupert said.

Joshua tried to stand up straighter and stop his voice from warbling.

"So ... um ... Dedecus was angry at the village and God for treating him badly, and the Creativity Stone magnified that rage and caused him to attack us."

Everyone was silent for a moment. Then as if with a flip of a switch, everyone broke into arguments, and Rupert yelled at Joshua for allowing such a thing to happen.

Don tried to defend him.

Marvin shook his Bible and yelled at Joshua for insinuating it was their fault Dedecus attacked.

Freda was handing out an "I told you so" to everyone, saying the Judges of Mercy were wrong, and they should've killed the product of sin when he was a baby to avoid the judgment now cast upon them.

Joshua stood in the middle of the room. He hoped no one noticed the sweat stains developing on his shirt. His parents would've known how to handle this meeting.

"Would everyone shut up!" Sharon yelled. Once everyone settled, she turned to the wild-haired man, Jerold, who had sat quietly in the corner. "You've been studying the effects of this stone for the past four days, correct?"

Jerold stood, and papers dropped from his lap, but he ignored them. "That is correct. The Creativity Stone, as this juvenile has referred to it, is a fascinating anomaly I could spend centuries studying. Instead, Dedecus took it. However, based on my observations and sensors, I've been able to study the unique energy that comes from the stone. What I found most interesting is my analysis of the sword he seemingly created. While maintaining that specific energy between its atoms, the sword itself seems to be a sword. Something, I can assure you, is scientifically impossible."

"But he did it without any effort," Don said.

"Exactly. And now that I've heard more of the circumstances, I'd love to study where the stone was first discovered as well as you, young Joshua." Jerold turned to him.

"Me?"

"Precisely. From all appearances, it seems that while the stone's destructive capabilities cause only minor entanglements between the object and energy, its creative capabilities seem to have a very different effect. It actually changes the molecular structure and stores the energy inside the object itself. If my hypothesis is correct, your life being restored likely brought drastic changes to your body, even if the extent of those have yet to reveal themselves."

"Anyway, Gent." Freda rolled her eyes. "I'm sure we're all worried about another appearance of that monster. Do you have a solution?"

"Well, I have several fascinating theories, which is why I'd greatly appreciate the inspection of Joshua here, but—"

"Would you quit rambling old man?" Freda slammed her hand against her chair's armrest. "Give us a solution."

"A solution? I don't have one. And *if* my theories are correct, it seems that all of us except Joshua would be at the complete mercy of Dedecus."

Except me? He did a mental scan of his body. He felt fine. Great even. Was there something wrong with him?

"So that leaves us with only one option." Marvin stood. "573 people died four days ago. This was a terrible tragedy, albeit one that could've been avoided," he said, pausing to glare at Joshua. "Not only has the whole village been destroyed, but it's entirely possible that Dedecus could come back and attack again, something Gent here says we have no way to defend against. As my wife said, we're suffering God's wrath at allowing the sin of our people to fester like a weed. And when weeds have overtaken the garden to the extent where nothing can be planted, all that can be done is plant a new garden.

"You all know our history. We came from a corrupt world that God had turned his back on, and now we see him turning his back again. If we stay here, we'll become like the world we left—corrupted and sinful—a world where cursing, drugs, divorce, atheism, and having sex out of wedlock are all commonplace. In recent generations, we've seen a turn toward this as the mercy followers push further extreme, accepting wicked behaviors in the name of love."

Don stood. "We are not blindly accepting behaviors."

"In previous generations," Marvin ignored Don, "having sex outside of marriage would be taken care of swiftly. But as the clothes get shorter and shorter, and the weekly celebrations thrown by the Judges of Mercy grow wilder and wilder, God grows more disgusted with us."

"Nothing bad happens at those parties," Don shouted. "They're simply a fellowship opportunity."

Marvin glared at Don. "No, it's clear that—"

"Just get to the point, Marvin," Sharon said. "We're not here to rehash old debates."

Freda stood, ignoring her husband's protest as she took over what he was trying to say. "Before all of this happened, Jerold and the other scientists discovered another planet that is suitable for life. So, we're going to leave this place and settle there, using the same teleportation device our ancestors used to get here. I think we can all agree that the Judges of Mercy's faulty theology was what led to this, so this new village will have much stricter laws. Now, I know that this seems like a drastic step, but I see this new place as God giving us redemption for our corruption and sin. And just as the fig tree in the good book was cursed and withered, so will we if we don't bear the fruit of holiness."

Everyone remained quiet for one long moment.

"That is the most preposterous thing I've ever heard!" Don yelled. And once again, the council plunged into loud arguments.

Joshua stayed quiet.

"You must hold them together," the angel's words came back to him. "After Dedecus's attack, many of them will try to leave, but you must stay. Then, God will redeem, and blessings will flow into the land he's given you."

Everything the angel had told him was now happening. But the thought of arguing with the Judge of Justice prevented his mouth from opening. Each council member was older, smarter, and more experienced than he. Why couldn't God use one of them? Joshua wasn't great at giving amazing speeches or inspiring people. He was awkward and shy. He'd never be able to convince the Judges of Justice,

Rupert, or Sharon that they were wrong when his parents had tried for decades and couldn't get them to budge.

What's wrong with moving? It could make things easier since they wouldn't have to worry about Dedecus coming back or about having to clear the mounds of rubble that would take weeks to clear before they could actually start to rebuild.

A memory came back to him. Every child in Fides went through a dedication ceremony where they would dedicate their lives to Jesus, sing a song that spoke to them about God and their journey, tell everyone their testimony, and be baptized. During Joshua's, when he was fifteen years old, he'd stuttered and messed up both the song and his testimony.

His dedication ceremony was supposed to be a time of celebration and holiness. But it had been ruined. He would remember that day as the first time he knew he would never live up to his parent's legacy or be the great leaders they were. That night he'd asked if it were possible for someone else to inherit the role of judge. *You will be an amazing leader, my son,* his mom had said with confidence in her voice.

But he hadn't even been able to stop his best friend.

Joshua stayed quiet as Marvin, Don, Sharon, Rupert, Freda, and Jerold argued for several hours, their differences and lack of respect for each other ripping at the seams of the already-tattered tapestry of Fides Village.

CHAPTER 18

WHITE MOUNTAIN RANGE, NOVITAS—
DAY 4, YEAR 371

What have I done?

Dedecus stood atop a mountain, his entire body shuddering violently.

You're a murderer. The village was right about you. I never should have trusted you, Joshua's voice said. At this point, he couldn't really tell whether he was hearing things or if Joshua was actually there.

I was always there for you, always loved you, but what you've done is unredeemable, Joshua's voice said.

"Wait, I can fix it!"

It's too late for that.

Ever since taking his revenge on the village four days ago, he'd been up here, unable to stop the violent shaking that had taken over his body. He tried to calm his body and mind, but the Creativity Stone that pulsed inside him only amplified his emotions, and right now, his emotions were pulling him in every direction imaginable.

Remember the first time we all met? He heard Joshua say. *I was ten years old, and my parents were worried about me because I would never leave the house and had no friends. So, they said I wasn't allowed to go into my room until I tried to make a friend.*

Dedecus tried to smile at the memory they'd retold countless times. "Just after my parents had died in an avalanche, the Judges of Justice said terrible things about my parents at their own funeral. To get revenge, little ten-year-old me threw rocks at their window, but the rocks bounced off because all I could find were small pebbles from the gravel path." Dedecus's trembling began to subside a little.

Yep, but you didn't realize Namid was the only one in the house at the time, and she took it upon herself to defend the house. They were painting one of the rooms yellow, so she decided to dump the paint out the window and onto the attacker. Of course, you were too far away from the window to get hit, but she didn't know that. Meanwhile, I was walking past the house and heard the rocks smacking against the window. Not knowing what to do, I hid in the bushes outside the house so the attacker wouldn't see me.

"That didn't work. Namid was up in the second-story window and saw someone duck behind the bush, so she dumped the can of bright-yellow paint all over *you*. You looked like a yellow crayon. I heard the commotion and went to check it out while Namid came down to confront her attacker. And that's how we all met and quickly became friends."

I was so embarrassed, and it took me a week to get the paint out of my hair.

Dedecus's vision started to clear. He could see the clouds above him and the peaks of mountains and tops of palm trees spread out below him.

The voice grew cold and emotionless. *If I could take it all back, I would.*

"You have no idea what I've been through! I was ten years old when Marvin walked up to the pulpit at my parents' funeral and told me they got what they deserved, and I should've died with them just because my parents had me before they got married." He'd never set foot in a church again.

But you had me. You had Namid. We loved you and were there for you.

"Don't pretend you had my back. Remember when we were eleven? We were playing tag together, and I was having a good time for once. Then I crashed into a cart of fruit, and suddenly everyone yelled at me and called me a black mark on their hypocritical perfection. I stood there sobbing, and what did you do? Nothing. In fact, I can't think of a single time you defended me. You've always been too much of a coward to do anything."

You're calling me a bad friend? That's ridiculous, considering you just murdered my parents.

His best friend's face flashed through his mind, the Creativity Stone creating every horrible detail of the image. Joshua stood there, broken and covered in dirt and tears, as he looked up at Dedecus's triumphant glow after watching the life of his parents being ripped away from him. He'd never seen Joshua look like that before. He was completely destroyed—a feeling Dedecus knew well.

Why would you do that to me?

"I ... I never ..." Dedecus collapsed to the ground.

Adrenaline from the stone sped through him, and he shot back up.

"No! Finally, you understand what it's like to not live in your perfect little bubble of happiness. What you're feeling is just a tiny sliver of what I've experienced for the past eight years. At least you still have your little village of hypocrites."

The image of Joshua standing before him opened his mouth to respond.

"Enough!" Dedecus screamed. A blast of energy shot out from his body, shattering the image of Joshua and creating a mini avalanche of rocks sliding down the mountain.

"I have the Creativity Stone now. I refuse to be the orphan trash or the black mark."

He thought about staying in this world and making them bow down to him. But as wonderful as making them grovel at his feet and serve him would be, he couldn't bear the constant memories of always being the outcast, and he didn't want to be trapped inside the laws of nature that guided this universe.

Instead, he would create a new world—a world of true perfection. He could create a world that was anything he wanted, where the only limit would be his imagination. A world where he was the one and only god, and he would never be judged or treated as an outsider. He would be worshipped and adored by his creation.

His body became very still, and the agonizing memories fled to the far corners of his mind at the thought of what he could do, the thought of what he could become.

For the first time since he'd arrived at the mountain, he grinned. He was finally ready to begin.

"Goodbye, Josh. I'm sorry."

Then he struck his palm on the ground, and a tunnel of light and wind enveloped him.

A bolt of power shot out of him, creating a creature to guard the mountain in case anyone came looking for him. Whoever came up here would get quite a nasty surprise.

Then he disappeared from the world and universe into a new universe he would create himself.

For now, emptiness and blackness surrounded Dedecus. He grinned at the thoughts of what his world could be—at what he could be.

What colors would he use? What kinds of animals would he create? Would there be strong gravity on the planet, or would everyone just float? What kind of people would he create? Would there be big deserts, oceans, mountains, or forests?

Everything and anything was possible. From the stars to the stones, he could create them all in his image. His only limit was his imagination. And he couldn't wait to get started.

CHAPTER 19

RIVER OAKS, HOUSTON, TEXAS, EARTH— NOVEMBER 10, 1971

Steven Waters pulled up next to the Lamborghini in the driveway of his parents' mansion in River Oaks.

Only his father was there. His mother had probably gone out to get another facelift.

The house was three stories high and full of rooms they never used. It was surrounded on all sides by flowers and perfectly trimmed bushes that made him sneeze. Steven had nearly choked the first time he'd heard the price tag of this place. Growing up, he'd only invited a friend over once. He'd known that friendship was over as soon as he saw the look of envy in the other boy's eyes.

He got out of the car and slogged over to the door.

I'm just here to see Lisa. That's it.

He opened the door and shut it quietly behind him.

The sound of his father's voice in the office down the hall made his stomach churn.

He quietly crept upstairs and down the hallway. He knocked softly on a door.

The door swung open wide, and his little seven-year-old sister stood there, a huge grin on her face.

"Steven!" she shouted and ran to hug him.

"Shh, I don't want Dad to know I'm here." He squeezed his little sister tightly.

His parents had always only planned to have one kid, but then all their friends had two, and so when Steven was sixteen, they'd had Lisa.

"I missed you so much. Daddy said you were a traitor, but I knew you'd come back."

Lisa was the greatest gift God had given him during his late teens. His father was always in court, meeting with clients, or drinking. His mother was always working in the garden, throwing parties, or getting another facelift. So that left him to raise Lisa, a job he loathed at first but which quickly became the highlight of his life. To her, he wasn't a failure and didn't have to be anything he wasn't.

"I'm sorry it's been too long. But I'm here now."

"Are you staying forever?"

He bit his lip. "You know Daddy doesn't want me here."

"But I do." She stuck out her lip.

He bent down on his knees and pushed her pigtails behind her shoulders. "I came to say goodbye." *Do not cry. Do not cry.* "I'm going to go away for a while."

She blinked and tilted her head. "But where are you going?"

"It's hard to explain."

"Will you be back for my dance recital next week? Mommy's been having me practice really hard."

He sighed. "No, it's going to be a lot longer than that."

"Oh, well, can I come with you?"

The laws of the New Day Separatists came to mind. *Remember to cast out the defiled.*

Was Lisa defiled? He felt nauseous thinking about anyone calling his precious little sister defiled. Surely, they wouldn't label her that way.

"No, you have to stay here."

She started to cry. "No, I hate it here. It's been no fun without you."

He pulled her into another hug. Her teardrops dripped onto his shoulder.

"What are you doing here?" a cold voice said.

Steven was ripped away from Lisa and thrown into the railing along the hallway balcony.

His father, dressed in his normal black suit, glared down at him.

"I was just—"

"I told you to never show your face here again. We have a pristine reputation that you nearly ruined."

Lisa walled and ran to Steven "Daddy, stop—"

"Quiet! Go to your room." He picked her up and put her in the bedroom, slamming the door behind her.

Is that the last time I'll get to see my little sister's face?

His father grabbed Steven by the collar and yanked him up. "Look what you've done, upsetting her like that. Now get out."

Anger isn't righteous. Anger isn't righteous. Whenever he felt something bad like anger, he would shove it deep down inside him, never to be seen again. But hearing Lisa's crying behind the closed door, he snapped.

"What have *I* done? *You're* the one who left me to practically raise her. *You're* the one who kicked me out of the house just because I'm not a part of your cult of atheists who think they're better than everyone else. *You're* the one who cares more about your wretched image than doing what's right or actually caring about anyone."

His father took a step back.

"How does it feel to be on the receiving end of an angry rant? Not good, huh? Well, now you know how I've felt every day of my life when all I wanted was to be acceptable in your eyes."

"I—"

"No, I'm tired of your excuses. You want me to get out? Fine. Then I'll leave. And you'll never see me again."

Steven pushed past his dad and stormed down the stairs. He opened the door to see his startled mother, who was starting to look like one of those creepy china dolls she kept buying Lisa. Lisa always hated those dolls.

"Steven?"

He brushed past her and got in his car. He yanked the car into reverse and shot out of the driveway.

He gave one more glance at his childhood home and family before he drove off for good. His mother was still looking at him in surprise. His father—that man was no longer his father. He was just Harold. Harold was standing at the door with an expression Steven couldn't place. He thought it might be regret, but that was impossible. Harold's motto was *regrets are for losers*. And peeking through pink curtains on an upstairs window was a little girl with red hair and pigtails.

"Goodbye, Lisa."

CHAPTER 20

HOUSTON MEMORIAL PARK, HOUSTON, TEXAS—
NOVEMBER 12, 1971

Harold Waters shoved his foot down on the gas pedal, pushing his Lamborghini to eighty-five miles per hour. The speed limit was seventy, but he'd gotten out of countless tickets with his smooth talking and connections.

He hadn't told anyone where he was going. But through his network, he had been able to figure out the New Day Separatists had some big meeting at Memorial Park. And he was sure that his son would be there.

Something had snapped in him when Steven had yelled at him two days ago. He was normally too busy to sleep much, but for the past two days, he hadn't been able to sleep for a very different reason. He couldn't get his son's face out of his head.

He'd pulled out an old photograph album and stared for hours at pictures of Steven as a baby. There were very few of him in it; he'd always been too busy to spend time with his son.

A visionary, they'd called him. Magnetic and irresistible. He'd risen quickly through law school and accepted a job at a prestigious law firm. Between his persuasive tongue and his eye for advancement and deals, he gained a fortune in the time it took normal people to use the bathroom.

But does any of it matter? He didn't like these thoughts he'd been having ever since his son had stormed past him. Now he could only pray—another thing he never did—that it wasn't too late to save the relationship.

Harold slammed to a stop at the entrance to the park. In front of him, barriers and government vehicles blocked off the sidewalk. Government officials canvased the area. He leaped out of the car and knocked over the barricade, aiming straight at the man with the most stars on his uniform.

"What is going on here, general?" he asked.

"Sir, this is a government operation. Please step back behind the barriers." The man had a horrendous black toupee on that didn't match his gray facial hair.

"I will not. My name is Harold Waters, and I am a very important lawyer. My son is—" his voice caught in his throat. *What's happening to me?* "My son is Steven Waters, and he was supposed to be here at this park for a meeting."

The general gave him a second glance. "Is your son one of the New Day Separatists?"

The New Day Separatists were a fringe cult of orthodox Christians who were unsatisfied with society and wanted to remain pure. Harold's law firm had taken one of their leaders, Jefferson Gent, to court several years ago, and Harold had represented the case. It had been a job he'd eagerly taken.

He wished he hadn't. Something had changed in his son when he watched the trial. Suddenly, Steven was no longer interested in following him around or being a lawyer.

Harold sighed. "Yes."

"I'm sorry, sir. They're gone."

"What do you mean they're gone? There were a hundred of these fanatics that were supposed to meet here today, and you're saying they just disappeared?"

The general glanced back and forth. "Yes, that is what I'm saying. Their leader, Dr. Gent, is a crazy scientist, and he built some kind of portal device. Now he seems to have taken all of them off to some other planet, where they're supposed to set up their own world."

"No. That's ridiculous." Harold rushed past the man. The field was roped off, but he knocked it down. *There has to be a clue, something that will lead me to Steven.*

He noticed several large areas where the grass had been pressed down. They must have brought a lot of supplies with them.

From behind him, the general said, "Sir, if you'll just come with me."

"No." He dropped to his knees. He couldn't remember the last time his custom-tailored pants had touched the ground, but who cares about pants?

"I'm sorry, Steven, please forgive me."

As Steven stepped into their new world, Novitas, he was awed by its simplistic beauty. They were in a large clearing covered in grass, and up above, a yellow sun was high in the green-tinted sky. Surrounding them on one side was what he assumed to be a forest, but one unlike anything he'd ever seen.

Ignoring the others carrying boxes of supplies and dragging sheep, pigs, cows, and other animals that had made the trip with them, he raced over to the trees.

They looked like palm trees with tall green branches jutting out the top that blocked out most of the sunlight and created a dark and mysterious look to the forest. On the tree trunks were what looked like green hairs about an inch long.

Steven stroked the green hairs and grinned. Something as simple as a tree had become wondrous. The small hairs were soft and tickled, like a feather.

He turned around and stared with wonder at some towering white cliffs. They shimmered in the sunlight, standing as towers of protection over them.

Then a thundering waterfall caught his attention. The falling water was a clear but shimmery, sparkling, emerald green. The water crashed down from the cliffs and fed into a small river that traversed the edge of the clearing.

Jefferson Gent stood by the river where he'd stuck some sort of metal device into it that looked out of place with their new pastoral surroundings.

"The water's safe," Jefferson declared to those gathered.

He spun around, arms wide, beaming at the incredible new world they had the joy of exploring.

Lisa would love this place. The thought faded his smile, and he dropped his arms.

He missed his little sister. He even missed his mother and father.

This would pass, though, he assured himself. He didn't know most of the people, so he would simply have to make new friends.

I'm doing the right thing.

Novitas would be perfect, free from all the sin and evil that corrupted everyone, his family included.

"Waters, quit standing there gawking and help."

The time for sightseeing and reflection was over. Steven sighed. "Coming."

CHAPTER 21

FIDES VILLAGE, NOVITAS—DAY 6, YEAR 371

Joshua sighed and stared at himself in the mirror. He looked ridiculous in his father's suit they'd salvaged from the rubble of his house. His father was six feet tall, while Joshua was only five-foot-four. The entire thing engulfed him, and his fingers barely poked out the sleeves. Yet somehow, the tie around his neck threatened to strangle him.

The suit wasn't the only thing that didn't fit.

Today was his appointment ceremony. A day of celebrating the new judge. Normally this would involve a huge celebration in the church where everyone attended. But the church had been destroyed, and over half the village had chosen to boycott the ceremony, refusing to acknowledge the boy who'd played a part in destroying Fides.

Not even Namid would be there. His only remaining friend had been forced to join her parents in the protest against him.

"I am proud to receive the honor of being your newest Judge of Mercy," he recited into the mirror. His speech needed to be perfect. Maybe then they'd finally respect him.

He glanced behind him in the mirror where his dad should have been standing.

He could almost see his dad's smile and hear him say— I'm so proud of you, son. You'll do great today!

But, imagining what his dad would say wasn't the same as hearing him say it.

Joshua turned from the mirror. "Let's get this over with."

He walked to the door of the makeshift hut they'd thrown together to allow people to change without being seen naked since most buildings and homes had been destroyed.

He opened the door and was greeted by a couple hundred people lining the path. Several clapped for him while the rest just stood there, watching him.

"Coward," someone in the back of the crowd yelled. Everyone else stayed silent.

Joshua glanced up and bit his lip. Above them, the sky was yellow and filled with troubling, churning clouds. The sky on Novitas was always a light green with at most a few clouds. Something seemed wrong, but, of course, nothing was normal anymore.

Don and Sharon came up to him. Normally the whole council and other judges would be there to welcome him and officiate the appointment. But half the leaders were dead, and Rupert and the Judges of Justice were boycotting.

Don put his hand on Joshua's shoulder. "You look great, just like your dad."

"Have you seen the sky? I've never seen it that color before," Joshua said. "Maybe Jerold would have an idea about what's going on."

"It'll be okay. We'll figure it out later. But right now, it's your big day, and nothing will ruin it."

Nothing except my parents being dead, my best friend becoming a murderer, half the village hating me, and ominous clouds in the sky.

A deep crashing noise filled the air as fingers of red-tinted light made webs across the sky. Four bolts reached down and slammed into the ground. One immediately in front of them on the path.

Joshua's eyes went wide, and the hairs on his arms and legs shot up.

The ground in front of them was burned and smoldered.

People screamed and ran.

"Dedecus is back!" someone yelled.

The clouds swirled above them, a deep red that blocked out the sun.

"What is that stuff?" Joshua cried.

"It's lightning," Don grabbed his arm. "Something that was apparently common on Earth, but we've never seen here before."

"What do we do?"

"We need to get the people to safety."

More bolts shot across the sky as torrential rainfall crashed down on their heads, instantly drenching them.

Joshua pushed his wet hair out of his eyes and glanced around frantically. They had no shelter to protect them from the rain or strange bolts of energy.

Lightning lit up the sky again, allowing him to see better. But, unfortunately, the hospital was too far away. The best option was getting everyone into the palm forest, the tall canopy of trees would protect them, and the long leaves would keep them from getting too wet.

"Everyone, get to the trees!" He yelled as loud as he could to be heard over the downpour.

They ran to the forest and crowded under the palm trees near the edge.

What if Dedecus has come back? What if he attacks again and kills us all?

A bleating sheep ran past them. They'd probably been frightened by the lightning and had broken fences down— and after all that time they'd spent collecting all the animals after the first attack.

Lightning flashed again, illuminating more figures running toward them.

Gent ran up to him and shook him. "You foolish boy, what are you doing?"

"I—"

"Did you not learn anything about Earth? Lightning is attracted to the highest object. So, by having people stand under trees, you're practically inviting the electricity to cook us."

Lightning flashed again, striking from the sky and slamming into one of the trees above them. It was instantly charred and sent the person clinging to it flying backward.

"What have I done." Joshua ran to the man.

He appeared to have been electrocuted. His flesh was sizzling, and he had no heartbeat.

Jerold grabbed Joshua's shoulder and pulled him up. "Forget him unless you want everyone but you to join him."

Everyone but me?

The sky lit up again.

"What do I do?"

"There are caves near the bottom of the Pearl Cliffs. We need to get everyone there. And we need to crouch low as we run."

"Everyone, follow us," Joshua yelled.

They ran. The ground was muddy, and the river had swollen to twice its normal size, spilling out onto the grass. Lightning flashed all around them.

"What is causing this?" Joshua shouted to Gent as they ran.

"The energy frequency appears to be the same as the Creativity Stone. However, the only way for me to verify involves holding a big metal rod into the sky."

"So, Dedecus is back."

Joshua stumbled forward, nearly tripping in the mud. The lower half of his suit pants were covered in mud.

"Not necessarily. It seems more likely that since he left this world to create his own, but there still appears to be a tether between the two places. The incredible amount of power he's using wherever he is—is creating chaos in our world."

They were almost at the caves. But if the downpour didn't stop soon, the caves might start filling with water and drown them. Joshua decided to keep his mouth shut, though—his decision-making had already killed one person today.

"So, this will continue?"

"There seems to be a high probability of intermittent storms. Whatever he's doing over there must involve a ton of power."

Joshua tried to push the water out of his face. The giant suit felt like a large weight pulling him down. He dropped the outer coat into the mud and ripped off the tie.

He'd had no trouble listing all the horrible things that could happen during his appointment ceremony. But a massive storm and another one of his mistakes causing the death of someone; that hadn't been on the list.

They poured into the caverns at the base of the Pearl Cliffs. They were too small for this many people, but they had no other options. They pressed in and hunched together.

Whispers surrounded him. They were talking about him.

Joshua squeezed his eyes closed. I am proud to receive the honor of being your newest Judge of Mercy.

CHAPTER 22

TRANSCENDENCE

In the beginning, Dedecus created the heavens and the earth.

Dedecus grinned. He liked the sound of that.

Surrounding him was empty nothingness. While he could feel the Creativity Stone pulsing in his chest, his eyes registered nothing but darkness; his ears picked up less than silence. While he could mentally feel his body, no movement registered. He tried to put his hand on his face but couldn't seem to find it and couldn't even tell if his hands were responding to the command from his brain.

He tried to inhale air into his lungs, but this place had no air to take in. However, the stone in his chest seemed to take care of providing for his needs.

What comes next? Ah yes. "Let there be light." He couldn't tell if he said it or only thought it, but the effects were immediate.

Red energy from his chest exploded outward, causing his body to lurch. His eyes were filled with blinding red light.

His other senses returned as well. Turning his head, he looked out at the ocean of red energy enveloping him and tingling against his skin. His form was back, and he placed his hand on his chest.

And the earth was formless and void.

"Well, let's see what we can do about that."

Dedecus held out his hands, and red light streamed out, collecting in a tight, bright ball that blazed with heat.

"Agghh," Dedecus cried out, and he dropped his hands to his side. The energy that had filled his cells when he first touched the stone had left him. The Creativity Stone still pulsed within him—but fainter now. An incredible amount of power was needed to create. He felt the need to rest.

Once he'd regained his strength, he held out his hands again and continued working.

A second stream of power flowed out of him and surrounded the ball. The color of the enveloping energy slowly changed to gray and solidified. A small rock with heat inside it now floated in the vast expanse. More layers of energy coated the rock, expanding it until it stretched about a mile across the void. A layer of dirt covered the rock.

A gravitational pull tugged up from the ground, and his feet landed on the cushioned surface.

I can't believe I'm doing it! He leaped into the air like a child, and the gravity pulled him back down much quicker than it would on Novitas since he was so close to the center of gravity.

He looked out at the red energy filling the horizon. It twinkled like stars.

Dedecus grinned.

What did those foolish stories say God created man out of? Ah yes, dirt.

He grabbed some dirt off the ground and threw it out in front of him.

The dirt expanded and transformed into bones and flesh. A body formed. Arms, legs, and a head shot out. Features grew on the man's face as he landed on the ground.

His eyes were hollow, and his face looked plastic. Dedecus shuddered. He'd have to get better with that.

The naked man's creepy face twisted in pain, and he clutched at his chest. His eyes bulged, and his skin turned purple. The man fell backward onto the ground—dead.

Dedecus grimaced. "Whoopsies—probably should've started with making some breathable air."

He kicked the dead man's foot. *Rookie mistake.*

But he would get it right. And it would be glorious.

CHAPTER 23

WHITE MOUNTAIN RANGE, NOVITAS—DAY 6, YEAR 371

Grass and rocks crunched below Adia's feet as she made her way up the mountain. Her feet ached from the desperate journey she was on. Her heart pounded, echoing in her chest that felt empty and hollow. She couldn't understand why she was hiking up the mountain, but she continued to ascend.

The sky above her was a dark yellow, and rain poured down on her head, but she ignored it.

She'd made this trip before with Lincoln. They'd had a beautiful time together. Even though exhausted by the time they reached the top, they'd laughed so much that day. But now, she was left with this frantic attempt to reach the top once more.

She tripped on a revealed tree root and went sprawling to the ground, but as the gash on her hand spilled out blood, she could barely feel it. Her nerves were completely numb to pain, for nothing done to her physically could hurt more than the emotional pain she felt every second.

She needed to make it to the peak where Lincoln had been alive, and she'd been happy. She pulled the picture of her and Lincoln out of her pocket. They stood atop this same mountain, delighted and in love.

Lincoln had chosen the easiest mountain for them to climb that day, for which she was grateful. Well, one side was easy; the other side was more of a rocky cliff than a slope. She'd always thought it looked as if someone had taken a giant chunk out of it. Maybe a giant was hungry or something.

She got back to her feet and headed higher.

The wind whipped around her. The clouds darkened and cast a gloom over the world. The rain drenched her, and she pushed her soaking, black hair out of her face. Blots of energy shot across the sky. The word lightning came to her mind, although she couldn't remember where she'd learned it. Her heart beat faster now, but she continued to walk onward.

She could not stop. She would not stop.

And then she was there. Standing at the peak, looking out and seeing the other mountains and the forest surrounding her. She'd longed to be back up here—as if the beauty of the place could bring back Lincoln, but what had once been beautiful was now dark and stormy.

She ignored the huge droplets of rain that fell from the now reddish-yellow-tinted sky as she panted hard from the climb.

She took out the rumpled picture again and held it against her pounding chest.

Standing at the edge of the mountaintop, she stared over the edge of the cliff and down toward the rocky bottom.

Lightning flashed in the distance, illuminating the scene around her for a few seconds before plunging the world back into reddish, murky darkness.

She'd fought against the storm her entire life. The wind of unworthiness had whipped against her, knocking the breath out of her. The rain of sorrow beat viciously on her head. A torrent of depression had overtaken her and

124

threatened to drown her at any moment as she struggled to keep her head above the thoughts.

Lincoln had been her lifesaver. Now he was gone, and she had no reason to fight anymore.

Images rushed her mind in that moment, each fighting for dominance in her broken mind. The memory of when she had first met Lincoln. He'd stared at her for a long moment before saying, "Wow, I think you're the most beautiful girl I've ever met."

The memory of them praying together for her parents as he tried to help her forgive them.

The memory of their nicknames for each other—He-Bear and She-Bear.

The time sixty years ago when he'd put that wedding ring on her trembling fingers and kissed her. The ring was made of blue copper, the rarest stone on Novitas. Lincoln had paid a fortune for it. He said her joy outweighed the cost.

She remembered him telling her about God's love.

They were all supposed to be beautiful moments, but they were more reminders of what she'd lost—her everything, her reason for living.

Her tears mixed with the rain that drenched her entire body. She slowly walked to the edge of the cliff and looked down at the sharp rocks far below. With just one single step, the fall would kill her before she ever knew what happened.

"God ... if you're there ...then prove it ... give me a reason to fight ... rescue me from this storm inside me ..."

She waited for several moments, not really expecting anything to happen but throwing one last desperate attempt in the air in hopes that Lincoln was right and that somehow God did care about a broken woman.

Nothing happened, though. She thought she heard a voice in the wind, but it was gone before she could tell.

The rain still poured.

The wind still whipped.

The darkness still surrounded her.

"I'm sorry, Lincoln."

She took the step forward and stopped fighting.

CHAPTER 24

EMERALD WATERFALL, NOVITAS—DAY 7, YEAR 371

Joshua sat on the rock at the bottom of the waterfall where he'd fallen, died, and was brought back to life. Yesterday's storm had washed away all proof of it. Now it was hard thinking that it was not all just a dream.

If only it were just a dream.

Now he'd had to sleep outside on the ground because his house had been destroyed, and his parents were dead.

The council continued arguing about what should be done until long after yesterday's meeting was over. Joshua had been quiet for most of it. Everyone else but Don had also agreed to leave Fides.

He glanced up at the sun. Today's council meeting was probably soon. He didn't move.

The waterfall dumped thousands of gallons of water on the ground every hour, slowly eroding the hard stones and making a path through them over hundreds of years. He wished he could stay here forever, watching the water slowly carve its way into the rocks.

The storm had caused the river to swell, flooding the area. If another storm came soon, flash floods would cause even more destruction. Lightning had struck the grain silo in the eastern fields destroying much of their crops. Now he didn't even know if they'd have enough food for everyone.

"Mind if I join you?"

Joshua turned around to see Don standing on a rock a few feet away. Before he had a chance to respond, Don came over and sat down beside him.

"You doing okay?"

Joshua squeezed his eyes shut. "Oh, yes, I'm doing fine. I'm handling everything just fine."

"I'm sorry about your parents. They were amazing people." Don put his hand on Joshua's knee, and Joshua flinched slightly as a mallet struck the dam inside him that he was trying to keep together. "Shouldn't you get going? The meeting is starting soon."

Joshua kept his eyes clenched tightly to keep the tears in. "You're supposed to be there too—we can walk together."

Neither moved.

Joshua's butt was getting sore from sitting on the rock.

"Mind if I tell you a story about your father?"

"I really am—"

"Your father was such an amazing man. He would always chase where the spirit led, zealous to follow its lead out of his love for God. I never felt good enough to be in the council, but your father brought me up higher."

Joshua pressed his fingers to his temples. He wanted to run into the waterfall and disappear.

"To me, he was larger than life, so full of energy and passion. Which is why it was such a surprise when he told me something."

Joshua opened his eyes and looked at Don.

"He confessed his own insecurities. He said his big ego and passion would keep him from being the leader Fides needed. He said everything he did made things worse and divided Fides further."

Joshua stared at Don. "He was a great leader, though."

"I told him that. But do you know what he told me?" Don gave Joshua a soft smile. "He told me that you were the kind of person Fides needed."

"Me?"

Don nodded. "He said Fides needed a leader who was eager to listen instead of getting into a yelling match. Who was confident in the truth but willing to come together in unity."

"But what if ..." Joshua averted his eyes. "What if I'm not confident in the truth?"

"What do you mean?"

"Everything is so confusing." Joshua shifted on the uncomfortable rock. "Everyone seems to have a different argument for who God is. I know my parents loved God, but who are we to just ignore all the verses the Judges of Justice talk about. God isn't some free spirit who doesn't care what people do and just wants everyone to be happy. But on the other hand, I've seen what they do to people like Namid. The judge's law crushes people, pulverizing their will to live because they know how unachievable redemption is."

Don was silent for a long moment. "I see what your dad meant."

"Huh?"

"When people are passionate, they tend to get a little extreme with what they know to be true. We've got a lot of passion—we need someone who can bring us somewhere in the middle. Because yes, God is love, but what does that really mean?"

"I can't do what you're saying, though. I couldn't stand up to the others in the council meetings. And ..." Joshua closed his eyes. "I'm responsible for over five hundred deaths."

"You're putting way too much blame on yourself." Don stood and grabbed Joshua's hands, pulling him up too.

"You've been through a horrible loss and are trying to climb a mountain with a ton of weight you were never meant to carry."

"And how exactly am I supposed to just deal with it?"

"That's the point. You're not. Give the fear, the shame, the unworthiness, and the guilt over to God and let him deal with it. I promise you that he can handle it."

Joshua looked up at the cliff he'd fallen from. "That just seems too easy."

"I didn't say it was." Don stood. "But will you let him forgive you?"

Joshua raised his shoulders and let out a long breath. "My dad really said that I'm the kind of leader Fides needs?"

"He did." Don smiled. "And I happen to agree with him."

Joshua remembered the angel's words. If he was called to hold the village together, he needed to do something to get their attention.

"Now, are you ready to head to the meeting?" Don asked.

"Not yet. I think I know what needs to be done." He took off toward where Namid's house used to be. "I'll meet you there," he called back to Don, who was still standing by the waterfall, grinning.

Joshua smiled. What he was planning his father would have thought of—something bold and against decorum. Maybe they were more alike than he'd thought.

CHAPTER 25

THE CABIN, NOVITAS—DAY 7, YEAR 371

Absolute darkness surrounded her, and ... the smell of steak? Adia opened her eyes and looked around, trying to comprehend what her eyes were seeing.

She lay in a modest, simple cabin on a cozy leather couch with a warm, hand-woven, white-and-yellow blanket over her. The verse in 1 Peter 5:7 was stitched on it: "Give all your worries and cares to God, for he cares about you."

She sat up. Her back was sore, but otherwise, she was fine.

It hadn't been a dream. She was sure of that. She brought her hands to her face and dropped her head into them.

How am I alive?

She looked around at the cabin. It looked like it had been taken out of a fairytale. Unlike houses in Fides, this one looked like it had been built out of Earth trees, very unusual considering how few they had.

How did I get here?

Hundreds of family portraits and pictures of different families laughing and having fun were on the walls around her. She wasn't sure who lived there, but they certainly knew a lot of people.

She smiled at the rich smell of food cooking in the kitchen.

"Dinner will be ready in a minute," a man called from the other room, startling her.

She slowly pulled the blanket off to the side and got up, much to her stiff bones' complaint. As she walked across the room to the kitchen doorway, the floorboards creaked slightly.

As she was about to reach the doorway when an older man stepped out, carrying a plate and a tray. The man was tall with shoulder-length, mixed dirty-brown and gray hair.

"Oh, sorry, I was just—"

The man laughed warmly. "I know you must be confused right now, waking up in a strange cabin with a strange man bringing you food."

"How did I get here? And where ... is *here*?"

"I'll tell you everything while you sit back down and eat. The food's getting cold, and you must be starving." The man smiled again. His whole face lit up from his dark, tanned cheeks to his warm, hazel eyes.

Her stomach growled in agreement, and she sat down on the couch. He placed the tray of food down in front of her.

"Wow! I haven't had steak with steamed vegetables since I was little. It was my father's and my favorite meal. How did you know I liked it?"

"One question at a time," he said with a smile in his voice as he came back from the kitchen with another plate of food on another tray. He set his food down and pulled up an armchair that sat next to the window.

"First off, I found you lying unconscious at the bottom of a mountain in that huge rainstorm last night, so I brought you back to my cabin so you could rest and recover. You've been unconscious for most of the day. It's getting dark now."

"Who are you?"

"I've gotten a lot of nicknames, but you can call me Emeth."

"Hi, Emeth. I'm Adia. Sorry for asking so many questions, but where are we? I've never seen this place before."

"You're good. I'm sure I'd have lots of questions too." He smiled. "We're on the other side of the mountain range from Fides Village. I love this area's peace and quiet. Although, my door is always open when someone comes along."

"But wait, that fall should have killed me. How did I survive? I'm only a little sore."

"It seems as if God was watching over you after all." Emeth laughed again.

What does he mean by after all? Does he know what I did?

She brought a forkful of food to her mouth. Her taste buds were instantly rewarded with a rich flavor even better than what she remembered as a child. It distracted her from her confusion and questions.

She immediately devoured the food as if the first meal she'd had in years.

"Don't eat too quickly. You don't want to give yourself a stomachache later." Emeth laughed warmly. It seemed like one was always prepared in his throat, waiting to be let out. He took a small bite of his steak.

"Now, tell me about yourself, kiddo. What were you doing up on that mountain in such a bad storm anyway?"

She swallowed the food in her mouth, stared down at her plate, and then looked back at the stranger sitting across from her and thought about lying to him. But she could sense he could see into her heart and would know she wasn't honest. She also felt that he would understand.

"I ... I was tired of fighting, tired of the pain and the depression. I just wanted to escape it all. So, I tried to end it ..." she said, unable to say the word *suicide*.

"You might not believe me," he said, "but I've been where you were before. One night, I was sitting in a garden, and the pain of what I was going through at the time was just too much. I begged God to take it all away—to change what I knew was about to happen."

That story sounded familiar, but she couldn't place where she'd heard it. "Wow, really? You just seem so ..." she paused, unsure of what to say.

"Put together and at peace?" He smiled.

"Yeah, that. What did you do?"

"Well, the answer to that is both simple and complicated. For it's much easier said than done. I surrendered and trusted God. I said, '*Your will be done.*'"

"But how can you do that? How can you trust a God who could allow you to reach that place?"

"That moment was hard. Probably the hardest thing I've ever had to do. But life really is all about trusting God, knowing that whatever happens to me, God has a plan for my life."

"Yeah, I've heard all that before, but that's a lot easier said than done."

"I suppose you're right," he said with a grin. "One thing that helps me do that, though, is to look outside myself at the beauty of the world that surrounds us. Look around at these pictures hanging on the wall at the love and joy of these people and families. They remind me that there's more to life than what I'm going through, that while there will always be evil, pain, and darkness, love and joy will still remain."

He paused for a moment, and they listened to the birds chirping cheerfully outside before he continued. "God has a perfect track record."

"What if you can't think of anything good in your life?" Involuntary tears came to Adia's eyes. "What if everything and everyone has shown you that you're stupid, ugly, and worthless?" She had begun to yell, but she didn't care. "All my life, I've felt as if I was drowning. The storm and waves ripped at me and stole the air from my lungs. Eventually, I became tired of fighting. And now, the only person who actually thought otherwise and offered me an escape from the storm is dead. He's dead because of what one man's rage and anger at the world that you call so beautiful had done to him."

She lay her head on the armrest and sobbed. Her tears slid down the tan leather. She might have survived last night, but that still didn't change anything about her circumstances.

For a long moment, she abandoned herself to sobbing.

She heard the soft strumming of an acoustic guitar, but she didn't look up.

> What a friend we have in Jesus,
> All our sins and griefs to bear!
> And what a privilege to carry
> Everything to God in prayer!
>
> Oh, what peace we often forfeit,
> Oh, what needless pain we bear.
> All because we do not carry
> Everything to God in prayer!

Adia stopped crying as she listened to the words of the song and Emeth's beautiful, rich voice that seemed to carry a thousand harmonies all at once.

> Have we trials and temptations?
> Is there trouble anywhere?
> We should never be discouraged.
> Take it to the Lord in prayer.
>
> Can we find a friend so faithful?
> Who will all our sorrows share?

Jesus knows our every weakness.
Take it to the Lord in prayer.

Memories of singing this hymn in Sunday school and in church flooded her mind. Memories of being comforted as a child that Jesus could be the best friend she didn't have. Memories of leaning on Lincoln as they sang the words together, and he would squeeze her hand.

Are we weak and heavy-laden?
Cumbered with a load of care?
Precious Savior, still our refuge—
Take it to the Lord in prayer;

Do thy friends despise, forsake thee?
Take it to the Lord in prayer;
In His arms He'll take and shield thee.
Thou wilt find a solace there.

More memories continued to flow of her long-forgotten elementary school teacher, who would sit with her and patiently teach her things she thought she was too stupid to learn. Memories of Lincoln encouraging and inspiring her to push herself.

She had always felt that God had abandoned her and that no one truly had loved her. *But maybe ...*

Blessed Savior, Thou hast promised
Thou wilt all our burdens bear;
May we ever, Lord, be bringing
All to Thee in earnest prayer.

Soon in glory bright, unclouded,
There will be no need for prayer—
Rapture, praise, and endless worship
Will be our sweet portion there.

"I ... I always thought that because I wasn't as smart or as pretty as those around me and because my parents weren't as loving and because I struggled with depression, that God had ... that God had ..." her brain struggled to come up with the word.

"Abandoned you?" Emeth continued to softly stroke the guitar strings. "Everyone seems to think being a Christian means you won't ever have depression or anxiety or struggles. They seem to think that Jesus is a get-out-of-anything-free card that will make everything perfect. But that's just not the case. We're humans, and the world is not perfect. Because of that, there will always be something to cry about. And it is okay to cry."

"But ..." she let the words trail off.

"What makes us Christians is we realize God is crying with us and is wrapping his arms around us in a loving hug. What makes us Christians is we know we don't have to stay in that place of darkness."

"I believe in God ... but how do I do that? What do I do when the depression threatens to overwhelm me?"

He smiled as he quietly strummed the guitar and sang the answer once again.

What a friend we have in Jesus,
All our sins and griefs to bear!
What a privilege to carry,
Everything to God in prayer!

Oh, what peace we often forfeit,
Oh, what needless pain we bear.
All because we do not carry
Everything to God in prayer!

"Jesus truly is a loving friend," he said. "Take your pain to him, allow him to use it to make you stronger, and always remember to be thankful for what he has done. Even when you can't think of anything, I promise you ... there's always something to be thankful for. By having a thankful heart, you'll begin to focus on the good. You'll begin to see more and more things to be thankful for."

Who is this man who seems to see into my heart?

CHAPTER 26

FIDES VILLAGE, NOVITAS—DAY 7, YEAR 371

Marvin tapped his foot loudly on the floor as the council waited.

"Can we go ahead and start already, Don? I think we're all ready to vote on this especially important issue," Freda said. "It's already been an entire week since the attack. Who knows when another storm is going to come, and I've listened to you children squabbling for the past three days. Let's get on with it."

"Shouldn't we wait until Joshua gets here to take a vote?" Don asked.

"If that child is going to be late, then that just shows how unfit he is to be here." Marvin was tired of catering to a spoiled child's schedule. "You're only here because of his parents' ancestry anyway. You live in a broken-down shack and depend on others to survive. You're hardly fit to help lead this village."

"Stop it, you two," Sharon snapped. "I'm tired of listening to your constant bickering!"

Joshua ran into the room, his clothes and hair all wet. "Sorry I'm late guys, I needed some time to think and pray."

Marvin glared at this boy who had no business being here, and when Joshua was unable to return the eye contact, he received guilty satisfaction from it.

Joshua hurried across the room to his seat. Everyone sat in silence as his squeaking chair echoed loudly off the wooden walls.

"All right, now that we're all here—"

"Since some of us decided to take a swim," Marvin muttered as he glared at a puddle of green water forming under Joshua's seat.

Don glared at Freda and continued, "Over the past several meetings, we have discussed the Judges of Justice's proposal that we relocate to another world, and unless anyone else has an argument to present, I believe the time has come to vote."

Clearing his throat, Joshua pushed the damp hair out of his face, stood up on shaky legs, and addressed the council. "Actually, I have something to say."

"Oh, it looks like the mouse is finally speaking up," Rupert muttered.

"Shut up, Rupert," Don said. "He has more of a right to speak than you do."

Joshua cleared his throat again.

Marvin felt bad for the kid. He didn't belong there, and everyone knew it.

"I've been listening to you guys argue for days, and your differences are glaringly obvious. Rupert thinks he's better than everyone else because he's a warrior. Don doesn't have much money, so he constantly has to fight for respect. Marvin and Freda see themselves as the wisest and most holy. And Sharon just doesn't like anyone. We're supposed to be an example to the village, but instead, we argue and berate each other because we each think that we're superior."

"That's a very nice speech," Freda said, interrupting him. "But what does this have to do with leaving Fides and setting up a new world?"

"I'm getting to that."

Marvin watched Joshua very closely, confused as the boy's shaking began to subside.

"You seem to think we're supposed to be perfect, but only Jesus is perfect. You seem to think we're all called to be exactly the same, that we're all called to be you." He looked into each face as he spoke. "And yet, all we're supposed to do is be united in love, not a diamond that people will see and never be able to live up to. A little while ago, Don asked me a question about what love was. I don't have an answer yet, but I do know that what we've been doing isn't love."

Marvin rolled his eyes. Love meant correcting one another. And that's what he was doing. It was everyone else who refused to receive his love.

Namid slipped quietly inside the room, carrying her violin, battered slightly from the attack but still playable. She was supposed to be back at the house. Marvin clenched his fists.

"Now tell me, how are we supposed to examples of God's love when all they see us do is argue and fight. How are we supposed to do so when we run away and don't trust in God's promises. God pointed this land out to our ancestor Jefferson Gent. He and the others found refuge in this beautiful land we now call home. But now, we're just going to run away in fear instead of trusting that God can do something good through this, no matter how awful it is? Are we going to let fear and division destroy everything we've built?"

Joshua signaled Namid, and she played a slow and haunting melody on her violin.

Marvin glanced over and saw Freda's face flushed red. Her fingernails dug into her chair.

He looked back at Namid, but she refused to make eye contact.

God, please, no.

He took Freda's hand and squeezed it tightly.

"I want to sing you guys a song—a song that tells our story."

Before anyone could respond, Joshua began to sing,

In the beginning, God made us,
And he said, "It is good."
He gave us passions, pieces of his glory,
And he said, "It is good."

But somewhere along the way
What was good became hated.
What was celebrated became cursed.
Lines were drawn, divisions made.
The rich against the poor,

Strong against the weak,
Warriors against the thinkers,
Old against the young.

Marvin glared at Joshua. He wasn't some villain trying to divide everyone—he was merely a father and a leader called to protect his people from corruption and ungodliness.

We all think that we know best
But have just a small piece.
Instead of letting go of our pride,
We let our differences divide.

Our differences become a chasm,
But we were all created unique.
Instead of one part in a complex body,
We're separate and on the attack.

Marvin scanned the room and saw Don was grinning and Rupert was leaning back in his chair, looking bored. Beside him, Freda was still glaring at their daughter, her nails making permanent dents in her chair.

He glanced over at his daughter. Her jaw was set, her eyes staring directly at him, pleading for him to listen as she played the beautiful notes on her violin.

But aren't the rich called to help the poor?
Aren't the strong called to protect the weak?
Aren't the thinkers to inspire the warriors?
Aren't the young called to learn from the old?

Sharon cried softly. He couldn't believe some song was swaying her.

It is the story of the poor that needs to be told.
The humility of the weak needs to be learned.
The courage of the warriors needs to be admired.
The passion of the young that needs to be encouraged.

Marvin's heart fluttered. Somewhere deep inside him, Joshua's words pulled at him. If only it were as simple as coming together in unity. The poor boy was terribly misguided. He never wanted to be the divider, but he had to stay firm in the truth. The Bible said false prophets would come to tempt them.

Marvin clenched his jaw. The boy might be too far gone, but was his daughter?

Will we follow God's plan
And say it is good?
Or will we draw the lines
And scoff at his love?

When the song came to an end, everyone remained silent for a long moment.

Freda stood and marched to the front of the room where Joshua and Namid stood. Marvin followed her.

"How dare you conspire with this child!" Freda shouted at Namid as she ripped the violin from her hands and broke it in half, throwing the ornately carved instrument to the ground in pieces.

"I did it because it was the right thing to do," she said. "You two have always taught me that we must work for perfection to get to Heaven because God hates us, but you're wrong. God doesn't hate us for our sin, and we can't just go run away."

Freda drew her hand back and slapped Namid across the face, knocking her to the ground next to her broken violin and leaving a giant, red handprint on the left side of her face. The loud smack of flesh hitting flesh and the thud of Namid hitting the hard ground echoed around the room.

Tears flowed down Freda's face as she held her hand, "We love you, daughter. We want you to be in Heaven with us. Don't you see that we're doing all of this for you?"

The walls that kept any emotion from entering Marvin's heart—the walls his parents had taught him to erect since he was a child—cracked. His shoulders slumped as he watched his only daughter on the floor crying. He had tried so hard to teach her the truth. Didn't she know the seven remembrances he'd given her and everything they'd done was because they loved her?

What have I done to deserve this, God? his heart cried out. *What unrepented sin have I done that would cause my only daughter to choose evil.*

"We don't care what you decide—we're taking as many as we can and leaving this cursed planet," Marvin said.

Rupert stood from his seat and walked to stand by them.

At least someone was with them.

Marvin held out his right hand and offered it to Namid to help her up.

Please, take it.

Namid only glared at them.

"Are you okay?" Joshua asked as he bent to help Namid to her feet.

"I've been better," she said, grimacing.

"I should never have asked you to come. I'm so sorry." Joshua said.

"Don't be sorry. It's not your fault. I should've stood up to them years ago. I'm tired of my parents spreading fear and casting judgment on me and on everyone else."

"I did everything I could for you, daughter." Marvin's voice cracked. "I tried to love you by showing you the truth. But if you choose to spit in the face of our love, we will leave you to God's punishment."

Namid closed her eyes but remained where she was.

"Fine. You're too far gone." Marvin did as his father had taught him. He straightened his back and held his head high. Doing anything he could to keep from crying like his beloved daughter.

Namid picked up her broken violin and shook it at them. "You can flee in fear if you want, but I'm staying here and trusting in what God's going to do. And not the God of fear and judgment you guys preach about." She glared at her parents, "but the God who has been whispering words of love to me since I was a child."

Freda trembled slightly as she picked up her Bible from her chair. When she looked back at him, her eyes were bloodshot.

"Fine." He pressed his lips together. "Tonight, we'll gather up supplies for the journey. Tomorrow, we'll make an announcement and leave with whoever still follows the truth."

Marvin grabbed his wife's hand and turned his back on Namid.

He started walking quickly, with Rupert and Freda close behind. He glanced back, but Namid hadn't moved. He slowed but kept walking.

"Please, God," he whispered. "Don't make me spend an eternity without my only daughter."

The door was only five feet away, but the journey seemed to take forever.

He reached the door and paused for a second, then he pushed it open and walked out.

Only Freda and Rupert were behind him as the doors shut with more finality than he thought possible.

Don made his way to the center to stand with Joshua and Namid. "That was beautiful, you two. You did all you could." He put his hand on Joshua's shoulder. "Your parents would be so proud of your creativity." He turned to Namid. "And your bravery is greater than anyone I know."

Sharon then stood and came to the three of them, her eyes still red from crying, "I'm sorry for always fighting with you guys. Your parents were amazing people, Joshua. I didn't agree with them on most things, but they loved God. And I might have been a little too hard on everyone." She turned to Namid and put a hand on her shoulder. "Are you okay, darling? That hit looked painful."

Her face had a bright red handprint where her mother had smacked her. "Yeah, I'm okay ... I'm pretty used to it by now."

"We had no idea."

Joshua hugged Namid tightly. "I'm proud of you," he said to her.

Namid smiled. "I'm proud of you too."

Now, they had to stop the rest of the village from leaving.

CHAPTER 27

THE CABIN, NOVITAS—DAY 7, YEAR 371

Adia never liked the quiet. She always had tried to fill it because it made her uncomfortable and fidgety.

But she sat with Emeth in silence for several minutes and stayed still.

She'd never met someone like the mysterious man sitting across from her. A man who seemed so wise. A man who always had a smile on his face but wasn't afraid to face the sorrow.

"I always thought God wasn't listening to me, and I definitely never thought he'd respond," she said more to herself than to him.

"You have the Holy Spirit within you. He's constantly whispering words of wisdom and absolute love. But most of the time, we're too distracted by our lives and struggles to listen. So we focus on the distractions around us instead of the only one who's bigger and more powerful than anything we face. When we do focus on God, he'll be faithful to show us his love and remind us of his goodness. And that's why it's so important that we're always thankful. It brings our thoughts to God and helps us to focus on seeing what he's doing in our lives."

An ornate, hand-carved grandfather clock chimed from the corner of the room, signaling eleven o'clock at night.

The man yawned and stretched. He set down his guitar and stood up from his plush chair. He grabbed the trays and took them to the kitchen.

Adia looked out the window at the golden moon peeking above the trees, its light sparkling off the damp ground.

"It's getting pretty late," he called out from the kitchen, "and you have a long trip back to the village tomorrow, so we should probably turn in for the night."

Adia yawned and laid back down on the warm couch, pulling the hand-woven blanket with the verse *Give all your worries and cares to God, for he cares about you* over her. The blanket was soft and warm and felt like a hug.

"So, I'm heading home tomorrow?"

"I'll pack you plenty of food and water for the trip, but they need you there." He came back into the room and flipped a switch to turn off the light.

"Why would they need me?" If she weren't so drained, she'd have laughed at his statement. Yes, God might love her, but that didn't mean she was any use to the people in Fides Village.

She had another fifty years of life ahead of her without purpose.

"God has a plan for you. I'm hearing him say that he wants to use you to help those most broken and lost. All your life, people have said you were stupid and couldn't do anything, but God created you for a purpose, and he'll show you that purpose."

"I'll go back, but I doubt I could ever truly make the difference you seem to think I can."

He smiled at her. "Don't worry, kiddo, remember what we talked about. He'll give you the strength and ability to accomplish great things. You aren't who your father said you are, and you aren't who your teachers or peers or anyone else in the world said you are. You are a beloved child of God, and he has a purpose for you."

DOWNFALL

He walked over toward her, sat down in his chair, picked up the guitar once more, and softly began to strum the strings.

She closed her eyes and smiled. She still had no idea how she'd ended up in this cabin, and she probably never would. But that didn't matter as she listened to Emeth gently sing.

> God, my father, protect me tonight.
> Take my fears and throw away my fright.
> Warm me with your peace and love
> As I look out at stars shining above.
>
> You are stronger than my fears.
> You will wipe away all my tears.

Adia let the simple yet beautiful words flow over her soul as she slowly drifted off.

> You are so vast and immense—
> Creator of the whole universe.
>
> And yet you see me here down here.
> From your love, I will never disappear.
>
> I pray that as I drift into dreams,
> I will always stay in your peace.

Right before sleep overtook her, she once more glanced at the old man, who was filled with such love and wisdom. Maybe the faint light of the stars and golden moon coming in from the window behind her couch was tricking her, but she thought she could make out wounds in his hands as he was playing, the kind you'd get from having a nail pierce through them.

> God, my father, protect me tonight.
> Take my fears and throw away my fright.

Warm me with your peace and love
As I look out at stars shining above.

The next morning Adia awoke to bright sunlight streaming through the lace curtains in the window behind the couch. She sat up and saw a bag lying on the floor beside her.

She looked around the picturesque, rustic cabin once more and wished she could stay there forever.

The pictures on the wall smiled at her. One in particular she hadn't noticed the night before caught her eye.

Along with the hundreds of others was the picture of her and Lincoln on the mountaintop, smiling and hugging each other—the same one she'd had in her pocket.

She stood and walked over to where the bag was packed. On top lay a hand-drawn map giving her specific directions on how to get back to Fides. It showed her a path through the mountains so she wouldn't have to do too much climbing. A cave or something on the side of one of the mountains had been circled with a red pen.

She wasn't sure why it was marked, but the path he'd drawn for her led right past the cave, so she figured she'd check it out on her way back. After all that had happened, she had no idea what could be in the cave, but Emeth had marked it for a reason, and she trusted him.

On the back of the map, he'd written her a note.

Had to get an early start this morning, but I know we'll see each other again. In the bag is plenty of food and water for your trip back, but feel free to take the blanket you were using or anything else you need.

—Jehovah El Emeth

CHAPTER 28

FIDES VILLAGE, NOVITAS—YEAR 2

Steven shifted on his feet in the hot midday sun. Esther had gathered the entire village to the center of town for some kind of ceremony, although he was uncertain for what.

They'd been working tirelessly for the past year to plant crops, build shelters and buildings, and turn this land into their home.

The palms, what they'd taken to calling the trees, made excellent logs for building. Since there weren't any branches on the palms, all that had to be done was strip off the hairs, a surprisingly easy process. As a result, they had begun a large pile of palm hairs to be used for building fires.

Esther stood on the church steps, staring out at the crowd. Her daughter sat on the ground beside her. Esther was a widow whose husband had died four years ago, right after she gave birth.

Now, most of the planned buildings and homes had been completed, with the beautiful and ornate church looming over everything else.

Esther cleared her throat, and everyone instantly quieted. Jefferson might have gotten them to Novitas, but it was clear who was in charge.

"I've gathered you all here today because we need to make a decision." Her eyes searched the crowd, landing on him. He shuddered under her gaze. "You, why did we come here?"

"Me?" Steven looked around. His lungs constricted.

Esther gave an exasperated sigh. "Yes, you, come on. We don't have all day."

"Well, we came because the world was evil and corrupted. We wanted to separate ourselves from sin."

She nodded once. "Good."

She took her eyes off him, and he could breathe normally again.

"So, if that is the case?" she continued. "What are we to do when sin enters this, our new world?"

Everyone was silent.

"Come on, people, this isn't that hard. We've spent countless time and resources to get here. Should we just let sin infect us like it did Earth?"

Several noes came from the crowd.

"Then we need to root it out. We need to curse the fruitless fig tree just as Jesus did." Esther gave a slight smile as the group nodded. "It has come to my attention someone has sinned, and sin cannot go unpunished." She pointed at someone near the center of the crowd. "William Larson, please come up here."

Everyone near the middle stepped away like the parting of the Red Sea. The only one left was a little boy and his parents. The boy was no older than his own sister Lisa. He clung to his mom tightly.

Steven bit his lip.

"William Larson, come up here now." Esther's voice grew harder.

The boy slowly walked toward Esther.

"Young William. Yesterday your parents contacted me about something you said to them. What did you say?"

152

"I ... I don't know what you're talking about." William's voice squeaked.

"Did you or did you not say the "f" word to your parents yesterday?"

"I—"

"This is a simple yes or no question."

Steven's pulse quickened. *Where is Esther going with this?*

"Yes, but—"

"And can anyone tell me what Exodus 21:17 says?"

"Now, wait a minute." William's father took a step forward, his face pale. "You can't be serious—"

"Can anyone tell me," Esther rose her voice, talking over the man, "what does Exodus 21:17 say?"

"And he that curseth his father, or his mother, shall surely be put to death," someone in the audience supplied.

"No!" the boy's mother screamed. "You can't! It was an accident."

"Luke 6:45," Esther said. "An evil man out of the evil treasure of his heart bringeth forth that which is evil; for of the abundance of his heart his mouth speaketh."

Steven felt nauseous. *She can't be serious.*

"In biblical times, the punishment of sin was death through stoning. We left Earth because we were disgusted with sin. Will we turn a blind eye to it now?" Esther picked up a large stone from behind her.

William looked at his parents with tears in his eyes. "Mom, Dad?"

William's mother fell to her knees and wept. His father closed his eyes and turned away.

Steven was going to throw up. *God, this can't be right. This boy can't be older than eight.*

The laws of the New Day Separatists came to mind. *Remember to remain pure in all thoughts and actions.*

Remember to cast out the defiled. Remember to enact what others deserve.

Steven wanted to be good and follow the law God had given them, but how could this be good?

About half the people nodded with Esther and found stones. Others turned away. But no one said anything.

Esther grabbed William's arm and gave out a little scream. He tried to pull away, but her grip was iron. Finally, he stopped fighting and stood there, weeping.

Do something! Something within him screamed. Steven closed his eyes.

The sound of a stone smacking against flesh echoed in the air, followed by louder wailing and crying.

Steven stumbled away as the lunch he'd had earlier rose into his throat.

Another stone hit William. Then another. He could only whimper now.

What if that was Lisa? Steven lurched over and threw up.

Another smack of stone against flesh came from the gathering. Then the whimpering stopped, and all was silent.

Steven took off running into the dark forest of palms, crashing through the underbrush. He didn't know where he was going, but he had to get away.

All he heard from behind him was dead silence.

CHAPTER 29

FIDES VILLAGE, NOVITAS- DAY 8, YEAR 371

Joshua stood with Namid and Don off to the side of a large crowd of people who had gathered at the Judges of Justice's order.

Freda and Marvin stood, their shadows looming over the people of Fides where the steps of the church used to be.

Marvin held the portal creator their ancestors had used to get to Fides. A medium-sized, bulky device on wheels, with a screen and several knobs and buttons along the top and side. A pair of antennae jutted awkwardly out from the top, and a ton of wires stuck out haphazardly from behind.

"People of Fides," Marvin said in a loud voice. "We have become a corrupt and evil people who have allowed sin to fester in our streets and hearts for far too long."

Silence instantly fell over the crowd.

"You all saw for yourselves what happens when we allow sin to fester. If we had cast out or killed that byproduct of lust and evil, Dedecus, like the Lord had insisted, we wouldn't be picking up the pieces of our village. But instead, the Judges of Mercy welcomed sin in and allowed it to grow. Now, we all must pay the price of them allowing corruption."

Joshua averted his gaze as Marvin glared at him.

"What do we do, Joshua?" Don asked him.

"I don't know," Joshua said. His shoulders slumped, and he stared at the ground. The confidence he'd felt so strongly yesterday at the meeting was gone.

Namid gripped Joshua's hand. "We have to do something."

"There's nothing we can do."

"We all remember what it was like in the world we came from," Marvin continued his speech. "In that world, the name of our Holy Lord was used as an insult and to show scorn. In that world, even the faithful had become corrupted by their sins of idolatry, sexual evils, and lustful hearts."

About half the villagers nodded at the judge's words. Ronald, Regina, and Rupert glared at Joshua.

"Looks like someone took their self-righteous pills this morning," Don said quietly.

"We came to this world and built Fides because we were horrified by the evils of society on Earth," Marvin said. "However, we have compromised our beliefs and have grown lazy in our discipline. This attack was a message directly from God, telling us he sees us and is very displeased with us. If we do not take a drastic step, his wrath will return and destroy us completely for our foolish indolence."

Freda sighed. Shoving her husband aside, she cleared her throat and spoke up. "Basically, what my husband is droning on and on about is we are going to use the same portal we used to get here to leave Fides to start a new world where we will be more diligent and less tolerant to the sin that has destroyed our village. We tried and failed to make Fides a place that would please God, but because of our laziness and mercy," she scowled at Joshua, "it's now a pile of rubble. We will leave this broken place to create a world that's perfect in God's eyes."

"No!" Joshua cried out. He squeezed Namid's hand once, then let go and marched to the front where the Judges of Justice stood. "We can't just leave this place. Fides is our home, and God has given us this land to build on and protect."

"But what if Dedecus comes back?" someone in the crowd called out.

"And what about the storms?" someone else said.

"Then we'll deal with it together."

"You were friends with that monster!" Ronald shouted.

"Dedecus isn't a monster. He just—" As soon as the words left his lips, he knew he'd made a mistake.

"My family is dead because of him, and you defend him?"

"Yeah!"

"This is all your fault!"

"This is what showing mercy got us!"

"I bet he still wants to show mercy to that monster!"

"Hey!" Namid shouted from the back of the angry crowd. "This wasn't Joshua's fault or Dedecus's or God's. All of you people did this. You were so worried about being perfect and holy that you forgot the greatest and most important commandment that Jesus taught—to love God and love each other. And because we didn't show Dedecus love, he attacked us."

"How dare you!" Freda glared at Namid.

"I am proud to say I was friends with Dedecus. Maybe if more of us had been, none of this would have happened."

Freda rushed toward her daughter.

"Leave her alone!" Joshua ran toward Freda and shoved her away from Namid.

Freda stumbled backward, tripping on her long dress and falling on her back. The thud of Freda hitting the dirt silenced all of Fides Village.

Marvin charged at Joshua. "How dare you shove my wife!"

"I just—"

Marvin punched him in the gut, knocking the wind out of him, and Joshua fell to the ground. His left hand landed on a sharp rock that stabbed into his flesh.

Dust swirled around Joshua as he let out a shrill scream. He'd gotten cuts before but whatever was happening to him was not normal pain. Every nerve in his hand felt like it was on fire. He grabbed his left wrist and tried to stop the shaking so he could inspect the wound. He wiped the blood away and saw smooth skin.

What's happening to me?

Marvin helped Freda back up, and she tediously brushed herself off, removing any speck of dirt from her dress.

"You've all heard what this pathetic little boy has to say," Freda said. "He wants to receive Dedecus with open arms after what that monster did to us. If this is what mercy is, I want no part in it. If you want to stay here with this foolish boy, then stay. Everyone else, follow my husband and me into a new and better world—one where we will not allow mercy to ruin and corrupt us."

Joshua tried to shake off the pain but stopped. "I'm not saying that Dedecus doesn't deserve some kind of punishment, but—"

"Oh, would you just shut up! We all know you don't deserve the title of judge. Would you stop pretending and let the grownups talk?" Freda said.

"Leave Josh alone!" Namid ran at her parents.

"We loved you," Marvin said with tears flowing down his face. "I don't know what I did to fail you, but if you choose to side with this Judge of Mercy, then you are not our daughter."

Marvin and Freda turned from Joshua and their daughter and stepped to the front of the crowd.

Marvin picked up the portal creator and pressed a button on the side. In a bright flash, a swirl of colors erupted from the device and shot out in front of them. On the other side through the portal was a sandy desert as far as they could see, the sun—bright and harsh.

Get off the ground and stop this.

"Follow us, all who are righteous and holy, into our new world," Marvin called out.

Without another glance at the daughter they were abandoning, the two of them stepped through the portal and into the desert.

A large group of devout followers of the Judge of Justice's teachings followed them through the portal first. Some stopped to glare at Joshua while others looked back at the homes they were leaving behind.

Many more followed, carrying in their arms or in carts the few possessions they had left.

Joshua recognized many of the people leaving, Rupert and his family, the guy that Namid's parents had been planning to have her marry, the town architects who designed all the additions to the village, a bunch of his classmates and their families, even those Joshua recognized as members of his parents' church. They all followed Marvin and Freda into the desert.

Regina laughed as she went through the portal, never looking back.

The sky grew yellow as clouds formed quickly. *Not again.*

One young woman sobbed openly as she watched her husband, children, and parents abandon her to follow the Judges of Justice.

Joshua lay unmoving on the ground. He closed his eyes, unable to watch as hundreds left.

I need to stop this. Just say something. Anything.

The angel had told him to hold Fides together, and yet before his eyes, he watched them being torn apart. He'd tried but failed them. He failed Fides. He failed his parent's legacy. He failed God.

I'll probably be the only one left.

Suddenly, someone laid a gentle hand on his shoulder. He opened his eyes and quickly closed them. Namid. What must she be going through as she watched her parents abandon her? He should do something to try to comfort her and encourage her, but he couldn't even manage to be a good friend.

The worst part was now he had to figure out a way to go forward, to stand in front of the villagers even while knowing he'd failed them miserably, and to lead Fides ... or what was left of it anyway. And now they were about to have another storm. How was he supposed to flip the perspective of this?

The swirling wind of the portal stopped, and they were gone.

Joshua couldn't bear to open his eyes and see what was left.

CHAPTER 30

WHITE MOUNTAIN RANGE, NOVITAS—DAY 8, YEAR 371

Adia wiped the mix of rain and sweat off her forehead and stopped to pull out the map, trying to shield it from the rain. She was almost at the cave Emeth had marked for her, and darkness crept closer. Maybe that's why he marked it for her—so she'd know of a safe place to stay for the night where she wouldn't have to worry about the storm or tree bears coming into her camp for food.

She'd always been terrified of tree bears as a child. They were gray and brown nocturnal bears that were expert climbers and usually slept on the top of palms. They were hungry scavengers who weren't afraid of humans or anything else that got in the way of their growling stomach, and their stomachs were always growling. They would eat just about anything—dead or alive.

When she was little, she used to be scared to go out at night because, in her mind, she was the perfect size for a snack. Her father's response was to "grow a spine."

She slogged forward down the path. The pack on her back and her thoughts competed to outweigh each other.

Arriving at the cave, the entrance was small but noticeable and was covered in palm leaves. After pulling the leaves to the side, she stepped inside, eager to be out of the rain.

A small stream of waning sunlight filtered in through the entrance. She could barely see anything, but she could make out a lantern next to the opening. Setting her pack down, she picked up the lamp already filled with palm hairs and stared at it.

How did this get here?

She lit it, and light filled the cave, which was about the size of a bedroom. She gasped as she read the words painted in green across the back wall: *Happy Anniversary, Adia.*

She took a step forward and nearly tripped over a thin wire that had been set up about a foot off the ground. The trip wire activated more lanterns across the room, and music began to play.

Adia cried as the song from her and Lincoln's wedding played softly. This was where Lincoln had been planning on taking her as a surprise for their anniversary. He must have planned to take her here to have dinner and to dance together to their wedding song.

How he had gotten hold of a music player was beyond her. While her uncle had tinkered with a design for a new one, the only music players in the village had been brought with them from Earth over three hundred years ago. They were priceless and treated with the utmost care. He must have made some kind of deal with the council.

In the center of the cave was a table draped in a white cloth where they would have sat to eat dinner together. Surrounding her on all sides on the walls were pictures of them together. Pictures from their first date, from their wedding, from dates and anniversaries, to them sitting on the couch together. Lincoln had loved taking pictures of the two of them. Adia was pretty sure the cameras her grandfather had designed were his favorite inventions. Now those photos surrounded her on all sides, enveloping her in their memories.

Adia let out a laugh.

The orchestral music rose and fell gently. She closed her eyes and pretended Lincoln was standing beside her. Every year, on their anniversary, they would play their wedding song and dance to it together. He was gone now, and their anniversary had passed, but she would still have their dance.

Taking Lincoln's imaginary hand, she twirled around and danced to the music, following Lincoln's lead. She could almost feel him beside her, leading her in the dance they'd shared every year. She could hear him singing the song to her to remind her of how much she meant to him.

> God gave me you;
> God gave you me.
> So forever, we'll dance
> Into eternity.

Adia smiled at the countless memories she'd forgotten— memories of Lincoln leaning in and whispering those lines to her as he squeezed her tightly in his love.

The song ended. She opened her eyes and noticed an envelope sitting on the table. In Lincoln's messy handwriting that only she knew how to read were the words: *to my beautiful she-bear*, his pet name for her.

Adia tore open the envelope and tried to wipe away the tears in her eyes to read the letter.

Dear Adia,

Over the past couple of months, I have watched as depression, discouragement, and self-pity have once again attacked your soul. Ever since you were little, you've always thought of yourself as stupid and unworthy of love, but when I look into your stunningly beautiful eyes, I see a woman who I am madly in love with; a woman who is filled with compassion and kindness;

a woman who would make any sacrifice for those she loved; a woman who is absolutely hilarious without even trying to be; a woman who is beautiful and brilliant in her own special way; a woman who has a childlike excitement and wonder over the smallest things; and a woman who I will love and protect for all of eternity.

You are so much more than what your father and mother said you were. You are more than what your teachers labeled you as; you are more than society judged you to be; and you are more than just my wife. You are a daughter of the almighty God and a princess in his everlasting kingdom. You are cherished and loved for all eternity.

Even if something happens to me, I want you to know God has incredibly amazing things planned for your life, and you should never give up on them or on him. Because as much as I love you and want to take care of you, he loves and cares for you infinitely more than I ever could. So, no matter what happens today, tomorrow, or the next day, remember you are loved so much more than you could possibly imagine, and you do have a purpose.

You are the light of my life,

Lincoln

Adia clutched the letter against her chest. Then, after several seconds, she released her grip and let the paper lay back on the table.

The storm still raged outside the cave, but inside she was safe and warm.

As she sat in the cave he'd spent weeks preparing for her, Adia smiled. Closure washed over her. Lincoln sitting beside her, pushing her forward into the next chapter of her life, even if it meant without him.

"All right, God, I will never forget this love Lincoln and I shared, but if I'm still here, then that means you still have a plan for me. I'm ready to follow you, God, wherever you lead and whatever you have next for me. I'm ready."

She wanted to stay in this moment forever, and yet she knew an end was near. The hour was growing late, and not only had she been walking all day, but she still had several hours of walking to do in the morning to make it back to the village.

"Goodbye, Lincoln."

Yawning, she went over to her backpack and removed the blanket from the cabin with the verse from 1 Peter 5:7 stitched on it. She read it out loud, "Give all your worries and cares to God, for he cares about you."

She went around and turned off all the lanterns. She laid down on the hard ground against the back wall beneath her husband's words *Happy Anniversary, Adia* with the blanket draped over her.

After only a minute or so, her mind was filled with beautiful dreams of dancing with Lincoln to their song all night long.

CHAPTER 31

FIDES VILLAGE, NOVITAS—DAY 12, YEAR 371

"It is genuinely quite stimulating, I must say. To think your body has seemingly absorbed its energy and been permanently affected by the Creativity Stone. And yet it seems to show no signs of decay."

Joshua only half-listened as Jerold Gent rambled on while inspecting some of his skin cells under a microscope. The process of scraping off skin cells had caused a burning pain in his nerves. Something was seriously wrong with him, but there were so many things to worry about, he was having trouble focusing on one at a time.

"The cells themselves do not seem to be going through their normal decay process either. The energy seems to have slowed down their aging process, and when they are damaged, they send out a pulse that speeds up recovery. What I would be most curious about is what this did to your hair. While hair on the head is dead in a way already, would cutting it, or your fingernails for that matter, bring the same result?"

The worry at the forefront of Joshua's mind was the storms. There had been two storms so far, causing electrical fires and flooding. While the flooding did help some with cleaning up the debris from the attack, it also hindered

"No."

"It seems to have had no ill effect on you."

"What exactly did that thing do to me?"

"Seriously?" Jerold let out a dramatic sigh. "Have you not been listening to anything I said? Dedecus used the stone to heal you and bring you back to life. That energy has literally filled your cells."

"So, what you're saying is whenever I get hurt—"

"Your cells recover almost instantaneously. While we obviously wouldn't test the limits, it seems you can essentially heal yourself. It also seems to have slowed down your body's natural aging process, so you will likely live well past a normal life span."

"So, I'm invincible?"

"Not invincible, but when you do get hurt, you will heal almost immediately. Although, as I'm sure you noticed, said healing process seems to cause you extreme pain."

Joshua rubbed his temples. He should be more excited— he was practically a superhero like in the Earth stories. But all he could think about was the energy coursing through him—the same energy Dedecus used to kill Joshua's parents. *Can I even trust myself? What if it's doing to me what it did to Dedecus?*

"Joshua, come quick!" Namid ran into Jerold's makeshift research lab. She grabbed his arm.

"What is it?"

"Another storm. It hasn't started raining yet, but lightning struck the cow pen and started a fire."

They ran out of Jerold's hut.

Lightning lit up the murky sky, and thunder shook the ground.

"We have to get everyone to safety," Joshua said.

"The caves again?"

"No, Jerold worked with the blacksmith to design lightning rods. We've only installed them on the hospital so far, so get everyone there."

"Got it. Don is in the Eastern Fields putting out the fire from the lightning strike. You see how he's doing, and I'll get everyone else to safety." Namid raced away.

Joshua ran to the Eastern Fields, calling out to everyone he saw to go to the hospital.

A strong wind slammed into him, nearly knocking him over. The wind was worse than it had been the previous two times. The clouds seemed to swirl in the sky like someone was mixing a pot of some really nasty soup.

The smell of cooked beef came to his nose as he neared the Eastern Fields. Hopefully, some cows survived.

Don ran up to him, sweating and panting. Several others followed behind.

"Good, you're here," Don said while catching his breath. "We put out the fire and kept it from doing too much damage. But if more lightning strikes, we'll be in trouble."

Joshua's head pounded. He had too much to worry about.

"What should we do?" Don asked.

"The safety of our people is what's most important. Get back to the village and help Namid get everyone to the hospital."

"What about you?"

"Well, apparently, I'm invincible, so I'll stay here and protect the food supply if more lightning hits."

"You're what?"

"Never mind, just go."

Don left with the other guys, headed in the direction of the village.

"Okay, I got this. If lightning strikes the barn or silos, all I have to do is get to the well. And if rain comes, then the fire won't matter. But what if I have to get the animals to higher ground?"

He ran forward in no particular direction.

The wind was getting stronger, whistling through the air and blowing leaves and hairs off the palm trees. And whoever was mixing the soup pot in the sky was stirring awfully fast.

The sound of sheep and pigs reached his ears. They sounded as nervous as he was.

"Joshua Waters!"

Joshua swung around to see Namid racing toward him.

"What are you doing here?" he asked.

She approached him. "What are *you* doing here?" she put a finger on his chest. "You think I'm just going to let you risk your life out here? We're supposed to be partners in this leadership thing."

"It's too dangerous for you out here. I'm the only one who can do this. I talked to Jerold, and he said I'm invincible."

She stared at him. "What are you talking about?" Her curly brown hair flew in every direction.

"When Dedecus—" Joshua looked up. "What's that?"

He pointed at a huge swirling mass southeast of them, about a mile or so away. It looked like a funnel of wind that went from the sky down to the ground.

Namid turned around and stared. "Run!" She grabbed him and shoved him in the opposite direction from the gray, swirling funnel.

"What is that thing?"

"It's a tornado. Another Earth thing. It's like a tunnel of wind that destroys everything in its path."

The massive gray whirlwind came closer, flinging around everything it touched. It took a palm tree and ripped it right out of the ground. The tree joined the funnel of wind, flying upward before being spit out and becoming a flying projectile, crashing into several other trees.

"How did people survive on Earth?"

"I have no idea, but we have to get out of here." Namid grabbed his hand.

The wind seemed to blow in every direction at once. Joshua glanced from Namid's face to the tornado to the barns to the village.

"Someone has to protect Fides." He tried to pull away from her, but she gripped his hand. "I'll stay here and protect our crops and animals."

"You don't stop a tornado. You just pray it doesn't destroy everything. So, what are you trying to prove here?"

"I'm just trying to be a good leader. I've failed at everything else—just let me do this. I need to prove to everyone I'm worthy of being their leader." His voice grew quiet. "To prove to myself I can do it."

"You can be a good leader by leading by example and by not being an idiot. We have to get everyone to the hospital and get away from all windows. If we hide in the center of the building, we should be safe."

"But—"

Namid ignored his protests and ran toward the village, still holding his hand in an iron grip. He stumbled after her.

They reached the crowd of people streaming toward the hospital. A couple people looked his way, but most ignored him.

"Good. You got him," Don said when he saw them.

Is that how they see me? A little kid who has to be watched?

"It's coming closer," someone yelled.

Everyone ran to the hospital, crowding through the double doors.

A frazzled nurse tried to direct everyone, but chaos reigned.

He should be doing something to lead everyone, but nothing he could do would be of any consequence.

DOWNFALL

All they could do was ride out the storm and pray the tornado didn't hit them.

Joshua's list of worries kept growing, as did his headache.

CHAPTER 32

THE CABIN, NOVITAS—YEAR 2

"Just great." Steven scanned the evening sky for any sign of where he was. The nauseous horror at witnessing the little boy's, William's, stoning had been replaced with an urgency to find his way back to Fides.

He had wandered aimlessly through the forest until he came to a mountain range. Then hoping to get high enough up over the trees to find the village, he'd gone up a small animal trail. That had been over two hours ago. Now he couldn't even tell which side of the mountain he was on.

His feet ached, and his stomach grumbled, but he ignored it.

Lord, is this punishment for not being willing to enact your justice?

He scanned the tops of the palms in front of him for any signs of human life, then put his hand over his forehead to block out the sun and squinted at the horizon. A small column of smoke rose lazily above the horizon.

Thank you, Lord. Grinning, he ran down the side of the rocky mountain toward the smoke.

He raced through the palms. Compared to trees on Earth, the beauty of these kinds of trees afforded him plenty of walking space under the large leaves high above.

A splash of color off to his right caught his attention. About ten feet away was a gravel path with flowers of every imaginable color growing along the sides.

Who did this?

He walked toward the path and stepped over the flowers. The path curved around trees, winding around to avoid having to cut down anything.

He walked down it, his shoes crunching against the gravel.

The forest thinned out, and he came upon a clearing with a vintage cabin that looked like it had come right out of an Earth magazine. However, unlike the distinctive look of the palms, this cabin looked like it had been made out of wood from back on Earth.

"What in the world?" *We must not be the only ones living on Novitas.*

The sound of whistling reached his ears, and he turned around. Coming down the path was a tall, older man with shoulder-length brown and gray hair. He held a hand-woven basket that he swung as he walked.

Steven glanced around, unsure of what to do.

"Hey, there." The man's smile lit up his whole face.

"Um ... hi."

"You came just in time for dinner." The man walked past him and opened the door to the cabin.

The smell of food wafted out of the open door, and Steven's stomach growled.

"I had to go grab some carrots for the stew, but it should be ready soon."

Steven followed the man into the cabin. The front room had a fireplace along the sidewall, a leather couch by the front window, and several doors leading to other rooms. Across all the walls were colored photographs of people and families. The clarity and definition of the pictures were like nothing Steven had ever seen.

The man went through a swinging door into the kitchen, and Steven followed.

The kitchen was surprisingly modern, with an oven, sink, refrigerator, and wooden cabinets that also seemed to be made of Earth wood.

"Um ... I don't mean to be rude, but who are you?" Steven leaned up against one of the cabinets.

"My name is Emeth." The man gave out a deep laugh. "Thought you guys were the only ones who lived here?"

"Well, yeah, kinda. Does this mean there are more people here?"

The man pulled the carrots out of his basket and washed them off.

He even has running water.

"No, just me. But I get around."

"You don't seem that surprised at seeing me, though."

"I make it a habit to expect the wondrous workings of God. Although, I'm always in awe of how he pieces things together." He grabbed a cutting board, peeled and sliced up the carrots, and dumped them into a large, black pot on the stove. "What are you doing over here? Isn't your village on the other side of the mountains?"

He knows about Fides. "Yeah, I just got lost."

"Well, you're welcome to stay the night. I don't get company often, but it's always a treat when I do." He picked up a wooden ladle and stirred the stew. "So why were you wandering about?"

The air fled Steven's lungs as an image of William's trembling body flashed in his mind. "I had to get away and think for a while."

The man nodded sympathetically. "I'd need to get away too from that bunch, too."

"They're not bad. They're just doing the right thing."

"Point me to a verse in the Bible that says to walk around with a stick up your butt."

"Huh?"

"Following Jesus isn't supposed to be a punishment. It's humanity that's stripped the gospel of its power and joy."

"But isn't that the whole point of religion? Acknowledging our wickedness and then being better? Are you saying we're not sinful and in need of transformation?"

"Of course." He pointed the ladle at Steven, and a large drop of stew broth landed on the floor. "But who exactly is doing the bettering?"

"What do you mean?"

"Well, take this stew, for example. Without these carrots, the stew would be less rich and full of the complexities that make it taste so good. We know this because of a recipe, and it's been proven by previous stews. Let's say the stew knew this. Could it force itself to have carrots in it or trick the people eating it into thinking there are carrots in it?"

"No, you had to add them."

"Exactly." He put the ladle back in the pot and continued stirring. "We have a recipe, too. It's called morality. We can make all the laws and insist on having all the ingredients we want, but that doesn't mean we have those ingredients. We can try with all of our might to make carrots or whatever else within ourselves, but that's not how it works."

"So, then, what's our job?"

Emeth's hazel eyes twinkled. "That's the beauty of it— we just have to say yes. There's nothing we have to do to earn grace—we just have to repent. The gift Jesus gave us at the cross was simple—freedom. We're just the stew for God to place his kingdom in."

"Someone else has to add those things." Steven crossed his arms. "So, are you saying that we don't have a choice in the matter?"

"Wow, you go straight for the holes in my analogy." He laughed. "Unlike stew, God's given us free will. He's given us all the ingredients, but it's up to us whether or not we want to accept them. And also, unlike stew, there's a lot we have to let God take out of us so that he can put his ingredients in."

"Yea, non-Christians are pretty messed up." He thought of his father, and he clenched the countertop.

"Christians too."

"Well, at least we're better."

"I don't know about that. Anger, unforgiveness, and pride seem to run pretty rampant in Christian circles." Emeth went over to a cabinet and pulled out two bowls. Using the ladle, he scooped stew into both.

"Oh, I don't struggle with that."

"Then why are your knuckles white? You're gonna leave a dent in my countertop."

Steven glanced down and released the wood.

"Christians are very good at hiding their sins in the effort to be perfect. And they see themselves as better because they've become masters at convincing themselves and others of that perfection." He handed Steven a bowl and walked into the front room with the other.

"So then what good is being a Christian if I can't be perfect? Doesn't the Bible say to be perfect?" He followed Emeth through the swinging door.

Emeth sighed. "I really wish they hadn't translated it that way. God doesn't want you to be perfect by the world's standards: he wants you to become mature. He wants you to get to the point where you're completely dependent on him." He grabbed an overstuffed chair from the corner and dragged it in front of the couch. He plopped down into the chair, setting the stew down in his lap. "And the point of being a Christian isn't to be perfect."

Steven sat down on the couch. *The whole reason I became a Christian and came here was because I wanted to be better than my own father.*

"The point of being a Christian is to acknowledge our imperfections. To realize how much we need God and release everything to him. He doesn't want us to judge or punish each other for messing up. Every human but Jesus deserves death. But Jesus was the one who took that punishment."

"I'm pretty good, though, much better than a lot of people at least."

"Pride and anger are just as bad as any other sin. You should be able to see the consequences of those just by looking at your friends in the village."

Steven shifted uncomfortably on the couch. "That's not exactly what I meant."

"Of course, it is. You long so much to be good to please your father and God that you can't recognize you're just as bad as every other human on Earth, Novitas, or anywhere else." He took a sip of stew. "But the only way you'll be able to surrender all of that anger is by recognizing it in the first place."

"I'm not that angry." Steven stared down at the steam rising from his bowl.

"How did you feel when your father quit paying for your piano lessons because you messed up the first time you played for his friends? How did you feel when you were expected to take care of your little baby sister when you were only a teenager because your parents were too busy? How about when you wanted to be a writer until you failed that English test and vowed you'd never write again? Or, more recently, how did you feel when your dad disowned you for becoming a Christian? Or when he ripped you away from Lisa? Or when you saw that stoning earlier today?"

How did he—

"How would you feel if I told you that despite all his faults, your father did try to love you the best he could?"

His hunger forgotten—Steven set his bowl down on the floor. An ache gnawed at his gut, an ache he'd tried his entire life to ignore. "If my father loved me, then he wouldn't have treated me like a failure. All I wanted to do was prove to him that I was good enough to be loved by him." *Anger isn't righteous. Anger isn't righteous.*

"If all your dad knows is being treated like a failure, if all he knows is 'you are what you do,' then how was he supposed to treat others any differently?" Emeth leaned forward and put his hand on Steven's knee. "Your dad is a broken man who spent his entire life trying to prove to others and to himself that he was anything else."

"But that doesn't excuse what he did to me or to Lisa." He clenched his fists so tightly they hurt.

"Of course not, but what if God has something better for you than that anger gnawing at you. What if God has something better for him?"

"He doesn't deserve it." Steven didn't like the words coming out of his mouth. He'd spent a lifetime avoiding them. But he knew they were true.

"Neither do you."

Hot tears came to Steven's eyes.

"Seeing our real selves is not fun. We're a broken and bitter mess of unforgiveness and twisted motivations."

"What am I supposed to do with it?"

"Give it to God. The way he works doesn't make sense to our brains. But, by recognizing our faults, we see our need for God. Then, if we let him, he can take away that anger and teach us to forgive. Once we do that, he can begin to teach us about his love, his joy, his peace, and so much more." Emeth picked up a carrot chunk from his bowl and popped it into his mouth. "And this stew tastes so much better with carrots than without it."

"So, what do I do?"

"Release the anger, release the bitterness, release the striving toward perfection." He gestured at Steven's hands. "Your knuckles are white from squeezing them so tightly. What would happen if you opened your hands?"

Steven opened his pale fists, and his hands shook. His vision blurred as the familiar tightness in his chest dissipated.

The man got up from his seat and sat next to Steven, putting his arm around his shoulders.

Steven wept. He wept for his childhood, for Lisa, for the little boy who had been stoned, but most of all, he wept for his dad. He leaned against Emeth—the mysterious man who seemed to know Steven's own heart better than he did.

"This step is never fun, but it's always good."

"I ... I forgive you, Dad," Steven whispered.

CHAPTER 33

TRANSCENDENCE

"Okay," Dedecus pressed his fingers together, "let's try this again."

His last two attempts at making people hadn't gone great. The first one died instantly due to a lack of oxygen. The next one had stood there like a robot, unable to process his surroundings. Dedecus then created a sword and quickly put him out of his misery.

Maybe I just need a blueprint.

Dedecus thought of his mother. He barely had any memories left of her, but he would never forget her rounded face with a slight amount of baby fat on her cheeks. Her cheekbones were high and met with a small, pointed nose. Her lips were plump. Yellow specks dotted her brown eyes. She had a huge forehead she always hid with bangs.

Her voice was gentle with an alto pitch. When angry, it became pinched and went up an octave. She had a donkey laugh that made anyone who didn't know her turn their heads and anyone who did know her join in on the laughter.

"My sweet little D."

Dedecus swung around. "Mom?"

There she was, standing in his world, exactly as he remembered her.

"You're here." His voice cracked.

Without hesitation, he grabbed her and squeezed her tightly, like he did when he was little and a villager had been mean to him.

His mom looked around. "Where are we? How did we get here?" She looked closer at him. "And when did you get so big? You were nine." She tilted her head. "No, ten."

Dedecus stepped back, unsure of how to tell her.

"Why can't I remember anything past you being ten?" She started breathing faster and looked around frantically. "We were in the village, no ..." her eyes grew wide, and her voice became monotone. "We were mountain climbing. It was a beautiful day, and we were making our way back down. Then, suddenly, I heard a large crack and a moaning sound. Rocks slid all around us, once solid holds became loose in the torrent of stones sliding down the mountainside. I cried out and grabbed for my husband, but he's disappeared." A single tear runs down her cheek, but she must not notice it.

He had to stop this somehow.

"I tried to grab onto something. My hands were bloody as I slid down. Faster. Faster." She held up her shaking hands and stared at them. "The sun above darkens, and I look up. A boulder. A boulder slams into me and ... and I—" Her gaze jerked to him. "I died. What is this place? Why am I alive? What did you do to me?"

"Relax, everything will be okay. I brought you back to life."

"No, you didn't." She placed her hand on her chest. "I can feel my heartbeat, but I know I'm not alive. I'm a copy, a fake. Your mother died."

Dedecus swallowed hard. *What's happening?*

His mom ran her fingers through her hair and pulled. "I'm dead. But I'm alive. I'm just a corpse." She paced back and forth.

"Stop, please," he cried out. He only wanted his mom back. This wasn't supposed to happen.

"So, I'm a fake. A copy. Then what am I?"

He had to stop this. He shot out a burst of energy from his hand to get rid of her. Nothing happened. She didn't even notice.

"Do I even exist? What's my purpose? Why am I here? I'm dead." Her eyes were cold and lifeless.

He tried again to destroy his creation, but she didn't react. It was like when he'd attacked Joshua.

She stumbled over to him and fell to her knees. "Please." Her voice warbled. "Kill me. Take this pain away."

"I ... I'm trying."

He'd destroyed lots of things, but nothing he created seemed affected by the stone's destructive capabilities.

She grabbed his cloak and shook it. "Kill me. Kill me. Kill me." She chanted over and over.

He shot a bolt of power out of his hand at the ground beside them. A black snake flicked its tongue and slithered around in the dirt, testing its new surroundings. Then, it shot out, latching its fangs into his mom's flesh. She instantly fell backward, dead.

Dedecus clenched his fists and tried to scrub the horror from his mind.

The snake slithered closer to him, its black eyes locked on him.

"No, stop." He shot his power at it, but it was unaffected.

The snake lunged at him. Poison dripped from its extended fangs.

He dodged. How could he kill the snake?

He threw a wild bolt into the air.

A giant bird now flew overhead. Its feathers ruffled as it dove down and snatched the snake in its knifing claws big enough to carry off a human. The bird threw the snake into the air and snapped it in half with its two-foot-long beak. The bird circled above him, munching on the snake.

Dedecus breathed out a sigh of relief. If he couldn't destroy anything created with the Creativity Stone, he'd need to be a lot more careful with how he used it.

Pain flashed into his shoulders as his feet were lifted off the ground. He looked up. His bird's sharp claws had latched onto him. Apparently, the huge bird was still hungry.

A sword formed in his hand, and he hacked at the claws digging into his skin.

Letting out a screech that shook the planet, the bird dropped him. He lay sprawled out in the dirt.

Dedecus jumped up and healed his wounds while the bird flew circles over his head.

He flung disks of energy into the air that formed into solid rocks floating there. Dedecus leaped up, using them as stepping-stones into the air. He jumped toward the bird, sword extended.

It dodged him.

He fell back to the ground.

A stream of lava shot out of his palm, flying into the air and making an arch over the bird. Drops landed on its feathers, and it screeched.

Fully enraged, the bird did a nosedive toward him. Its long beak was open, ready to devour him whole.

Once close enough, Dedecus grabbed the top of its beak and catapulted himself upward. He did a summersault midair as the bird flew under him. Then, with all his might, he slammed his sword into its chest. Blood erupted everywhere, and he held the sword in there and twisted.

The bird screamed and thrashed wildly in the air, but Dedecus used the sword hilt as a handle and maintained his grip.

They crashed into the ground. He lurched forward into the dirt.

After a long moment, Dedecus stood and wiped the sweat and blood from his forehead.

He looked around. The lava had spread out, burning into the dirt. The dead bodies of humans and animals littered his planet. This was not supposed to happen.

He thought back to his mom's words. She needed a purpose, an intelligent designer, a god. But looking around at his universe that was supposed to transcend the broken creation God had given them, his place was even worse. He was going to have to step up, big time.

Dedecus clapped his hands together. "Let's get to work."

any rebuilding effort and had damaged both the food silos and animal pens. Based on Jerold's advice, they'd put bags of gravel and rock around the fields to prevent too much damage to the crops. But he felt like he was running blind, unable to stop or fix the damages caused. Already a handful of people had died.

"If we could find a way to collect this energy, it would be quite beneficial. With its seemingly endless reservoir supply, we could power our generators without the need for solar energy."

The next biggest worry was Namid. While she kept saying she was fine, she had started snapping at people and would randomly get angry at small things. She needed to deal with her parents leaving, but she kept insisting she'd already dealt with it.

This led to worry number three. He was sure everyone was regretting staying on Novitas with him. He was a failure, and the storms kept coming. Why wouldn't they regret not leaving with the Judges of Justice? He needed to figure out some way to make Fides worth it. If not, they could have another revolt.

Jerold had stopped talking and was staring at him expectantly.

"Oh, I'm sorry, what did you say?"

Jerold sighed. "Have you heard anything I've said? My question was, do you think we could get a hold of the Creativity Stone? Based on what it's done to you, I'd love to—"

"No," Joshua said loudly.

"I was merely—"

"No, the stone is the cause of all of this. The attack was less than two weeks ago. Are you already forgetting what that thing did to Dedecus?"

"But the potential scientific breakthroughs."

CHAPTER 34

FIDES VILLAGE, NOVITAS—DAY 13, YEAR 371

"I dug around in the rubble of my house," the woman complained, "and couldn't find the antique dolls my grandmother gave me. That man must have stolen them."

"I would do no such thing," the accused man replied. "Why would I want your creepy collection of dolls?"

Namid took a sip of water and tried to shake away her headache. As the Judge of Justice, her job now was to settle any disputes. But with everything going on, how in the world was she supposed to care about some woman's assortment of dolls?

"They're valuable! My ancestor brought them from Earth with her."

"Your ancestor must have been as crazy as you to waste her time with those things," the man said.

Namid glanced at the long line of people waiting to bring their case to her. How was it possible that even with most of the village either dying in the attack two weeks ago or leaving with her parents five days ago, that so many people still needed to talk to her.

"Well, you were the only one who knew they were valuable. If you didn't steal them, then who did?"

"You've bragged about those raggedy things your entire life—everyone knew about them. But I can promise you that anyone with a brain would take one look at those things and keep walking."

No wonder my parents were so cranky all the time. She frowned. She didn't want to think about her parents.

"How dare you, I'll have you know—"

"Enough!" Namid got up from her chair and walked to them. "If you haven't noticed, the flooding from that second storm moved a lot of things. I'm sure your dolls will turn up somewhere, and I'll make sure they get back to you."

"But—"

"Case dismissed." She sat back down.

Sharon, who took turns with Don in assisting her, shoved the two along as they continued to argue.

Namid gazed at the long line waiting for her.

Sharon walked back over. "Next up—"

"No!" Namid stood. "Please, no more."

Everyone looked at her, confused. They still had at least an hour of sunlight left.

"I mean, I'm done for the day. I'll hear the rest tomorrow."

Chaos erupted as everyone tried to talk over one another about how important their case was.

"I will deal with it tomorrow. Goodbye." Namid walked away as fast as she could.

Joshua walked up to her, smiling and holding something in his hands. "Hey, Namid, I brought you some—"

"Not right now."

"Oh, I'm sorry, I just knew you were moderating today and figured you might like ..." He bit his lip. "Never mind—it was dumb."

Namid sighed. Somewhere buried beneath everything she had to deal with, her heart fluttered. "Thank you, but I need to be by myself for a while."

Joshua stared at her for a second. "Oh, I understand. I'll deal with the mob." He gave her a smile.

"Thank you. I'll be on Peaceful Plateau if another disaster comes."

She walked past him without waiting for a response.

All the thoughts in her head felt like millions of invisible wasps stinging her. She needed to get away from everything. The best place to do that was Peaceful Plateau.

She made her way up the path along the Pearl Cliffs. It started out as the same path leading to the caves they'd discovered, but this one branched off and led to the top of the cliffs instead of to the waterfall.

Peaceful Plateau had been given its name by the New Day Separatists who settled Fides. People said it was impossible to not find peace while surrounded by the pinnacle of God's creation.

She reached Peaceful Plateau and sat down cross-legged in the lush grass.

The Emerald River ran alongside her, sparkling in the evening sun.

A golden-tipped butterfly landed on her knee.

"Hey there, little guy."

She extended her finger out to the butterfly, but the movement caused it to fly away and land on a Decus flower not far away.

She looked out at the grass and flowers waving slowly in the wind while butterflies jumped between flowers. It was simple and beautiful.

Up there, Namid's head slowly cleared. Finally, she was able to think without all the chaos surrounding her.

How did my parents do this every day?

She grimaced. She didn't want to think about her parents. But how long could she avoid it?

Her parents had abandoned her. They chose to run away in fear of God instead of trusting in his promises. Now she was expected to pick up the broken pieces of their lives and rebuild. But the pieces were so small and shattered that the task would be impossible to put back together.

Was that really what God wanted? For them to be stricter and for her to be alone?

Remember the consequences of your failure.

Remember to remain pure in all thoughts and actions.

Remember that God is found only through the law.

Namid reached into her pocket and pulled out the cross necklace her parents had insisted she wear. After the attack, she'd gone back to the cave and found it. The sharp edge cut into her skin as she clutched it.

Remember to stay modest to keep others from sin.

Remember to cast out the defiled.

Remember to enact what others deserve.

Remember, you're never good enough.

Tears came to Namid's eyes as memories played through her mind. She once tried to sign up for a dance lesson, and her parents had broken her ankle, so she couldn't dance. Another time, she made a birthday card for Dedecus, and when they discovered it, they burned it in the fireplace. How could she forget coming downstairs to see her parents sobbing because their messed-up little daughter couldn't seem to do the right thing?

Then every new year, she'd get the list of every sin she'd committed in the past year, a tradition that started with the first Judge of Justice. And the finale of it all ... her father's face as he turned away from her a week ago, left Novitas, and sentenced her to be an orphan.

She opened her hand and stared at the necklace, wanting to chuck it as hard as she could. Wanting it to be lost in the rubble of her childhood.

Another golden-tipped butterfly landed on her, bringing her back to her surroundings.

A different memory came into her mind, one that took place on Peaceful Plateau.

One night when she was thirteen, she was sitting about where she was now, gazing at the stars and feeling small, puny. Her mother had given her a long lecture, ending with a beating, saying she must stop dancing, that God hated dancing. Namid wasn't sure why she loved to dance but twirling and swaying to music made her heart soar like everything was right with the world, even though it wasn't.

"God?" she had cried out as she stood on the plateau overlooking the village that night. "I want to follow you, but why can't I do anything right?"

She hadn't really expected a response; why would God respond to her anyway?

"Who do you say that I am, daughter?" a voice came to her on the wings of the wind. She had looked around for where it came from but couldn't see anything. The voice came from all directions at once. "Who do you say that I am, daughter?"

God didn't speak to people anymore unless they were holy, and she definitely wasn't.

But then who was it?

"God?" she asked tentatively, feeling silly.

"Who do you say that I am?"

"You are the Great Judgment, the one who has given us the path to follow and rebukes those who don't. Is that why you're talking to me?" Her hands shook, and she wrapped her arms around herself. Her parents had always told her if she didn't act more holy, she would face God's wrath. And now that wrath would come upon her.

"Do not fear, my daughter," the voice said softer, warmer. "I am not who you have judged me to be. I am unconditional, never-changing love."

This couldn't be God.

"I am God; the one who created you, the one who died for you, the one who watches over you, the one who longs to spend time with you."

Namid clung to his words. She didn't understand the theology of what was happening, but all she could hear was that the God of the universe wanted to spend time with her.

She could almost feel herself standing taller.

A childlike giggle filled the air around her.

"Would you like to dance?" the voice asked.

And with that single question, music permeated the air, surrounded her, and cascaded through her soul. She had no idea if it were only in her mind or if other people could hear the music too, but she didn't care.

She took a step forward and danced awkwardly. But quickly, she became more assured with her steps. She did an arabesque, spun around five times, and leaped through the air.

Then lyrics came with the music. She wasn't sure how it was possible, but her own voice was singing, even though she couldn't sing and wasn't singing. She continued to pour everything she had into the dance.

All my life
I've been told
I'd never be enough.

All my life
I have learned
To fight for goodness and love.
But now ...
But now ...

DOWNFALL

She leaped into the air and spun. The music washed through her soul and scrubbed away the pain, frustrations, and fear completely.

> I rest in your arms, Abba.
> I lay at your feet, Abba.
> I dance in your joy, Abba.
> I bask in your peace, Abba.

> When I fall down
> And my hope seems lost,
> You pick me up
> And around we spin.
> You sing over me
> The song you wrote for me.

Namid smiled at the vivid memory of when her life had changed completely. Being up on Peaceful Plateau brought that feeling back, that she was loved. The song that had played that night long ago came to her mind, and she hummed it.

She had found God that night—she danced with him and let his love fill her. But she wasn't thirteen anymore.

She should try to think more positively, but how? What were they supposed to do now?

Her shoulders drooped, and she let the cross necklace fall to the grass.

A voice pierced through her sorrow and self-pity.

"My daughter, who do you say that I am?"

She jumped and looked around for who had said that. "God? Is that you?"

"Who do you say that I am?"

"You are my God, the one who created me and loves me. I know who you are, and I've turned toward you, repenting and receiving your love. But ..." After a pause, she continued. "But I don't know how to get through this."

"Would you like to dance with me?"

A melody came rushing through the air, slow and sweet, filling her soul and making her smile. The song she had danced to five years ago—the song God had created especially for her.

She stood and tried to dance, but she couldn't get into the music and felt awkward and clunky as she stepped forward, then back, then did a spin.

"I can't, God."

"Here, let me help you."

Namid closed her eyes and took a breath. She started to dance again, but this time was different. Instead of dancing by herself, she could feel God guiding her steps. He was right there with her and leading her in a dance more beautiful than she could have possibly imagined.

The lyrics came, once again, with her voice singing them even though her mouth was closed.

> You hold me tight.
> You take the lead.
> You spin me round and round.
>
> I follow you.
> I trust your lead.
> I close my eyes and dance.
>
> And now ...
> And now ...
>
> I rest in your arms, Abba.
> I lay at your feet, Abba.
> I dance in your joy, Abba.
> I bask in your peace, Abba.

She smiled, and tears cascaded over her face once again, but this time they were tears of gratitude and joy. Her Creator knew her intimately—he knew how to help her.

DOWNFALL

When I fall down,
And my hope seems lost,
You pick me up
And around we spin.
You sing over me
The song you wrote for me.

She might never see her parents or the people who'd
left with them again or never get back all the people they'd
lost to the attack. She might never get her friend, Dedecus,
back. The storms might still come. The village might never
be able to go back to what it was before.

None of that mattered.

She was dancing with a God who loved her for who
she was, a God who'd created her and had a plan for her
life. She looked down at the cross necklace and considered
throwing it away. Instead, she picked it up and placed it
back on her neck, a forever reminder of the kind of person
she didn't want to be.

I rest in your arms, Abba.
I lay at your feet, Abba.
I dance in your joy, Abba.
I bask in your peace, Abba.

You're my father, God.

CHAPTER 35

FIDES VILLAGE, NOVITAS—DAY 20, YEAR 371

Joshua pushed his blond hair out of his eyes for the hundredth time. He stood on a makeshift stage in front of the couple hundred people gathered at the town center.

"I want to thank all of you for your hard work. Because of *all* of you, we have finally cleared the rubble and are ready to begin building!"

The crowd let out a whoop.

It had been eight days since the tornado hit. They considered themselves lucky it passed around the village and didn't hit the hospital. Since then, the sky had been clear and sunny with Fides' normal sixty-five-to-seventy-degree temperatures. He constantly prayed that the storms were over and he could keep the promise he just made about rebuilding.

"If you're like me, your body probably wants to pass out for a year or two."

The chuckles from the audience lifted his confidence.

"But we've worked hard, and to celebrate, Namid, our new Judge of Justice, thought that we needed a party."

The center of town—not that there was much town left—had been decorated with anything colorful that could be found in the wreckage. Stringed lights hung across the sky from the few remaining buildings, creating a web of yellow over their heads to contrast the greens and yellows of the clouds during the sunset that evening.

"Tomorrow, we'll begin the process of rebuilding Fides. Although, since we've lost all our architects, I'm not really sure what we're going to do ..." What was wrong with him? Who mentions something like that in a speech? He needed to get back on track.

Joshua cleared his throat and looked around at the faces of Fides Village. No one had been left untouched by grief and loss over the past few weeks, but they were still smiling.

"We've faced a lot of loss, and no one would blame us if we just curled up into a ball and gave up. But even when everything crumbles around us, we'll find a reason to celebrate. Even when darkness surrounds us, we'll still find a reason to rejoice in God's provision and love! No matter what's happened or what'll happen next, we, as the people of Fides Village, will show the world that the devil hasn't won!"

The crowd cheered, and the band behind him started to play an upbeat song. The lead singer was singing something about hope. Some of the villagers danced around while others went to the snack table or sat on benches.

"Ooh, I love this song!" Namid twirled around, immediately putting everyone on the dance floor to shame as she got lost in the music.

Joshua tried not to stare.

An older woman he didn't recognize came up to him as he hopped off the stage.

"Can I talk to you for a minute?" She had to shout to be heard above the band, so they walked off to the side and sat down on one of the benches.

"My name is Adia, and I heard you mention that you needed an architect."

"Oh, you're Jerold Gent's daughter."

Adia fidgeted. "Yeah, that's me. Anyway, about the architecture."

"Yeah, we need one. Your father is better with tech than design. Everyone skilled with that kind of thing was either killed in the attack or left with the Judges of Justice.

"Well, technically, that's true, but before I met my husband, Lincoln ..." she looked down and bit her lip as her eyes grew misty. "He ... um ... he died in the attack."

"I'm so sorry." He'd had a lot of conversations like this since the attack. He flinched and prepared for the onslaught of accusations.

Adia took a deep breath. "It's not your fault, and don't let anyone tell you otherwise. I know you were friends with Dedecus, but he made his own choices."

Joshua tried to keep from crying.

"Anyway, before I met Lincoln, I studied to be an architect. I'm not great at it, but I'm pretty decent at drawing up blueprints."

"Wow! That would be amazing. I've tried not to stress about that, but no one I've talked to has any idea how to design a building."

Adia laughed. "Well, God said he had a purpose for me, and I guess this is it."

"Thank you, you'll be carrying on the Gent family tradition of keeping this village's gears running."

"Well, I don't know about that. But I'm happy to help." Adia looked off to the side as if preoccupied with her thoughts.

The song the band was playing wound down, and Joshua couldn't help but look over at Namid.

Everyone else danced and had a good time, but no one could dispute who the best dancer in the village was. Namid was born a dancer. Everything within her moved to the music, from her light brown hair to her soft and graceful hands to her long, flowing skirt to her quick feet. They all flowed together in a perfect display. She was the embodiment of whatever song they played and perfectly reflected the energy and soul of the music through her dancing.

"Ooh, so the Judge of Mercy has got a little crush."

Joshua darted his gaze back to Adia and really hoped he wasn't blushing.

"Oh, please, everyone in the village knows you two like each other."

"What do you mean?"

"Now I get why you guys couldn't be together before with the whole Judge of Justice versus Mercy rivalry that's been going on, but her parents left, so it's okay now."

Joshua was so surprised by Adia's forwardness. He could only stare at her and blink.

"You guys have been friends forever. She gets you out of your shell. You're a safe person she can depend on compared to all the gunk in her life. Plus, you two just look adorable together."

"How ... um ... do you know about all this?"

"The boy who would one day become the Judge of Mercy befriends a disgraced orphan boy and the girl who would become his political rival. That gossip has been going around for years. It has to be the worst-kept secret in the whole village."

"I didn't know. I thought we did a pretty good job of hiding it."

"Well, everything worked out, and now's your chance to act on your feelings."

Okay, now Joshua was sure he was blushing. He didn't even know this woman who gave him relationship advice.

Suddenly, Namid turned to look at him with her hazel brown eyes, and he tried to make his heart beat normally.

Namid stopped dancing, looked over at him, and walked toward where they were sitting.

"She's coming over. What do I do?"

Adia grinned like a little girl as he shifted awkwardly. "She already likes you, so just be yourself."

"Hey, guys, whatcha talking about?"

Stop blushing, be confident. "Nothing. I'll tell you later."

"Well, if you don't mind, I think it's time you joined me in a dance."

Joshua started to say something, but she grabbed his hands and pulled him to his feet before he could.

"Just because you're now a leader doesn't mean you can't have some fun," she said as she dragged him out to where the people were dancing. "Plus, we're actually co-leaders, and as your co-leader, I order you to dance and enjoy yourself."

"Oh ... um ... I don't think so ..." he stuttered out as she pulled him to the center of the dance floor.

"Last week, you tried to stare down a tornado."

"Yeah, but that was different. I can't dance."

"Oh, come on, everybody can dance. Just follow my lead, and you'll be fine," she said, laughing as she twirled around.

The song ended with the lead singer holding out a long, high note as Joshua was about to awkwardly attempt to follow Namid's expert moves.

"Darn, I guess I won't be able to," he said and tried to maneuver away from the dancers and back to the safety of his seat.

"Don't be silly," she said, laughing. "They're about to play another song."

After everyone clapped for the band, they started back up with an upbeat and energetic song.

Namid danced around wildly, grabbed his hand, and spun him around as she twirled.

Joshua clumsily followed her moves and tried not to trip on his own feet or run into anyone else on the crowded street. For a moment, he forgot about everything else as he concentrated on dancing.

Namid pulled him close to her and whispered in his ear, "Dancing is about having fun, so stop trying so hard, smile, and stop looking like you're constipated."

She grinned at him, and he couldn't help but laugh. After that, Joshua loosened up a bit as they listened to the upbeat music and continued to dance.

> Oh, when I dance with you!
> My world starts changin'.
>
> Yeah, when I dance with you!
> There ain't no feignin'.
>
> 'Cause, when I dance with you!
> Ain't no doubt remainin'.
>
> And so, I dance with you!
> Ooh oh, oh, oh, oh.
>
> And so, I dance with you!
> Ooh oh, oh, oh, oh.

The lights blurred around them as Joshua and Namid danced together.

> It might be crazy—
> Awkward, just maybe.
>
> But when that first note plays
> My heart's set ablaze,
>
> And so, I dance with you!
> Ooh oh, oh, oh, oh.
>
> And so, I dance with you!
> Ooh oh, oh, oh, oh.

The song ended, and Joshua tried not to show his nervousness as he leaned in to kiss her. Slightly to his surprise, she warmly kissed him back, and their lips and hearts joined together. They stayed in that moment for a beautiful glimpse of eternity.

A couple people cheered, and soon the whole group clapped. It took Joshua a minute to realize they were all cheering for him and Namid.

He blushed awkwardly as Namid shrugged and laughed. Normally, he'd be incredibly embarrassed by the attention and eager for the moment to end, but he stared into Namid's deep hazel eyes, and she stared back into his. He wished that this moment and this night would never end. He wished they could stay there forever, dancing together in celebration of the new thing God was doing in their lives.

CHAPTER 36

FIDES VILLAGE, NOVITAS—YEAR 2

Steven ran toward Fides with the morning sun in his eyes. Ever since last night at the cabin, something had changed. For as long as he could remember, a familiar tightness had settled in his gut. He'd always labeled it a desire to be righteous and better than the father who'd hurt him. But now, he wasn't so sure what it was.

Either way, the tightness had fled, and whenever it tried to return, he would repeat what Emeth had taught him.

I forgive because I've been forgiven. I am broken, but grace only requires repentance. He is working on me in his timing.

The forest of palms broke abruptly, and the simple wooden buildings that made up Fides Village sat before him.

They had been so foolish to come to Novitas to run from the suffering. How were they supposed to see God's plan of restoration if they ran away?

They still had the portal, though. He could wrap his arms around his little sister, Lisa, again. He could forgive his father in person. The thought filled him with equal parts of fear and joy.

He ran between houses, but no one was in sight. Either everyone was still asleep or at another town gathering.

What if they're stoning another person? The thought made him nauseous but wasn't his problem.

Jefferson Gent's house was near the center of the village—that's where the portal device would be.

Jefferson's house came into sight. It had been designed perfectly for water flow and looked more advanced than any of the simple wooden houses surrounding it.

He pushed himself harder.

Beside him was the town center by the church that had become the meeting place. Esther once again stood on the steps leading to the church below the large cross at the entrance.

A woman he didn't recognize stood beside her, seemingly small beside the looming presence of Esther.

Everyone had gathered around her, nodding at whatever she was saying.

He got to Jefferson's door and put his hand on the doorknob.

"I pronounce judgment upon this woman's head." Esther held up a stone. Even from this distance, he could see the red stains on the light gray rock. "Judgment so that my daughter, so that all of our children will be able to grow up in a pure world."

He squeezed the doorknob tightly. *It's not my problem. They would sooner stone me before letting me leave. This is my only chance to escape.*

He flung the door open and raced inside. In the middle of the front room, in a place of prominence like a prestigious trophy, sat the portal maker.

The device was oversized for the room, but Jefferson didn't seem to care. It was about three-fourths his height and twice his width with wheels thrown on the bottom. It had several knobs and buttons along the top and side. A pair of antennae jutted awkwardly out from the top, and a ton of wires stuck out haphazardly from the back.

He ran to the screen and fiddled with the knobs.

A woman's wail reached his ears, and he froze. *It's not my problem. It's not my problem. I never should have come in the first place. I was just running from my problems.* He went back to messing with the portal device, trying to make it work.

He was simply fixing their mistake in coming to Novitas. They shouldn't have run away in the first place.

And what are you doing now? The quiet nudging in his spirit immobilized him.

But Lisa, my mom, my dad...

What if I want to redeem Novitas too?

Smack. The sound of stone against flesh sent him flying into action.

The floorboards creaked under his feet as he reached the door.

Beside the door sat a broom. Not the best weapon, but it would have to do. He grabbed it and flung the door open.

The crowd had gathered in a circle around the young woman. She lay curled in a ball on the ground.

Steven held the broom in front of him and charged through the people.

A large rock flew toward the woman, and with reflexes he didn't know he possessed, he swatted it out of the air with the hard area of the broom between the handle and thistles.

"What are you doing?" Esther screeched like a bat. "The defiled must be punished."

"No! This is wrong. I will not let you harm this innocent woman."

"She is not innocent, and now neither are you." Esther grabbed a rock and flung it at him.

God, I'm going to need you right now.

Steven flung the handle around like a baseball bat. The chunk of stone connected with the wood and went flying through the air. It sailed past the gathering and landed in the grass.

"Get him." Esther's voice was flat, devoid of emotion.

Rocks flew at him from all sides, and he used the broom as a sword, striking the rocks and knocking them to the ground.

One almost hit him in the back of the head, but he ducked just in time. It flew past his head and rammed into another stone flying toward him.

"Get him!" Esther's voice had become a throaty roar.

He twirled the broom that should have snapped in half already and circled around the woman. Stones pinged off the broom like it was made of metal.

Sweat dripped into his eyes.

Esther threw a small boulder, and he held the handle in front of him with one hand on either side to deflect it. The stone connected with the broom handle, and while it fell to the ground, the impact cracked the broom in two, and wood splinters flew toward his face.

"Leave, save yourself." The woman looked up at him, and her blue eyes twinkled with tears. A large, red welt was on her shoulder from the first hit.

"I'm not going anywhere."

Steven used the broken pieces like clubs, swatting stones out of the air left and right.

A man and woman pushed through the crowd. Steven recognized them instantly as Mr. and Mrs. Larson, William's parents. They each held thick wooden boards.

"I stood by and watched my son die because of these people." He grimaced; his eyes filled with regret. But he held his head high. "I will not let another person die for Esther's wickedness."

"I'm wicked?" Esther glowered at them. "I am only following the law we all swore to uphold."

"Well, maybe God isn't found in your laws," Mrs. Larson said. "If he is, then he's not a God I want to serve."

Esther gave them a death glare, her nostrils flared, and she screeched, "Kill them!"

For a second, no one moved.

"Kill them!" Esther let out a guttural roar, spittle flying from her mouth.

The crowd grabbed rocks from the piles gathered for them.

Steven and the Larsons stood circled around the woman still curled in the fetal position.

Stones soared through the air toward them. The Larsons used their planks as shields. Steven continued waving the pieces of the broom around, swatting at anything that came near him.

An older woman named Olivia pushed through the mob. She held a metal baking pan in her hand. "I gave everything for the New Day Separatists because I was sick of hypocrites in the church. Turns out I joined the biggest hypocrites ever." She joined their circle.

Stones rained down on their heads.

Steven knocked down several more stones. He turned his head to see a gray blob headed right for his face. Before he had time to react, a baseball bat came out of nowhere and smacked it away.

Fredrick, a gray-haired man who'd been there the day he'd joined the group, held a metal bat in his hands.

"Thanks," Steven said through panting breaths.

"Thank you." Fredrick gave him a nod and joined the circle.

Rocks continued to come toward them, but they all fell to the ground.

The barrage slowed and then stopped.

"Why did you stop?" Esther yelled.

"We're out of rocks," someone said.

Steven let out a short laugh and looked around. "What's your plan now?"

"I knew you were trouble, Steven Waters. You're just as bad as your father." Esther seethed. "You might have survived, but I promise you will pay for this."

Steven ignored her and turned to the woman. She was short with curly brown hair and around his age. He stared into her eyes and held out his hand to help her up.

She took his hand and gave him a tearful smile. With all the adrenaline flowing through him, he hadn't noticed how beautiful she was.

"What's your name?" he asked as he helped her up.

"Hannah."

"Hi, I'm Steven." He wiped the sweat on his forehead away and smiled.

"You saved me. Why?"

"Because it's what God would have done."

CHAPTER 37

FIDES VILLAGE, NOVITAS—DAY 22, YEAR 371

Don wandered aimlessly in the Eastern Fields, feeling self-pity and hating himself for feeling that way.

Taking long walks had always been therapeutic to him, but today felt like an endless trudge.

He looked down at his tattered clothes that itched when he moved, reminding him of everything he wasn't.

"I miss you, Aaron," Don whispered into the breeze, which was hitting his face like someone's moist breath.

He couldn't believe the mighty Judge of Mercy, Aaron Waters, was dead. He'd often taken these walks with him. Sometimes, they'd walk in quiet contemplation, but they usually talked for hours without stopping, their voices filling the air with depth and life. But today, silence surrounded Don as he walked. The world itself seemed silent as if content to let the least qualified leader ever wander for eternity.

He wished one of the other leaders had survived instead of him to help lead the village through this difficult time. Walter had always been wise—he would know how to help Joshua and Namid to lead.

Don allowed himself a small smile. Joshua was going to become an amazing leader. He was the perfect blend of wise but understanding mixed with a bit of his father's unconventional creativity. He was exactly what the broken and divided village needed.

Unlike me.

What the village didn't need was a hot-headed poor man making decisions for them.

Don's smile faded as he trudged onward through the fields of silence. But the fields weren't silent. The wind carried the faint sound of crying to his ears, and he stopped.

Why was someone so far away from the village?

Don jogged toward the sound. Every yard closer brought the wailing louder and clearer. A little girl?

He stopped at a large pit he'd never seen before. About a hundred feet below him was a little girl he didn't recognize. She had short brown hair and was alternating between crying and hyperventilating. Her face was a bluish purple from lack of air and was streaked with trails of tears.

"Hello?"

The little girl inhaled sharply and tried to stop crying long enough to answer.

"Don't worry, I'll get you out."

Don looked around and tried to find anything he could use to pull her up.

The earthquake during the attack had created a sinkhole. He looked down at the ground beneath his feet. He should step away from the ledge so he wouldn't fall in too.

Suddenly, the ledge crumbled and was now behind him. Don coughed as dirt covered his vision, and he slid down to the center of the hole where the girl sat.

He pushed dirt out of his face and stood. "Well, that's unfortunate," he muttered.

The poor child cried uncontrollably as she shook.

"Shh, shh, it's going to be okay." He sat down in front of her and took her tiny hands in his. "What's your name?"

After several seconds of gasping, she pushed the name "Jenny" out.

"Well, Jenny, my name is Don, and I promise you I will get you out of here." He looked into her eyes and hoped he seemed confident enough to soothe the little one. "How old are you, Jenny?"

She held up five fingers. "I ... I th ... I thought no ... no one—"

"Well, I'm here now." Talking seemed to help her calm down and force her to take a breath, so he tried to keep her talking. "Where are your parents, Jenny?"

"The ... they died ... in the quake. So, I've been hiding out here from the scary light flashes, booms, and twisty wind. Then I fell in this yesterday."

Don could feel tears pressing on the back of his eyes. This girl should be playing happily in the fields, not living in them, hiding from some monster she was scared would kill her like he killed her parents.

"You're safe, I promise. You're a very brave girl, Jenny. We're gonna get out of this pit together." He squeezed her hand.

Jenny perked up, stopped crying, and let out a large hiccup.

He pushed against the dirt slope beside them, but it only gave a little bit.

"Okay, I think we can make it up." The edge of the pit was high above them, and they were too far away from Fides for anyone to hear their shouts for help. The fact that Don had found her was all God's doing.

He stood and looked down at Jenny. "Okay, I want you to hop on my back, and I'm going to try to climb this out of this thing."

Jenny stood and looked up at the dirt slope with wide eyes.

He leaned over and looked at her squarely. "I want you to repeat after me."

When he was little, his parents couldn't afford a powered generator, and at night their house was pitch black. He'd been scared of the dark, so his parents made up a song for them to sing together. The words didn't exactly fit, but he'd make them work.

> I'm not afraid of the dark;
> The dark's afraid of me.

Jenny repeated the phrase back to him as Don helped her get on his back. She wrapped her tiny arms around his neck and her legs around his chest as they kept singing.

> When I think I am alone,
> You're always holdin' me.

Don grabbed a handful of dirt above him and dug his feet in. Jenny squeezed his neck tightly as he began the climb.

> I'm strong, I'm brave,
> 'Cause I've got
> His strength.

The climb was slow, and every time either one of them shifted slightly, they slid downward. With every couple of feet he climbed, he lost at least half that much.

> Even when my fear is big,
> My God's much bigger.

Don was only a quarter of the way up and panted hard. But he continued to sing and climb.

> I'm not afraid of the dark.
> The dark's afraid of me.

When I think I am alone,
You're always holdin' me.

I'm strong, I'm brave
'Cause I've got
His strength.

Even when my fear is big,
My God's much bigger.

After the third or fourth repetition of the song, Don reached for the next fistful of dirt and gripped grass instead.

He quickly pulled himself up before more of the ground was swallowed by the sinkhole. Then, after getting several feet away, he let Jenny down, dropped to the ground, and wiped away some of his dirt-stained sweat with the thick grass.

Jenny bounced up and down. She bent down and hugged him tightly. "Thank you, Mister Don!"

"You're welcome." Don laughed as he pushed the sweat from his forehead and sat up.

Don blinked as suddenly words echoed around in his head.

I will use you to lead a powerful revival of faith through Fides. You will be a leader known for his steadfast faith.

Unsure of what to do with those words and too exhausted to do anything else, he turned to Jenny and said, "Come on, Jenny, let's get you back to the village."

"But what if that scary man comes back?"

"What does our song say?"

"Even when my fear is big, my God's much bigger."

"Exactly." He stood and took her hand. God wasn't only bigger than fear—he was bigger than Don's doubt and insecurities.

Although, the words *even though my doubt and insecurities are big, my God's much bigger*, didn't really work for the song. Don rewarded himself with a dumb grin for his dumb joke as he walked Jenny back to the village.

He looked down at Jenny. They'd faced so many problems lately that they'd forgotten about one very important one. What were they supposed to do with little kids like Jenny who'd lost their families either in the attack or the storms?

CHAPTER 38

FIDES VILLAGE, NOVITAS—DAY 30, YEAR 371

Sweat dripped into Namid's eyes, and she blinked rapidly. Then, she heaved with all her might along with the others to lift the support beam.

"All right, guys, we're almost there. Just push that beam into place, and this house will be done!" Joshua called out. He and Don held up a cross section as Namid, Adia, and many others helped push the giant beam into place.

They'd been hard at work to rebuild the village, a blessing in disguise because each of them was too tired at night to do anything but pass out.

Namid was especially grateful because it took her mind off how her parents and half the village had abandoned them. In some ways, she missed her parents, but she was also secretly thankful they were gone. They were the reason the village had always seen Dedecus as a curse of sin. Their cruel and unforgiving religion drove him to use the Creativity Stone.

But they were still her parents, and while they were wrong about God, they were only trying to do what they thought was right. That she was a little happy they'd left filled her with shame.

Her mind snapped back to attention as, with a giant heave, they finished pushing the beam into place.

Cheering, they stepped back to admire their work on the first rebuilt house. Nothing fancy or huge, but they'd built the one-story, cabin-like structure out of stripped palm logs, and they'd all worked together to build it. The effort had united what had been a broken village.

"Amazing job, guys. I'm so proud of all of you!" Joshua pushed his hair out of his eyes and beamed brightly.

The thirty or so sweat-covered people celebrated their hard work.

"After the attack," he continued, "We weren't sure if we'd be able to recover, but this cabin is proof that Fides Village is a fighter and a survivor. For as long as this cabin stands, Fides will look to it as a beacon of new beginnings and remember to never give up because God is with us, and with him, we can do anything!"

The people cheered and clapped.

Namid cheered the loudest, although more for Joshua than the cabin being finished. While they hadn't had much time to themselves, they'd grown closer in their relationship in the past four days than they had in the past four years.

She'd always been able to tell he had a crush on her for as long as she could remember. Even though he never said anything, he was always obvious and was bad at hiding his emotions. The way he smiled at her made her feel warm and giddy, but because of her parents, she'd refused to allow herself to feel anything for him in return. A friendship could be concealed, but dating her parent's worst enemy was a little harder to hide. Plus, she'd always seen him as a little too childish and cowardly—afraid to do anything out of his tiny comfort zone and always hiding behind his parents. But now, with his parents gone, he was becoming more confident in himself and in his leadership.

"I want to honor Adia. Without her designing the blueprints and making sure everything is safe, we couldn't have done this."

Everyone applauded and shouted for Adia, and she blushed awkwardly.

"I also want to honor Don. Without his oversight in getting all the logs cut and measured correctly, this cabin would never have gotten done."

"And let's honor Joshua, an awesome leader!" Don said.

Everyone hooted and roared in agreement. Even with all the chaos, people were beginning to accept Joshua as a leader.

The bright light of the sun suddenly grew dark.

Someone screamed, and Namid looked up.

As it had three previous times, the sky had grown a reddish-yellow swirl, and a rumble sounded above them.

Not again.

"Everyone, get to the hospital!" Joshua yelled.

Chaos erupted when those gathered ran west the hospital.

"Don, you find Sharon and manage everyone at the hospital. It's about to get very crowded there."

Even with the dread of what was to come, Namid couldn't help but appreciate Joshua's growth in leadership skills.

"Adia, you designed this cabin so that it would withstand another storm, right?"

Adia grimaced. "Well, yes, I think so."

The sky darkened further, and the wind began to swirl around them, this time worse than before.

"That'll have to do. This one seems to be coming rather fast, and if people can't get to the hospital, they'll have to shelter here."

Lightning flashed. Buckets of rain poured down on them, drenching everyone immediately.

"Namid, you take the south side of the village. I'll take the north side. We need to get everyone to safety. This one looks way worse than the other three."

Namid ran, and the wind pushed against her backside, helping her to move faster.

"A storm is coming!" she shouted as people streamed past her.

A little boy stood near the Emerald River, looking around frantically.

"Where are your parents?" She had to yell to be heard over the thunder.

"They—"

"Never mind. We'll find them once everyone's safe." She grabbed the boy's hand and joined the crowd running for the hospital.

At least, by now, everyone knew what to do. All she could do was pray everyone would make it.

"It's a tornado!" someone screamed.

Namid looked to the left. A massive swirling column, much bigger than the previous one, touched down close to them, way too close.

Jerold Gent was confident these storms had something to do with Dedecus using massive amounts of energy from the Creativity Stone. If so, whatever he was doing was the biggest yet.

"Take the boy," she said to the guy next to her. Joshua would still be on the north side near the Pearl Cliffs. She needed to find him.

Everyone ran faster, away from the tornado. Namid ran faster toward it.

Her hair whipped around wildly. She squinted into the darkness ahead.

She passed the twister, and it seemed to follow her. At least it wasn't headed toward the hospital.

"Joshua." Was she wrong? Maybe he'd gotten to safety, and she was the idiot running around in a thunderstorm.

"Namid, what are you doing?" Joshua emerged from the darkness to her left.

"What are *you* doing? You were supposed to go to the hospital."

"*You* were supposed to go to the hospital."

Lightning lit up Joshua's worried face. "I had to make sure everyone got away."

"Well, it's too late to reach the hospital now. The new cabin is closer."

They ran, their feet slipping in the mud. The gusts of wind grew stronger, nearly knocking them over.

They reached the cabin and barreled inside, closing the door securely behind them.

Joshua pushed his wet mop out of his eyes while Namid tried to catch her breath.

"What is with you lately? You go from being afraid of everything to running into a storm," she said.

The wind made a terrible moaning sound, and the house jumped like it had shifted off the foundation. *Will we be safe here?*

"You think I'm not scared? I'm terrified. But like it or not, I'm stuck with this healing power, and I'm more afraid of failing as a leader. I can't let anyone else get hurt again."

"A great leader doesn't risk killing himself for stupid reasons. We haven't tested how reliable and strong your power is. Besides, every time your body must heal, the pain is horrible."

"You think I don't know that? But which is worse—a flash of physical pain that lasts for seconds, or the pain that comes whenever I remember all of the people who have died because of me?"

A loud cracking noise filled the air. She looked up and saw one of the support beams breaking because it couldn't support all the weight it had been designed to hold. Without that crucial support beam, the house would collapse.

"We need to get out of here!" he said.

She threw open the door, and a gust slammed into her, knocking her backward and into Joshua.

"The tornado's right on us. What do we do?"

"I don't know." He was barely audible with the storm raging.

The roof collapsed. Wooden beams and planks were flung in every direction by the gusts coming off the twister in front of them.

One hit Joshua in the head, blood splattered from the impact, and he dropped to the floor.

He let out a scream and writhed in agony on the wooden floor.

Namid tried to wipe the blood away. *Please be healing.*

The wound healed—slowly.

The tornado got closer, and the walls began to crack.

Namid yanked Joshua to a standing position, grabbed his hand, and ran out the door.

She pulled him along, going as fast as she could without falling over as gusts of wind smacked into them.

"Hunch over. It'll help you brace against the force," Joshua said.

Namid glanced behind her. Joshua was fully recovered, and the rain had washed away the remaining blood.

They stumbled down the western slope away from the village toward the hospital, not yet in sight.

The Emerald River appeared before them, although emerald would no longer be the color to describe the murky waters rushing at twice the speed as normal. The river had swollen too large to jump over and was too fast to wade through.

"We'll have to go downstream to the bridge."

They stood at the bottom of a gully between two slopes separating the village from the hospital and the western forest.

"What about the caves at the Pearl Cliffs? Do you think we could reach those?" she asked.

Joshua shook his head. "Those are flooded by now."

God, please help us.

A sound similar to the waterfall reached her ears.

She jerked around and squinted into the murky darkness. Her eyes went wide.

"What's that noise?"

"Flash flood!"

CHAPTER 39

FIDES VILLAGE, NOVITAS—DAY 30, YEAR 371

Maybe Namid's parents were right, and we are being punished.

A torrent of water rushed toward them twice as wide as the river and well above their heads.

Joshua froze, fear becoming a cement that locked his muscles and joints.

"Come on!" Namid grabbed his soaked shirt and yanked him up the slope.

Joshua stumbled after her. But the water was moving too quickly.

The wall of water slammed into them.

Oxygen escaped Joshua's lungs as he flew backward and joined the current gushing toward the lake. Water pressed in on him on all sides. He became disoriented as water threw him in every direction at once.

He tried to get his bearings and find Namid. She was nowhere in sight.

He thrashed wildly, trying to reach the surface.

His foot found the bottom of the river, and he launched himself upward.

Breaking the surface, he coughed out water and flung his arms around, trying to stay afloat and gasping for air.

He latched onto a log gliding across the surface. His fingernails dug into the wood.

"Namid!" The last glimpse he'd had of her, the water was enveloping her. Where could she be?

Lightning flashed again, and he took advantage of the light to look all around. A glimmer of blue caught the corner of his eye. Her dress!

Forgetting about the log, he dove down after her.

He clawed through the water. His eyes stung as the murky surge clouded his vision.

Going deeper, he reached out and tried to get closer to her.

His lungs ran out of oxygen, and he needed to get to the surface. But he couldn't abandon Namid.

His left hand touched a strand of hair, and he reached out, grabbed a handful of hair, and yanked it toward him.

Sorry, Namid, but you'll thank me later.

With his right hand, he grabbed Namid's hand and thrashed upward. Her body felt like an anchor, but they slowly made it higher as he paddled upward and with the current.

His healing power seemed to be allowing him to last a bit longer without oxygen, which is probably the only reason he'd stayed conscious when the flash flood first hit. But it wouldn't last forever.

His head felt woozy, and his adrenaline faded. He needed oxygen—now.

His head broke the surface, and he inhaled sharply.

The storm still raged on but seemed to have died down slightly.

With all his might, he launched Namid upward. Her head emerged, and he grabbed her waist to keep her above water. She was unconscious—that is, he prayed she was only unconscious.

The current pushed them forward toward the lake. He paddled rapidly to keep them afloat.

Every second that passed, Namid grew heavier in his arms.

Lightning struck a nearby tree and lit up the world for a second.

A wooden structure loomed ahead. The bridge!

Water covered its surface, and some planks were missing, but the torrent hadn't yet broken the support beams supporting it.

He braced for impact. The water slammed his body into the beam, and he felt a rib crack.

No, not now.

Blinding pain flashed through his body as it struggled to repair the internal damage from slamming into the bridge.

His vision darkened, and he squinted, trying with all his might to keep from blacking out. He gripped Namid tighter in his right arm.

The water dragged his body down, trying to send him under the bridge. With his left arm, he held tightly one of the wooden poles from the bridge railing.

The pain in his chest lessened.

He tried to pull himself and Namid up the side of the rail, his weary muscles screaming at him. But, the water continued to barrel into him and push him down.

He dragged his leg upward and planted it against a beam. With all his might, he launched upward with his foot and yanked with his arm—and then vaulted up the side.

He draped Namid's body over the rail as he gasped for breath.

Before he could slow his heartbeat down, a crack sounded. The bridge began breaking up.

He hauled himself over the rail and held Namid's body in his arms. Water rushed around his calves. He trudged as fast as his waterlogged body could go.

Reaching the muddy dirt, he stumbled forward a few feet and then collapsed, still holding onto Namid.

"Please ... please, be all right."

He shifted and laid her body on the ground. She wasn't breathing and had gone way too long without oxygen. Her body had turned an unnatural shade of purple.

The water in her lungs was preventing her from breathing. Turning her on her side, he tapped on her back, trying to get her to cough up the water. Nothing came out.

Becoming desperate, he pounded harder. Nothing happened.

He turned her on her back and gave her mouth-to-mouth resuscitation.

The rain still poured down on them, but he ignored it.

He alternated between exhaling into her mouth and doing reps on her chest.

"Come on, you have to be okay."

He went faster, frantically trying to breathe life into her.

"Seriously, God? You can't take her away too."

His body drained of energy, and his eyes fogged with tears. He continued for several minutes.

His brain became hazy. He was going to pass out.

"Joshua?" A voice behind him reached his ears.

Joshua turned. Don ran toward him.

"Help Namid," he said as loud as he could, although it came out as a raspy whisper.

He collapsed next to Namid, still with one hand on her chest.

As the storm died down, Joshua passed out.

CHAPTER 40

FIDES VILLAGE, NOVITAS—DAY 33, YEAR 371

"Her brain went six minutes without oxygen," the doctor said. "Honestly, it's a miracle we were able to resuscitate her. Since we flushed the water out of her lungs, we've been able to get oxygen to her body, but her brain is completely unresponsive."

"God, please," Joshua whispered. His breathing grew heavy.

"It's been two days," the doctor said. "We were hoping for a miracle that she'd wake up, but it doesn't look like she will."

"If she wakes up, will she be okay?"

"Her body is fine, but her brain went too long without oxygen and is experiencing hypoxia. If she does somehow survive, she'll have extreme brain damage."

"She went after me. If I hadn't been so stupid during the storm—"

"She could still survive even with the brain damage, but only if she wakes up in the next few days."

"And if not?"

The doctor shifted and didn't look him in the eyes. "If not, she could have permanent damage to her reticular activating system, the part of the brain that's responsible for arousal and awareness."

"Meaning if she doesn't wake up soon, she never will?" Joshua grabbed Namid's hand from his seat next to her hospital bed.

"Yes, I'm afraid so." The doctor walked out of the room and shut the door behind him.

"Please, God," Joshua cried. "You've already taken my best friend and my family, but I need Namid ... I don't know if I can live without her. I think I love her. I tried to be the leader everyone expected me to be. I really did try to be this man of God who was confident and always knew what to do. But I failed, and every time I fail, you take away someone else. This is too much. I can't lose her too."

God was supposed to be all about making his children happy. At least, that's what his parents taught. There hadn't been much to be happy about recently.

Joshua tried to think of something to be thankful for or a Bible verse or piece of wisdom from his parents. How was he supposed to flip the perspective on this?

At least the hospital wasn't hit by the tornado or flash flood. The thought felt hollow. What good was a hospital when it didn't help everyone?

In Joshua's mind, the beeping of the heart monitor became a rhythm, and the annoying moan of the machines became a melody. Then, Joshua began to sing, trying to focus on God as words flowed out of his soul.

You are love, and you're faithful.
I've heard a thousand times.
You're good and so gracious.
I've said it all before.

But this doesn't feel loving;
This doesn't feel good.

He searched for a sign that the girl he'd grown up with—the girl he'd danced the night away with—was still in there.

But the loud groaning of the machines forcefully keeping her alive was the only signal he had to go by.

I cling to my pain,
My hands gripping tight.
I hold to my sorrow,
My knuckles turning white.

Joshua hadn't left Namid's side since he was cleared by the doctors himself.

His whole life revolved around watching Namid, listening to the annoying machines, and sitting in the uncomfortable chair next to her bed. His butt had gone completely numb from sitting there for two days without moving, but he ignored it.

Every time Don came to check on him, he tried to get Joshua to eat or to go get some sleep, but he'd refuse. Thanks to that cursed stone, his body would survive. This healing wasn't a gift—it was a curse. He would fight for everyone he loved, trying to keep them from being ripped away by God. But it seemed he would bury everyone he loved, and only he would remain.

If only there were a way he could transfer the energy restoring his body to Namid. But he'd talked to Jerold about it, and it would take years to create some sort of collection and transfer device. Even then, there would be no guarantee.

Don had also urged him to allow everyone to visit and hold a prayer vigil, but Joshua had refused. He didn't want a bunch of people trying to encourage him, trying to give him hope. The constant prayer thing never worked, for whenever things started to get back to normal or get better, another horrible, life-crushing thing happened. He couldn't take it anymore. He'd always had faith, and a month ago, he would have been eager for a prayer vigil, but now all he wanted was Namid back.

I want to surrender.
I want to rely.
But how ... But how?

How do I stop when I just feel pain?
How do I let go when I am so drained?

Someone knocked on the door, snapping him out of his song.

"I know you're worried about me, Don, but I'm not going anywhere," he said without lifting himself from the seat.

"It's not Don," a woman said behind him. Joshua turned around to see Adia, the woman who designed the blueprints for the house.

"What do you want?" he asked. His voice sounded hollow and monotone. He gripped the armrest.

I can't deal with this right now.

She cleared her throat. "I ... I wanted to apologize. I thought I could do it ... but I was wrong, I did it wrong, and now it's all my fault that Namid's in the hospital."

"Yeah, it is ..." he said. He was cold and harsh, but she had promised the cabin would be able to weather the storms. If she had designed it better, they could have stayed there during the storm and wouldn't have been out by the river. Namid wouldn't be clinging to life by a thread.

"I know I deserve your hate. I just wanted to tell you that I'm sorry ... I thought God was going to use me, but I guess I really am too stupid to do anything right."

Joshua ignored her. He should say something, but he couldn't bear to look at the woman who was at least partially responsible for Namid likely never waking up again.

He listened to her quiet sobs as she walked out and shut the door.

DOWNFALL

He leaned over and took hold of Namid's hand, begging God to save her life as he lost himself, his faith, and everything else in grief.

CHAPTER 41

FIDES VILLAGE, NOVITAS—DAY 33, YEAR 371

Adia ran from the hospital, her feet carrying her as far from Namid's dying body as possible.

"I'm really trying, God ... why can't I do anything right?"

She wanted to collapse, but her feet kept moving forward—to where? She had no idea.

"Why would you save me? I tried to do what you wanted, but I fail every time."

Emeth, the man in the cabin, said God was with her, that he would hold her and answer her questions. So, she waited for everything to suddenly make sense. She waited for God to tell her how she could fix this.

"Okay, be thankful. What is there to be thankful for?"

If only Lincoln would show up and hold her until everything was better, or if she could go back to Emeth and deceive herself into thinking she could actually have a purpose.

"Adia, is that you?"

Adia froze as the voice she had vowed to never hear again filtered through her brain.

No, God, please. I can't deal with this right now.

She quickly wiped away her tears and plastered on a smile before turning around.

"Adia, we're so glad you're alive. We were worried you'd been killed in the attack by that monster."

Kira and Jerold Gent stood there. Kira looked so relieved that she might cry. Jerold looked like solid granite.

"Hi, Mom, Dad."

"Why is it that you never come visit us, you ungrateful ingrate? We had assumed that you were deceased," Jerold said, something in his expression changing slightly in a way that Adia couldn't recognize. "But it seems as if you were simply avoiding us."

"I ... um ... figured you guys had left with the Judges of Justice." That wasn't a total lie.

"Well, we didn't. We couldn't leave knowing that you might still be here," Kira said.

Was that genuine care coming out of her parent's lips?

"Now, where's that oversentimental husband of yours? It's not proper for a lady to be walking alone at night," she said.

"He died."

"Oh."

Her father took a step closer, and she involuntarily took a step back.

"Our house is still in decent condition if you need a residence to stay in," he offered. "I have been working on various invigorating projects, but it seems as if you need habitation, so I will move those elsewhere. You are permitted to dwell with us for the time being."

"No, I'll be okay. I've got to get going now."

"Okay, well, you know where we live if you want to stop by. We would love to see you," Kira said.

"Okay," Adia said as she used every bit of willpower she had to hold back her tears.

Turning away from them, Adia quickly made her way down the path she was on, unsure of and uncaring about where she was going.

DOWNFALL

Tripping over a rock, she collapsed to the ground and lay there unmoving. She'd scraped her knee, but she didn't bother looking at it. A puddle of tears formed on the gravel path where her head was.

"Why are you doing this to me, God?" She turned over onto her back and stared up at the twinkling night sky.

Blood oozed out of the scrape on her knee, but no physical pain was worse than the pain in her head and heart.

"God, show me if you're even there. I can't do this anymore." She could feel herself being dragged down deeper into the stormy ocean of depression, so deep she wasn't sure she'd ever be able to reach the surface again.

What a friend we have in Jesus,
All our sins and grieves to bear!
And what a privilege to carry
Everything to God in prayer!

The beautiful melody washed over her. She looked around in confusion, then realized she'd wandered close to where the church once stood, and where they were now holding a prayer and worship service to pray for Namid and others still recovering from the attack.

Oh, what peace we often forfeit,
Oh, what needless pain we bear,
All because we do not carry
Everything to God in prayer!

"I've tried to be your friend, I've tried to pray and give it to you God, but—"

"Ma'am, are you okay?" A man raced toward her on the path. "Here, let me help you up."

Don helped her to her feet.

She didn't know him personally, but she'd seen him several times with the council.

"Are you okay? It looks like you've got a nasty scrape on your knee."

Adia had been trained since birth not to show weakness but staring at Don, a man who'd heard crying and left a service he was leading to help an older woman he barely knew—she broke.

Falling onto his shoulder, she wept. "No, I'm not okay. I've tried everything I can to be who God called me to be, but I'm just a stupid, worthless, pathetic, ugly girl."

The music continued to drift over the area.

> Have we trials and temptations?
> Is there trouble anywhere?
> We should never be discouraged.
> Take it to the Lord in prayer.

Don held her in his arms. "It sounds like you've gotten something mixed up."

Pulling back, she stared at him in confusion. "What do you mean?"

"You're trying to do something. You're trying to work to be Jesus's friend, to be worthy of love."

"Well, of course, I'm trying to do something."

"Maybe that's your problem. What is the beginning of the song they're singing?"

"What a friend we have in Jesus," Adia said, not understanding what he was getting at.

"Exactly. What a friend we *have* in Jesus. He *is* our friend, and he loves us no matter what. When he looks at you, he doesn't see a screw-up—he sees someone he created absolutely perfect."

"But how can he want to be my friend when I keep messing up? Maybe he created me perfect, but I'm certainly not like that now."

"You *are* perfect—perfect by his eternal, heavenly standards, not by the world's standards. Yes, you'll still mess up, but did you know that almost all of Jesus's closest friends while he was on Earth abandoned him when he died on the cross? And yet, he still called them beloved friends. He still had a special and important plan for their lives. All you can do is ask for forgiveness and then receive it."

Can we find a friend so faithful?
Who will all our sorrows share?
Jesus knows our every weakness,
Take it to the Lord in prayer.

"I thought I was doing what God called me to do. It all made sense because I had some experience in architecture, and you guys needed an architect."

"But did you ask God what he thought?" he asked her.

"Umm."

"It's something every single one of us is guilty of doing. We see a need, so we immediately think we're the ones called to fill it. But it's God's job to fill it. He'll lead our steps."

"I guess I need to work on doing a better job of that."

"It's not exactly something you work on, but just like everything, take it to the Lord in prayer. Would you like to join us?" He offered out his hand.

Taking it, Adia followed him to the makeshift church. She had a lot to give to Jesus.

A couple hundred people surrounded the four musicians who stood on a stage made from some old boxes. Some worshippers were on their knees crying out to God. Others with their hands and voices raised to the heavens. The scene was a stark contrast to the other times she'd been to church, where they all sat in an ornate building listening to a choir. This was simple, raw, and beautiful.

Are we weak and heavy-laden,
Cumbered with a load of care?

Precious Savior, still our refuge—
Take it to the Lord in prayer,

Do thy friends despise, forsake thee?
Take it to the Lord in prayer;
In His arms He'll take and shield thee,
Thou wilt find a solace there.

Blessed Savior, Thou hast promised;
Thou wilt all our burdens bear.
May we ever, Lord, be bringing
All to Thee in earnest prayer.

As she stood surrounded by the faithful who were giving their prayers as a simple offering to God, Adia could feel herself being enveloped by the Father's love. She smiled.

At that moment, the memory of everything Emeth had told her in the cabin rushed back into her mind.

Everyone seems to think that being a Christian means you won't ever have depression, anxiety, or struggles. They seem to think that Jesus is a get-out-of-anything-free card that will make everything perfect. But that's just not the case. We're humans, and the world is not perfect. Because of that, there will always be something to cry about. And it's okay to cry.

Soon in glory bright, unclouded,
There will be no need for prayer—
Salvation, praise, and endless worship
Will be our sweet portion there.

"All right, God, I'm still broken and messed up, but I guess you're not done with me yet. So, I give it all to you, God—everything."

She could feel God smiling over her as she surrendered the never-ending fight against her depression. But she wasn't surrendering to the depression. Instead, she surrendered the battle to God and let him fight and win the battle. He had already won it thousands of years ago when he breathed his final breath on a bloody cross and said *it is finished*.

Her shoulders lifted as she worshipped like she never had before—in earnest longing to be with God. Who could love her like her own father never could? Who had chosen her as a forever friend no matter what?

She couldn't wait to see where the Holy Spirit would lead her next.

> What a friend we have in Jesus,
> All our sins and grieves to bear!
> And what a privilege to carry
> Everything to God in prayer!

CHAPTER 42

FIDES VILLAGE, NOVITAS—DAY 36, YEAR 371

"It's been five days, and the swelling has only gotten worse," Joshua said, his throat closing up. "Even if she does wake up, will she ever be able to function normally?"

"Unlikely." The doctor walked over to Joshua and placed his hand on his shoulder. "All we can really do at this point is keep her comfortable and pray for a miracle."

"I tried praying, but it hasn't worked," Joshua muttered.

"Why don't you go home and get some rest? You haven't left this room in five days.

"Okay." Logic tried to enter Joshua's sleep-deprived mind as he stood, his legs asleep and not wanting to work, but his brain ignored it as he settled on a course of action.

"Hey, bud, glad to see you up," Don said, standing by the door. Joshua was tired of his fake cheerfulness and optimism, tired of seeing Don working so hard to exude hope, only to be betrayed by his eyes filled with worry. Although, maybe he was more worried for Joshua.

"Hey, Don, I think I'm going to go home and sleep. Do you have a pen and some paper? I'd like to write a note to Namid in case she wakes up while I'm not here." Joshua stared down, unable to look Don in the eyes

Don smiled. "That's a great idea. Let me grab it, and I'll be right back."

Joshua turned to Namid and kissed her on the forehead. "I'll be back, I promise. I have a plan." He bit his lip. "I won't lose you too."

A few minutes later, Joshua walked out of the hospital and toward the remaining silo that hadn't been damaged in the storms. He grabbed a few supplies then took off toward the Southern Forest.

If God isn't who my parents said he was. If he's really is this uncaring, he's not a God I want to serve.

He pounded through the forest, the water bottle at his hip smacking against him with every step. The palm trees blended together in a blur of brown and green as he jumped over logs that had fallen during the storms. He raced past startled squirrels, sleeping tree bears, and other critters. The palm hairs on the trees wiggled as he brushed past them.

His hair was once again in his eyes, but this time he didn't bother to push it out of the way. He kept running.

His lungs screamed for oxygen, and his muscles cried out for a rest, especially after doing nothing but sitting in a chair for five days and watching Namid fade away. But he shoved everything behind him, ignoring everything but his desperate mission. He was stuck with this power. Now, he'd put it to good use.

After several hours of running without reprieve, he finally made it through the forest and to the mountain range.

Dedecus had always loved one specific spot on top of a very tall, steep mountain. It had the nickname Mount Grave because anyone crazy enough to climb it was practically digging themselves a grave. Landslides constantly changed the landscape because little to no grass or trees could grow there to hold the gravelly rock in place.

Dedecus loved to climb Mount Grave and usually made a trip up it at least once a year. He did this because he liked doing things people think are stupidly dangerous, and upon reaching the top, the climber was rewarded with a breathtaking view and a sight of hundreds of miles in every direction. Joshua had always thought Dedecus would hate mountain climbing because his parents had died on a mountain, but he said it brought him closer to them.

Even though Dedecus loved Mount Grave, Joshua had never been up it, despite his friend's urging. He'd always been too terrified to risk his life going up an incredibly steep mountain where one wrong move would send him straight back down.

"I'm not too scared," he'd told Dedecus, "I'm just not stupid."

Joshua knew his best friend. If he were trying to get away from everyone, the first place he would think of going was Mount Grave. No one would ever be stupid enough to climb it, especially to go after him.

For the first time since he left Namid's bedside, logic finally broke through the wall of desperation and sleep deprivation that had held his mind captive as he stood at the bottom of the mountain.

Dedecus was no longer the best friend he once knew. But Joshua didn't care about the big possibility that Dedecus would refuse to help, that he'd laugh in his face or even kill him. Because if there could be even an outside chance Dedecus would use the Creativity Stone to heal Namid, he had to take it.

He was basically a hypocrite for doing exactly what he'd insisted Dedecus not do. At the very least, Dedecus would mock him for giving up his beliefs when things got hard—a prophecy from Dedecus becoming all too true—but that didn't matter anymore. God truly had abandoned him. He tried to be everything God called him to be, but every step of the way, he'd been faced with more loss.

Now he was taking matters into his own hands. He would find Dedecus and demand he heal Namid. The note he'd written to Namid in his horrible handwriting explained to her what he'd done and that he would be back soon. He had folded it and given it to Don, saying to give it to her if she had a miracle and woke up while he was gone.

Little did Don know it would be Joshua bringing about the miracle instead of God. After all he'd been through, he was ready to stop relying on God and do it himself. But, instead, all that his faith had gotten him was more pain and heartache.

So, he made up his mind, grabbed hold of a protruding rock above his head, and carefully pulled himself up along the face of the mountain.

As foolish as he knew he was being by giving up everything and chasing after the man who would likely kill him, he was still scared of slipping and falling. His healing power would likely protect him, but the horrible pain it caused wasn't something he enjoyed experiencing.

One handhold at a time, he inched further toward his destination. His hands sweated, and his exhausted body ached from the physical exertion he was putting it through.

Dirt and pebbles rained down on him, covering his already dirty hair and body from not showering since before that building collapsed on them.

After making it about only partway up, he came to a point where he couldn't find anything to grab on to.

All he could see was a small ledge about two feet above his head and to the right.

Calming his nerves, he found sturdy footholds and steeled himself for the jump.

The last time I had to rely on my ability to jump and latch onto things, I literally died.

He bent his knees, closed his eyes—which probably wasn't the smartest move—and leaped upward to reach the handhold. His arms flailed about as he tried to latch on to the tiny ledge.

Two fingers barely grasped his destination, but as he anxiously tried to get a better grip and pull himself up, the ledge gave way and came loose from the mountainside.

He slid down the loose gravel as a mini avalanche around him scraped up his arms and legs. He cried out in pain but had no choice but to ignore his injuries and frantically grab at anything to stop his fall.

The healing pain burned across his body. He did his best to ignore it.

His first two attempts only caused more gravel to join him in his fall, but he managed to grab a protruding rock and hang on on his third try. But, despite stopping his descent, he felt as if his arm were being ripped out of its socket.

Joshua cried out from the pain. Then, he pulled himself up and found places to put his feet and hands as he tried to slow down his panting breath.

"I can see now why it's called Mount Grave."

He checked his body for injuries, careful not to move too much and risk losing his foothold or cause another avalanche of rocks. He'd had a pretty bad gash on his left leg and was bleeding from where he'd hit a sharp rock. But both of those were almost completely healed.

While his nerves still screamed at him, the important thing was he was safe ... well, relatively safe.

A breeze hit his back, and he realized the back of his shirt was completely shredded from falling.

After taking a long sip from the water bottle he'd strapped to his hip, he took several minutes of much-needed rest.

He pushed the hair out of his face and slowly began his climb upward again.

He'd fallen about seventy-five feet and was now more exhausted than ever, but none of that could stop him. He was relentless in his goal to reach the top.

After several hours of climbing, he'd only made it a fourth of the way up the mountain. The sun was going down, and darkness was descending fast. He would be stupid to not stop for the night instead of climbing. How could he see hand and footholds without a light? To make matters worse, his adrenaline was all spent, and his body was at the point where he was about to collapse from exhaustion.

He'd stopped to eat before leaving but was hungry again and hadn't brought anything with him to eat. He could only imagine how much worse off he'd be if he hadn't eaten at all.

"Suck it up, body. I'm stuck with this healing power, so I'm gonna use it."

Joshua searched around for a place where he could rest for the night. Then, miraculously, although he wasn't exactly sure if he believed in miracles anymore, he spotted a small ledge that held a stunted and ugly-looking little palm tree he could lie next to up against the mountain with barely enough room to sleep safely if he curled up into a ball.

Carefully, he inched his way toward the ledge. He almost slipped again as what he thought was a firm foothold began to give out on him. So, he quickly shifted his weight to his other foot. He breathed a sigh of relief as he listened to rocks and dirt slide down the mountain, and he wasn't going with them.

He made his way to the ledge with the tiny, water-deprived tree. Finally, he pulled himself onto the ledge and took a long gulp of water from his bottle.

Normally, he would take forever to fall asleep in such an uncomfortable position on the hard, rocky ground, but nothing was normal anymore, and he quickly fell into a long and deep sleep.

CHAPTER 43

FIDES VILLAGE, NOVITAS—YEAR 6

"I can't believe we have to meet like this. It's ridiculous."

"I know. You'd think they'd let us use the church we helped build."

"All right, quiet down, guys." Steven looked around with pride at the thirty-two people gathered in his tiny house outside of the village.

They were few, but they were faithful. And despite everything, he loved learning more about God with each of them.

But as amazing as those thirty-two were, his house was tiny. He had long since gotten rid of the furniture in his living room so they could all fit. They stood shoulder to shoulder while Steven stood on a stool in the middle.

He'd been on house arrest for three years. If anyone outside of this group saw him, they'd flog him. But, as horrible as it was to never be able to leave, by the grace of God, he was alive. The group took shifts to guard his house, and aside from confrontations and jabs, the New Day Separatists hadn't hurt any of the others in his group.

"Tonight, we're going to be reading in John chapter 1, starting with verse 16." Steven had objected to leading their little grace church at first, but it really wasn't so bad. *At least it's better than listening to that poison being taught at the real church led by Esther.*

He'd hoped the man in the cabin, Emeth, would lead them. But when he'd gone looking for the cabin again but hadn't been able to find it no matter how hard he searched. So, the only conclusion he could come up with was that it had disappeared.

Everyone maneuvered around so they could all open their Bibles.

"And of his fullness have all we received, and grace for grace. For the law was given by Moses, but grace and truth came by Jesus Christ."

"Hear that, separatists—grace, not law." Laura Larson still had a hard time getting over the death of her son. "Say it with me, g-r-a-c-e."

Everyone chuckled.

"Amen to that," someone in the back said.

The door opened, and everyone turned to see who it was. From his vantage point on the chair, Steven could see Hannah. His heart started beating fast. Ever since he'd rescued her from being stoned, he'd had trouble getting his heart to beat normally whenever he saw her.

She wore a long-sleeved shirt which was odd since it was hot out, and she always wore short-sleeved shirts.

"Sorry I'm late, guys." She closed the door behind her. "The villagers stopped me."

Steven clenched his fists. "Why won't they just leave us alone?" he muttered.

"Yeah. It's not like we're bothering them." Madeline Peters had apparently heard him.

Steven turned his attention back to Hannah, who stood by the door. Her eyes were puffy, and she kept rubbing her left hand against her right arm.

"Are you okay? They didn't hurt you, did they?"

Those loyal to Esther and their legalistic interpretation of the Bible had never been nice to them. He'd go so far as to say they hated him and his followers. But aside from him, they wouldn't hurt anyone. *Would they?*

An image of the little boy, William, being stoned to death came to his mind. For a couple years, he'd tried so hard to erase that image from his memory. But now, he let it fuel him. He would not let anything like that happen again. Ever.

"Yeah, I'm fine." She brushed off his concern. "They just accused me of the normal things."

"Of being a hypocrite and a heathen?" someone in the back said.

"And a sinner who deserves damnation," Madeline said.

"Oh, and don't forget an irredeemable piece of trash," another person added.

Hannah let out a forced laugh. "Yeah, something like that." She made her way through the overstuffed room and reached him.

He smiled and bent down on the stool. "I'm sorry you had to go through that."

She looked at him like he was the only person in the room. His heart beat faster.

"I'm used to it by now," she said quietly, rubbing her right arm again.

He looked down at her sleeve, and his heart stopped for a second. Her rubbing had pulled the fabric up, revealing a bright red bruise near her wrist.

"What did they do to you?" His voice was louder than it should be, but he didn't care.

"It's nothing, I just um—"

"Did they attack you?"

All eyes were on them, but he couldn't take his eyes off the bruise. It was about the size of a small rock.

Hannah sighed. "Yes, okay? Is that what you want to hear? A bunch of guys confronted me while I was walking down the path here. They said God should have killed me when he had a chance. One of them threw a stone at my head, and I deflected with my arm. I'll be fine, though."

Steven's knuckles turned white, and he dug his fingernails into his flesh.

"This is what they'll do to all of us." Stan Larson shouted. "They won't stop until everyone joins my son, six feet under."

"Yeah," someone shouted. "When's the last time one of those pompous jerks helped us?"

"Instead, they kick us out of our own houses and make us build more outside the village."

"And poor Steven here has been trapped here for three years."

Steven remained silent. Staring at the bruise on Hannah's arm.

"And that church." Laura pretended to gag. "It's such an oversized eyesore with way too much gold and stained glass."

"And they won't even let us enter in? Instead, we have to meet in this dump the size of a shoe."

"We should just burn that thing to the ground," Stan said. "They deserve it."

"Maybe we should." Steven snapped his head up and stood on the chair. "Maybe we should! We've helped them, showed them kindness, and what has it gotten us?"

"Nothing!" the crowd shouted.

He hadn't been outside in three years. What he wouldn't give to be able to smell the sweet air, to feel the breeze, to go back up to Peaceful Plateau. Instead, he was stuck in this tiny house, unable to leave without being attacked.

"Exactly," he said. "They killed William. They've tried to kill me numerous times, and now you guys. It won't stop until we're all dead."

He'd told himself it was worth it. That he was suffering for the kingdom, and things would change. He could handle the persecution. He was fine if they didn't hurt anyone else. But now ...

Looking around at the faces of the abused, they felt the exact same way.

"Let's destroy that little symbol of perfection."

"Yeah!" Everyone shouted.

Stan grabbed silica stones off the fireplace mantle. They'd discovered that rubbing them together even slightly caused a ton of sparks. Stan put them in the basket of tree palm hairs. The hairs were highly flammable.

Someone flung open the door, and they poured out of the tiny house.

Hannah grabbed his arm. "Don't." The movement of her arm caused her to wince.

"I promised to protect you. I have to do something. If not, they'll kill you." Steven pulled away from her and ran to join the group.

He stepped outside and inhaled the fresh evening air, a luxury he hadn't felt in three years. Normally, he'd take the time to savor it. But his mind was elsewhere.

They ran as a group down the path from their mini offshoot of Fides. People got out of their way as they raced through the village and to the church.

"You want a stoning, then take this." Stan picked up a large rock and chucked it through the front stained-glass window in the front.

The rock slammed through the glass, shattering it into billions of pieces that fell to the floor.

Several others threw stones into the church windows.

Steven looked around, bracing for resistance. But anyone around had heard the commotion and wisely stayed away.

Steven grabbed the silica stones and threw the palm hairs across the front steps. Hannah had collected a huge basket of palm hairs from the forest palms so he could keep warm when it got cold. Now he would return the favor by saving her life again.

He slammed the silica stones together. Sparks rained down onto the hairs.

The sparks glimmered in the reflection of the golden cross on the front entrance.

The palm hairs instantly caught. They were engulfed in an inferno that spread to the wooden floorboards and doors in seconds.

"Get back!" he yelled.

They all ran a few yards away to be safe.

The doors were no longer visible as the orange and white flames spread to the front walls.

Those gathered cheered.

"What have you done?" someone grabbed his shoulder and spun him around.

It was Emeth. The man who'd first changed his life.

"What are you doing here?" Steven asked.

"What are *you* doing here?" he pointed his finger at Steven's chest.

"They've hurt us too long. We're giving them what they deserve."

"And what do you deserve?"

A mix of logic and dread trickled into his adrenaline-fueled brain. "We ... they ..." Suddenly, the arguments that had made so much sense a few seconds ago had fled him.

The man grabbed at his graying hair and pulled.

The church was fully engulfed in flames.

"Did you even check to see if anyone was in there?"

Steven's face paled. *God, what have I done?*

The sixth remembrance came to his mind, *enact what others deserve.* He'd become just like them: the judge, the jury, and now the executioner.

Steven looked back at the church. The flames had reached the ceiling. Any minute it would collapse.

Abandoning the celebratory crowd, Steven raced back to the church and up the stairs.

"Steven, where are you going?" someone called out.

He threw open the charring doors. It stung his hands, but he ignored it.

The flames couldn't catch him if he ran fast enough ... he hoped.

"Help!" someone cried out.

Steven raced down the aisle to the sound of the noise, covering his mouth with his shirt to keep out the smoke.

With a strength he didn't know he possessed, he threw over one of the pews and saw Esther cowering.

"Take my hand," he yelled over the roaring flames.

She turned to him. Under her was a little girl.

Lisa. No, not Lisa, another girl. He coughed. The smoke and heat must have been getting to his brain.

"I'll save myself, but get my little girl to safety," Esther said.

He'd heard that Esther had a little girl, but he'd never met her. She'd been very quiet about her personal life.

Steven grabbed the little girl into his arms, and she buried her face into his shoulder.

"Save my mommy." The little girl wept in his arms.

The ceiling cracked, and pieces of flaming wood rained down on their heads.

"I promise you both will make it." His skin felt red-hot, and his eyes burned.

He grabbed Esther's arm, and they ran. The area in front of them had mostly already been burned, which was a blessing.

The heat seared their shoes, and they sizzled.

Steven stumbled into the fresh air, coughing. Even though he was out of the fire, his skin felt like it was still burning. But he'd saved the little girl. He'd saved Esther.

Once they were a safe distance from the flames, he set the girl down. She ran to her mother and they embraced.

Lisa, his sweet Lisa. No, not Lisa.

Steven leaned over and shook his fuzzy head. Was there something he was supposed to be doing?

Esther looked up from her daughter. "You saved us. After all I did to you. Why?"

Steven's world faded away, and Esther ran to catch him.

"Grace," he whispered.

Everything disappeared.

CHAPTER 44

FIDES VILLAGE, NOVITAS—DAY 36, YEAR 371

Don stood atop a chair. The same chair Joshua had hopelessly sobbed in for the past five days. He looked around and smiled. The people of Fides Village stood shoulder to shoulder inside Namid's hospital room. The room was only big enough for about ten to fifteen people, but they'd removed everything that wasn't essential so they could fit more people in.

Over twenty people stood crammed into the tiny room. He wished he could fit everyone in the room, but dozens more were out in the hallway or in other rooms, praying and worshipping.

Despite any unworthiness, the devil tempted him. He could see the fruits of his faith right in front of him. While not everyone left in Fides Village was on fire for what God was doing, God was moving in the hearts of those faithful to stay, sparking revival and using him to speak to them.

"Do we believe Jesus is real?" Don shouted.

Beside him, Namid lay motionless. The only sound of life coming from her was the slow beeping of the heart monitor.

"Yes!" everyone shouted.

"Do we believe Jesus healed the sick?"

"Yes!" everyone once again called out.

"Do we believe he is still alive in us and that he said we would perform miracles too?"

"Yes!"

"Then let us all worship and pray together for this young woman, believing that God is truly who he said he is and will perform miracles!"

With one voice, Fides Village sang, declaring God's promise over Namid even though they had no evidence that anything would happen.

We don't have to wait;
You're already here.
We don't have to call;
You've already answered.

It didn't matter who was a good singer or who was completely tone-deaf. It didn't matter that they were all uncomfortable and hot in the overcrowded room. It didn't matter that there seemed to be no life left in Namid.

All that's dead within us,
All that has been lost,
We know you're restoring
With the power of the cross.

"Everyone make a shout of victory, for death has been defeated!" Don called out. And everyone responded with a roar that nearly shook the foundation.

Adia, who had been there praying with the group for three days straight, was undisputedly the loudest.

You're the answer.
You're the giver.
You're the healer,
For you are bigger!

That is who you are.
You are our Lord.

So, we don't focus on the healing,
But on the one who heals.

We don't focus on the provision
But on the one who provides.

They continued for several hours—late into the night, declaring their faith and God's promise over Namid.

You are faithful.
You're the beginning;
You're the end.
You're the author.

That is who you are.
You are our Lord.

So, we don't focus on the healing,
But on the one who heals.

We don't focus on the provision
But on the one who provides.

"Namid!" Adia suddenly shouted.

Everyone turned to see Namid sitting up with her arms raised in worship.

"Hey, doctor, you better get in here!" Don shouted over the throng of people.

Several doctors pushed their way through the crowd. "All right, guys," one of them said loudly. "Clear out of here. We need some room." He couldn't see Namid yet, so he looked at Don. "Is she gone?"

Don laughed. "Not exactly."

Don wished he had a picture of the doctor's face when he finally made it to Namid's bedside and saw her sitting up.

The doctors couldn't get through to the people that they needed to leave. So, they ran diagnostics in the crowded room. After about thirty minutes, they pulled the feeding tube out of her mouth, and she could finally talk again.

"What's the last thing you remember?" the doctor asked.

"The tornado was coming toward us so, we tried to get to the hospital." Her voice, dry and cracked from lack of water. "We reached the river and got caught in a flash flood. That's all I remember."

There seemed to be no sign of the brain trauma the doctors had insisted would affect her for the rest of her life. Her brain had been without oxygen for far too long, but God wasn't done with her yet.

"Wait ... Joshua." Her eyes went wide. "Where's Joshua? Is he okay?"

Don laughed again. "He saved your life. During the flash flood, he grabbed you and hauled you to safety. He's been sitting by your bedside for the past five days until this morning when I convinced him to go and get some food and sleep. You two really are crazy about each other."

Namid blushed, and everyone in the room chuckled softly.

"He gave me this note to give to you if you happened to wake up. I'd go get him, but after five days with no sleep, I think it would be best to let the Judge of Mercy rest."

Don handed Namid the note. Before she had a chance to read it, he turned and spoke to the crowd again.

"So often we ask God for a miracle, but like the nine lepers, we often forget to raise our voices in thanksgiving when we get a miracle. But not today. Today, we will be like the one leper who ran back to Jesus and thanked him for healing."

Namid put the note on the bed beside her to read later. And together, as a village, they all thanked God for once again doing the impossible.

We don't have to wait;
You're already here.
We don't have to call:
You've already answered.

You're the answer.
You're the giver.
You're the healer.
For you are bigger.

That is who you are.
You are our Lord.

So, we don't focus on the healing,
But on the one who heals.

We don't focus on the provision
But on the one who provides.

After the villagers left the hospital, Namid remembered the note.

She opened it, expecting to read about how Joshua couldn't believe he missed her waking up and how he couldn't wait to see her smiling face again.

> If you're reading this, Namid, then I've succeeded. You were deteriorating, and it looked like you'd never recover, so I did something very stupid. I chased after Dedecus. I know him, and I'm almost positive he'll be on Mount Grave. Since you're reading this, that means that I've succeeded in convincing Dedecus to use the Creativity Stone to heal you. I know what all your arguments against it will be because up until yesterday, they were my arguments too. But I had no choice. And soon, we will be back together, which will make it all better.
>
> I'll see you soon.
>
> Joshua

She missive many times, amazed that Joshua would do something so reckless and dangerous Joshua had always been a person who hated to leave his comfort zone with a passion. He was level-headed, logical, and strong in his faith. But, because of her, he would lose himself in this desperate quest.

Will I ever see him again?

Don had said Joshua left the hospital early this morning. No way could he have gotten through the forest and all the way up Mount Grave in only a day. That meant he hadn't reached Dedecus yet and was still on the mountain in a foolish and desperate mission to save her when she didn't even need saving.

God had healed her, and Joshua hadn't been faithful enough to wait for his timing. Instead, he'd tried to take it into his own hands and would likely kill himself or be killed trying to do something God had already done.

She glanced down at the IV still attached to her arm. No way would the doctors let her out of the hospital when hours ago she'd been clinging to life. God brought a full and instant recovery to her for a reason.

Namid couldn't let Joshua reach Dedecus. She had to figure out how to sneak out and get to him before he got to Dedecus.

CHAPTER 45

FIDES VILLAGE, NOVITAS—YEAR 6

"This man better make a full recovery, or it will be on your head." Then, the shrill voice of Esther entered Steven's consciousness.

"We're doing everything we can."

Steven's whole world was black. He groaned and shifted, sending waves of pain through his legs.

"Well, you'd better. If that man doesn't recover, you will experience my full wrath."

Steven opened his eyes slightly and squinted at the harsh light of day. He was in a hospital bed. The lights flickered overhead, and the sound of the generator they'd brought from Earth moaned outside. *How did I get here?*

Esther was standing outside in the hallway, yelling at a quivering, wide-eyed doctor.

"Yes, ma'am," the doctor said.

"Well, why are you still standing here? Get to work." Esther shoved the man, and he ran for his life.

Steven turned his head slightly. Hannah sat in the chair beside him. She had nodded off and had an adorable little snore that sent a flutter through his heart.

Esther turned to him, and her glare turned into an expression he'd never seen on her before. Worry maybe?

"You're awake," she said.

He lifted his head off the soft pillow and tried to move again, but his legs felt like they were on fire. He glanced down, but they were under the sheets.

He grimaced. What happened to me?

"Don't try to move."

"What," his voice was dry and gravelly. "What—"

"Shh, don't try to speak. It'll take too much energy." She stared down at him, tears gathering in her eyes. "That coward of a doctor will probably try to ramble around the truth, so I'll just give it to you straight. You have been unconscious for a day. You have two spots of third-degree burns on your legs, with second-degree burns surrounding them. You also suffered minor smoke inhalation damage. Your lungs and the rest of your body will be fine. But you may never walk again."

His eyes went wide. *What happened to me?* The last thing he remembered was being at his house, and everyone was gathered. Then Hannah had come in, and something had happened.

"But don't worry. I will make sure these doctors won't stop working until you regain use of your legs."

"Why—" He coughed twice. "Why are—"

"I'm helping you because you saved my life, and you saved my precious daughter's life. I might not agree with you on everything, but you proved to me what kind of person you are. You're a good man, Steven Waters."

The memories of the church flashed through his mind. They'd hurt Hannah. He had been angry for the mistreatment of him and his people. They'd burned down the church. But he'd gone in and rescued Esther and his little sister Lisa. No, not Lisa, another little girl, Esther's daughter.

Shame filled him, and his breathing grew fast. The blame belonged entirely to him.

"But I—"

"I know." Esther sighed. "Your followers told me everything. But after all I did to you, you saved my daughter and me. You risked your life for your enemy. And I—" She grimaced as if the words physically pained her. "I'm sorry."

Hannah stirred beside him.

"I'll be outside." Esther turned from him. "I need to have another chat with that doctor anyway." She left the room.

That poor doctor.

He turned his head toward Hannah. She opened her eyes and looked straight at him.

"Steven?" her voice wobbled.

The slightest movement drained him, but he slowly moved his hand across his bed and held it out to her.

She took it and started to cry.

He looked down at his legs under the covers.

Will I ever walk again?

CHAPTER 46

FIDES VILLAGE, NOVITAS—DAY 36, YEAR 371

Adia stepped out from Namid's room, grabbed a doctor's arm, and began dancing around him.

The startled doctor pulled away, and Adia laughed.

She still didn't know what God meant by loving the broken and lost like she'd been told at the cabin, but if God could perform miracles like the one she'd just witnessed, she was certain he could perform one for her.

She walked down the long hallway toward the door to go home and get some much-needed rest. Down the hall, she heard the cry of a little child.

From somewhere deep within her soul, she resonated with that cry. She was in a hospital, so of course, there would be lots of crying. But for some reason, she felt as if everything in her life had paled in comparison to that child's broken tears. As exhausted as she was, and despite the fact she probably wouldn't be helpful, she could feel her heart yearning to answer the cry.

Adia forgot all about going home to sleep and went down the hallway to see what was going on and if she could help.

A nurse came out of the room, hunched over slightly as if the pain of the past month was personally carried on her back. She had medium-length, stringy hair that looked like it hadn't been washed in days, and her eyes were tired and hard.

Adia went up to her and asked what had happened in the room.

"The woman in there just died. She had been clinging to life ever since the attack caused her home to collapse on her. Her husband passed away two weeks ago, also from the attack. Now we don't know what to do with their four kids."

"Are there any relatives who will take them in?" Adia asked.

"Unfortunately not. This has been a pretty common problem. There's really nothing I can do. I have got lots of other patients to deal with too."

Her heart went out to the clearly exhausted and overworked nurse who'd seen way too much death in the past month.

These poor kids were now orphans.

"I know it might be strange, but—is it okay if I go in and talk to them? Maybe I can cheer them up a little bit."

"Well, I doubt you'll be able to do anything but go ahead. If you'll excuse me, I've got other patients to attend to," she said as she walked down the hallway.

Adia knocked on the door. "Hello?"

She opened the door slowly and found four kids surrounding a hospital bed. The woman who'd just died must have been their mother. She was pale and lifeless but looked like she died peacefully.

"Hi, kiddos. I heard crying in here and thought I'd see if everyone is okay."

Of course, they're not okay. Why would I ask that?

The oldest one, who looked to be about twelve years old, stood up straighter and held her head high as if to convince Adia and herself that everything was going great. "Yes, we're just fine, ma'am."

The youngest, a little boy who couldn't be older than five years old, sniffled. "Mommy just died."

Adia tried to hide the tears at the sight of these kids. She needed to do something to cheer them up.

"Do you guys want to hear a joke?" she asked.

The youngest one perked up.

"What do you have left inside a gymnast when you take out the gym?" she paused for a second, laughing. "A bird."

They stared at her uncomprehendingly.

"Get it, a gym-nest."

One of the girls rubbed her puffy eyes, and the others didn't move.

What's wrong with me, their parents just died, and I'm telling jokes.

"Okay, so I'm no comedian." She bent down to their level and tried to get them to warm up to her. "What's your names?"

"I'm Fran," the oldest said. "And this is Jimmy, Merida, and Bennie." She pointed down the line at each child.

The littlest one, Bennie, clutched a worn and tattered stuffed bear. Then, he looked up at her with big brown eyes and said, "Are you gonna be our new mommy?"

"Be quiet, Bennie," Jimmy said. "We only have one mommy, and now that she's gone, Fran and I will take care of you." He put his hand on Bennie's shoulder and puffed out his chest.

Little Bennie's seemingly innocent question struck Adia in a profound way she'd never have expected. It echoed throughout her entire soul, but the voice had changed, from the little boy's voice high pitched and desperate voice into the voice of God.

Trust me, daughter.

Then Adia looked into the kiddos' eyes.

What was she doing? She doesn't know how to take care of kids.

"Well, I know that you four would do an amazing job at taking care of each other, but I recently lost my family too, just like you. So, I could really use some help from some big strong kids like you. So, I was thinking the four of you could come live with me, and we could help each other out."

"You're not our mom," Fran said. She reached out and took hold of her mother's lifeless hand.

"I would never try to take the place of your parents, but there are lots of kids like you who need a home now, and I was thinking of building a place for everyone. Do you think you would like to come help me?"

She had no idea where that thought came from, but as soon as she said it, she knew that was exactly what she wanted to do.

The second youngest, Merida, brightened up a little bit. "Will there be lots of toys and food?"

"Well, maybe not lots," Adia said, smiling.

How am I going to build, finance, and run an orphanage?

"Do you have kids that died like my mommy?"

Adia bit her lip. "Umm ... no. I never had kids. I was always afraid of being like my parents and messing up." Adia had no idea why she would tell them that. Too late to take it back now.

"You'll be great! You're nice and pretty," Bennie said as if that was all parenting required.

"Can we, Fran?" Merida asked, looking up at her big sister.

"Yes! I wanna go, too!" Bennie said, brightening up as he jumped up and down a little bit, still clutching his stuffed bear tightly.

"I guess so," Fran said.

Adia smiled. "Awesome!"

She stood and tried to process what had just happened.

Well, God, if this really is you, and you want me to start an orphanage to take in all these kids who lost their families from the attack, then you're gonna have to provide because I definitely can't do this by myself,

She walked out of the room. Maybe she could talk to the judges and council about getting funding for an orphanage.

God, help me to keep the promise I just made.

CHAPTER 47

MOUNT GRAVE, NOVITAS—DAY 38, YEAR 371

Joshua let out a long yawn and stretched. He struggled to climb out of the depths of slumber and tried to remember where he was.

He'd dreamed about being back at home with his parents, who were alive and well again. The dream had brought back a long-forgotten memory. They were all at the dinner table laughing as his dad tried to get out of eating the steamed carrots his mother had made. Unfortunately, they'd been cooked way too long and ended up being a gross, mushy mess.

In the back of his mind, Joshua heard rocks tumbling around him, but he was too caught up in reliving childhood memories to open his eyes and face reality.

His dad had always been the one messing around. He'd started a food fight, using his spoon as a catapult to launch his carrot mush at Joshua. Seeing the mush flying at his face, Joshua quickly ducked. The carrots missed him but smacked a framed family photo. It flew off the counter and shattered on the ground.

"How dare you, mister!" his mother had said, laughing through a fake frown.

Both he and his mom returned fire, smacking his dad in the face with their own carrot mush.

Joshua smiled at the memory. Then, he sat up and opened his eyes to the harsh sunlight of reality.

A jolt of adrenaline flooded his veins as he realized two important things. First, the sun was high in the sky, which meant for the second night in a row on this mountain, he'd slept way too late into the day and lost a lot of climbing time. Second, and more urgently, the ledge that had seemed secure last night was crumbling. If it tumbled down the mountain, he'd go with it.

It didn't matter how fast his body healed. He was limited. And falling off a mountain and being crushed by rocks would certainly cross that limit.

Joshua's fingertips shook, and he clenched his fists. Any wrong movement and the ledge would break off. He longed to go back to the peaceful and happy ignorance of sleep and his childhood, but he was stuck in the present. And now, he was facing a serious situation as the rock's foundation continued to crumble. The ledge was about seven feet long, and he had about three feet to walk to get to the actual side of the mountain where he'd be safe ... well, relatively safe.

His body was extremely sore from all the running, climbing, and healing over the past three days. But none of that mattered if he were dead.

"Can't I just get one break?"

He gradually shifted his feet and body into a position where he could stand, certain the ledge would crumble any minute and send him crashing back down the mountain.

He tried to slow his frantic breathing and ignore the rocks and soil shaking loose and falling down around him.

The ledge held firm for the time being. He let out a huge sigh of relief and almost smiled until he remembered he still had to make it off the ledge. Three feet to go.

"This can't be worse than lightning, tornadoes, and a flash flood." But, that line of reasoning did nothing to slow his pounding heart.

DOWNFALL

Joshua painstakingly inched his feet forward. A crack formed where the ledge began, and it took every ounce of willpower he had not to run as fast as he could toward the mountainside.

He took another step forward, pushed the dirty and sweat-drenched hair from his eyes, and listened to the rocks below him giving way. Finally, he said a desperate prayer as the crack widened.

He only had about a foot left to go, but it might as well have been a mile.

After calming his nerves again, he took another step forward. But this proved too much for the ledge, and it began to deteriorate faster.

He was about to take a swift and dangerous ride back down the mountain.

He eyed a protruding rock that would make a perfect handhold. Without a second to spare, he shut his eyes, leaped, and grabbed.

Joshua clung to the rock. His arm muscles quivered as he tried to hold his weight with one very tired and sore hand, but he quickly found footholds.

He opened his eyes again as the ledge behind him fell off completely and tumbled downward, crashing and breaking apart as it went.

He brushed the hair out of his face and smiled. Looking up, he found another handhold and grasped it. Slowly, he moved his feet up and continued what he'd been doing for the third day in a row—climbing toward the top to find Dedecus and save Namid.

As the hours wore on, Joshua stopped thinking about what he was doing—climbing had become animal instinct to him. His whole world became rock as he found handhold after handhold, foothold after foothold, and slowly inched his way up Mount Grave. His only rule was don't look down.

His head pounded from the altitude. The rocks seemed to dance back and forth in front of him. He shut his eyes to block out the visions. When he opened them again, the mountainside had returned to normal.

He was about four-fifths up the mountain and would likely make it up before nightfall. If he found Dedecus, would he save Namid? Dedecus could do whatever he wanted to him; all that mattered was that he could heal her.

"I'm coming, Namid," he said, his voice hoarse from lack of water.

A sharp rock stabbed into his hand, and the cut began to bleed profusely.

"Agghh." He tensed himself for the healing.

The nerves in his hand burned, and the pain spread throughout his arm. He gritted his teeth.

During his climb, he'd accrued many cuts and bruises all over his body and was learning to live with it. At first, the slightest cut would drop him to the ground, screaming and writhing.

The burning stopped, and he let out a deep breath.

He did his best to wipe off the blood on his tattered, sweat-drenched, and filth-covered shorts. He needed to be careful, or he'd slip on his own blood.

But as he strained to reach the next handhold with his left hand, the blood from the gash caused his right hand to slip off the rock. Panicking, he tried to grab onto something with his left hand, but he found nothing to hold onto as he fell backward.

He landed several feet below on his back and slid headfirst down the mountain.

"Ah!" He slowed his descent some by spreading out his arms and trying to grasp onto things as he slid down the graveled slope with nothing to hold on to. Joshua winced at the large gashes he was getting on his bare back.

The searing sting shot through his body. He couldn't tell where the cutting pain stopped, and the healing pain started. His scream pierced through the air.

Would the energy restoring him run out? Could it continue to repair damage from slamming headfirst into boulders at high speeds?

I'm going to die. I'm going to die on this mountain alone— without God and without Namid.

He flailed his arms around to grab onto something strong enough to hold him and stop his descent.

Something from above him grabbed hold of his right ankle. His descent stopped, but the action almost ripped his leg out of its socket.

Joshua pushed his elbows against the gravel and lifted himself to see who had saved him.

To his amazement, Namid was holding on to his leg, straining and trying to keep her grip on him without falling off the small ledge she stood on.

"Namid?" She was awake? And she looked completely healthy. How could that be? Was he in some sort of trance because of his lack of food and water? He blinked his eyes several times. "You're really here!" What was she doing on the mountain? He stared at her, unmoving.

"Are you just going to lie there like a dead fish making me do all the work, or are you going to help me save your butt—again?" she asked, laughing through her gritted teeth.

"Oh right, sorry." He flipped himself over onto his chest and found places to hold his hands. For the first time, he actually saw a bit of his blood that had painted a streak down the side of the mountain. He clung to what felt like a ledge with his left leg, which was still sore from when he hurt it two days ago, but then again, everything else hurt too.

"All right, I think you can let go slowly, and I'll turn myself around and then make it over to where you are," he said.

She slowly released the clamp she had on his right ankle, and he carefully turned himself around to face upward again.

"There's a nice-sized ledge with a little cave about fifteen feet up and ten feet to the right that we can stop at," Namid said through panted breaths.

He followed her.

Joshua's head felt woozy. Even with his healing, he'd lost a lot of blood on Mount Grave. Combine that with the high altitude and no food or water, his body felt like it was going to collapse.

They made it safely onto the ledge. Much like the one he'd slept by that first night on the mountain, but this one was a little larger and had a scraggly, stunted palm tree struggling to survive on it. Was that a small cave? What a relief that would be from the relentless sun and chilly nights.

They immediately peppered each other with questions.

"How are you here?" Joshua asked Namid. "You were unconscious?"

At the same time, Namid asked, "How could you have been so stupid?"

"How'd you find me?"

"Why did you think coming up here was a good idea? You're not invincible! You can't even rock climb!"

But all the questions Joshua had faded away. He felt his brain disconnect from his body, and he leaned forward. The world around him grew dimmer.

As he collapsed from blood loss, Namid's arms wrapped around him, keeping him from taking another trip down the mountain.

His world faded into blackness.

CHAPTER 48

FIDES VILLAGE, NOVITAS—DAY 38, YEAR 371

Don rubbed his temples and yawned.

The golden moon peeked out from the clouds, bathing the trees and ground with its light.

God had been moving in incredible ways over the past several days. Despite never feeling good enough to be on the council, to begin with, God had used him to speak to the people of Fides and restore something greatly needed—something they never thought they'd have again—hope.

Though the hour was growing late, they still had so much to get done.

"I just don't know—there's not much we can do about it," Sharon said, pacing back and forth.

"Well, let's look over the situation again. There has to be some kind of solution. We have twenty-seven kids who don't have a place to live—that's eleven families. Are you're sure there're no relatives we can place them with?"

"We've already been through this—between the attack, the exodus of over half of our people, and all the storms, all the kids with family have already been taken. Let's just wait until the judges get back, wherever those lazy children went."

"They just went through a traumatic experience. Give them some time, and they'll come back." At least Don hoped they would.

They'd searched everywhere for Joshua and Namid, but they were nowhere to be found. Every day, he had to fend off questions of where they were.

God, please let them come back soon.

"We've all been through a traumatic experience, but you don't see me running off." Sharon paced faster, practically running back and forth between the makeshift stage they were using for church and town meetings and a palm tree a few yards away. "What are we supposed to do when another storm hits?"

While they'd begun construction on a couple more houses, the one building they hadn't planned out yet was the church.

Don stayed quiet, unsure how to respond.

"Let's just make these decisions ourselves. If those kids want to run away, then they don't deserve to lead us."

"That's not our role, and you know that." Don sighed. "We're called to assist Joshua and Namid. We're not going to overthrow them because they're young and reckless."

"But have they done anything right to prove themselves as leaders? You and I both know that we would do a much better job. We have experience."

"They proved themselves by staying and fighting to keep the village together. They proved themselves by doing more than any untrained teenager should be expected to do." Don gave a half smile. "They're going to be incredible leaders, and it's our job to help them by sharing our experience."

"Whatever." Sharon rolled her eyes. "But that doesn't change our current problem. What to do with all those orphaned kids."

Don thought of sweet little Jenny hiding out in the Eastern Fields, terrified of Dedecus killing her like he killed her family. If he had enough to provide for her, he would take her in a heartbeat. But he was sleeping on the ground each night, living off whatever the villagers gave him.

"Well, we need to come up with something," he said.

"Then what would you—"

"Excuse me, I'm really sorry to interrupt, but there's something I wanted to talk with you guys about."

Don turned around and saw Adia walking toward them. She had her head down slightly and was biting her lip.

"What can we do for you?" Don smiled at her.

"Are the Judges around?"

Sharon sighed loudly.

"No, but you can talk to us about whatever it is."

"Okay, I know this might seem a little crazy, but I think God wants me to open up an orphanage or whatever you want to call it for all the kids who lost parents. I've been thinking about it, and while I don't have any experience taking care of kids, this is what God wants me to do. Now, before you say no, I've got a lot of vision behind it. Dedecus was an orphan, and if he'd had someone to love him, maybe he wouldn't have destroyed Fides. I want to make a place where every child feels loved and—"

Don let out a deep belly laugh that made his sides hurt.

Adia stopped and gave him a confused look.

"You're joking, right? Sharon, did you arrange this behind my back?"

He looked at Sharon. She had stopped pacing, and her eyes were wide. She shook her head.

"I know I'm not experienced," Adia continued, "and you might not want to put your trust in me, but maybe some of the experienced couples around the village can give me some pointers," Adia continued.

"You are an answer to prayer, Adia. We don't have a ton of available resources, but we'll do anything we can to help you get supplies and a place."

"So, you're saying I can do it?"

"Absolutely!" Don threw back his head and laughed. Then, he raised and arms to the sky and shouted, "Thank you, Jesus!"

God had provided, and he always would.

I can't wait to see what you do next, God.

CHAPTER 49

MOUNT GRAVE, NOVITAS—DAY 38, YEAR 371

Joshua woke several hours later to the smell of smoke. He looked around and realized he was lying in the small cave next to a backpack and a small fire.

He brushed his hair out of his face and tried to sit up, but the soreness in his back convinced him to lie back down.

"I wouldn't get up if I were you," Namid said with a guarded expression he couldn't quite place. "You've lost a whole lot of blood. I was worried you wouldn't wake up."

Joshua groaned and lay his head against the rocky ground. "What happened?"

"You fainted from blood loss and dehydration. Luckily, I wasn't as equally reckless as you. I brought a backpack with water, food, and matches."

"How are you here? You were unconscious. Brain-damaged. The doctors were convinced you'd never wake up again."

She sighed and went over to the backpack. "I'll tell you everything, and we'll trade stories. But first, you need to drink some water and eat something."

The mention of food stirred his starving stomach awake. "Deal," he said and laughed slightly.

After propping him up against the cave wall, Namid handed him a plate of beef jerky, carrots, cheese, and a water bottle. He quickly guzzled the entire bottle of water and devoured the food.

"So, I woke up three nights ago, only to discover that my boyfriend and the town's co-leader wasn't the one praying over me to be healed. Instead, Don and just about everyone else in the entire village were praying. I was told you'd left to get some food and sleep, but then I saw your note."

"Wait, did you just call me your boyfriend?" Joshua asked. They hadn't had a chance to affirm their relationship.

"Not for long if you do anything that stupid again!" she said as she smacked his shoulder.

He winced in pain.

"How could you abandon everyone that way and throw away your morals to run to Dedecus's to fix things when you were the one who was adamantly against using the Creativity Stone in the first place?" she asked.

Joshua closed his eyes tightly, unable to look at her. That's exactly what he'd done. "I thought I'd never see you again. I tried so hard to save you, but I failed. I thought this was the only way I could make things right."

"Did you even go to God?"

"I've always believed in the power of prayer, but God doesn't always heal like we want him to. I guess I thought—"

"But did you ask God?"

Joshua let out a long sigh. "I guess Dedecus was right about me and the perfect little life I had. I'm a hypocrite." He shifted and was rewarded with a sharp stab in his chest. His body wasn't happy with him either. He sat the plate down and looked at her. "I mean, he let my best friend betray me. He let my parents die. He let you almost drown. And he thrust me into leadership which led to the village getting divided and countless people dying. His plan for me seemed to be becoming a leader, which clearly I suck at—"

Namid placed her hand on Joshua's shoulder. "You're a great leader, Joshua Waters, and even before the attack, you were always the one reminding me God was more than the wrath and anger my parents taught. And for a while there, you were even a great Judge of Mercy. You stood up for what was right at the council meeting and were doing a great job directing everyone with the cleanup and rebuilding."

"I appreciate the encouragement, but in case you didn't notice, not only did that rebuilding project fail horribly, but I also failed miserably to keep the village together, I painfully failed to stop Dedecus, and I failed wretchedly to keep my faith up when I thought you were dying."

"Wow, that's a lot of negativity."

"You don't get it. I was all set to go to Dedecus and beg for your life. I was set to do anything he asked if he just would heal you."

They both sat in silence.

"I'm thinking about quitting completely," Joshua finally spoke up." I know that's never happened before, but I shouldn't be the Judge of Mercy or even on the council. Maybe Don should lead. He's a wiser and better man than dumb, little Joshie over here."

"I have no doubt Don would be a great leader—maybe we should have him become our pastor for the church—but he's not the one God's called to lead. For whatever reason, he's put you and me in those positions."

"Well then, you lead. I wasn't even smart enough to bring supplies with me on this trip. If it weren't for you, I'd be dead. You deserve someone better than me."

"Do you know why I like you?" Namid took her hand off his shoulder and placed it in his hand. "You showed me what it means to be good. Not a fake good like my parents preached. And not even the carefree and all over the place goodness your parents taught. But earnest, genuine goodness. You fought for people who didn't believe in you. You showed mercy while standing strong on the truth. You stared down a tornado to protect the food supply, so no one would go hungry. You risked your life, nearly drowning, just to save me."

The fire crackled beside them, warming his numb body.

"After all this, I think I'm starting to figure it out." she squeezed his hand.

"Figure what out?" Joshua cocked his head.

"Both of our parents are wrong. And you're only guilty of doing the exact same thing they did." Namid paused. "My parents tried to do everything in their own power to become the perfect Christians. They were afraid of God and believed the only way they could approach him was to become holy. So they put a ten-foot fence around God, adding all of these laws."

"Okay, but what does that have to do with me and my parents?"

"Your parents saw the flaws in legalism and knew it wasn't true. So they tried to do everything in their power to chase God's spirit. Running after his will like it was a mythical creature being hunted. But they ended up running away from God." Namid looked at him and gave him a half smile. "And you, my dear Judge of Mercy, were so afraid of failure that you tried to do everything in your own power to be the perfect leader. You heard from an angel what you were called to do, and you tried. Then when things didn't work out, you ran, disillusioned with God because he didn't do what you wanted him to do even though you never asked."

"Yeah, you got me." Joshua grimaced. "But I don't see the connection."

"You all did everything in your power to do the right thing but ended up further away from God."

Joshua sighed. She was right.

"Remember when I told you about how I danced with God?"

He nodded.

"I think what God is trying to teach us is to rely on him. What if following Christ is less about doing everything perfectly and is more about relying on him. Both sides have been running in the opposite direction when God seems to be somewhere in the middle, all alone. It's about a relationship." Tears came to her eyes. "It's about taking his hand and letting him lead."

"Look at God through the lens of his personality," Joshua said quietly. "It's something the angel told me that I didn't understand. We're running in opposite directions and doing everything ourselves because we haven't taken his hand. We haven't really learned who he is."

"And that's what God showed me when I heard him, and we danced together. I had to take his hand and let him lead as he told me who he was."

"I haven't been doing a very good job of that." Joshua stared at the ground.

"None of us have."

Joshua sighed, "I know you're right. I just feel like I don't deserve to be the Judge of Mercy."

"None of us are worthy of being judges. That's God's job to judge through a balance between both judgment and mercy. I've seen what happens when there's too much judgment."

"And what happens when there's too much mercy."

Namid touched the cross necklace resting on her chest. "I'm done being the judge, I'm done with the seven remembrances, and I'm done with this." Namid grabbed the necklace and ripped it off in one fluid motion.

The sharp edge of the necklace cut into her hand, and blood dripped to the cave floor. She stood and put the necklace into her backpack before sitting back down by Joshua.

"And I'm done being the Judge of Mercy. I want to rely on God's mercy before trying to dispense it out myself."

They stared at each other for a long moment as the fire crackled beside them.

"So, you think we shouldn't be called the Judges of Justice and Mercy?" Joshua asked, "You realize that's breaking a pretty major tradition."

"Yeah, well, everything else is changing. Why not this too?"

"Fair enough," Joshua said, laughing as he finished his food. "What should we call ourselves?"

"Ourselves? I thought you wanted to quit?" Namid said, grinning.

"You were right. While I still have much to learn and have a lot of apologizing to do, if God wants me to lead, then I'll follow his plan."

"Good. And I'm thinking we just call ourselves leaders. Who needs a fancy title?"

"Fair enough."

CHAPTER 50

FIDES VILLAGE, NOVITAS—YEAR 7

Steven inhaled sharply. Five months had brought him to this point. He sat up and leaned forward.

"Do you need help?" Hannah stood there beside him.

Most of the village had requested to be here. Word of his rescue of Esther had spread faster than the fire that burned down the church. The tiny detail that he was responsible for the fire seemed forgotten by everyone but Steven himself. To the village, he was a hero.

While they'd wanted to make a spectacle about it, he'd only said yes to Hannah being in the room with him, the girl who for some reason had chosen him despite everything.

"No, I need to do this." He gritted his teeth.

Five months of that horrible hospital bed. Five months of laborious exercises. Five months of pleading and begging God to heal him.

The healing hadn't come, at least not in the way he'd prayed.

The simple act of standing had become a monumental task. But after months, he was ready to do more than stand and take a step or two.

He slowly moved his legs out of bed so that they dangled off the bed in front of him. Seeing the charred pieces of flesh that were his legs still made him nauseous. They had slowly recovered and didn't hurt too badly most days, but he would be wearing pants from now on. The rest of his body had healed completely.

He pushed down on the bed and lifted himself, allowing his feet to touch the ground.

His calves quivered as he pushed himself up and stood.

He'd taken walking for granted for so long. But from the countless times of falling on his face in attempts after the burns along his legs, he'd learned to appreciate the skill.

He took one small step forward. Then another one.

Tears came to his eyes. He was doing it.

He stumbled forward several more steps. His legs started burning, but he ignored it. He would make it.

He reached out and touched the white wall. Sweat poured down his face as he turned around.

"You can do it," Hannah said.

God help me. God choosing not to heal him was something he was still learning to forgive. But when every step and every movement took all of his energy, relying on God had become second nature to him.

He took several steps. His legs shook back and forth, and he began to fall.

He reached out toward Hannah and fell against her.

She wrapped her arms around him, and he clung to her, breathing heavily.

She helped him turn around and get back into bed.

"I didn't make it," he said through panted breaths.

"No, you did. I'm proud of you."

Why she chose to stay with a man who couldn't even walk had bewildered him. But he was so grateful God had put her in his life.

The door swung open, and Esther marched in. "How'd he do?"

Esther was an enigma to him. She was still the same strict, blunt, and judgmental woman he'd first met seven years ago. But some of the ice had melted. She would take on an army to protect him, to protect any of those in Fides.

Hannah smiled. "He did great. He made it all the way to the wall and back."

Esther nodded once. "Good, then we can finally move forward."

Steven used the bed sheet to wipe the sweat off his forehead. "What do you mean?"

"Steven, you and I disagree on a lot. I follow the seven remembrances and the law because I want to honor God, and I've seen the consequences of sin. But you've taught me something; there are also consequences of ignoring grace. And based on your experience, you seem to have learned what happens when there are no rules."

"I probably would have used a different word than rules, but I get your point."

"I want to offer you a deal. Our village is growing, and we've needed to set up a structure for spiritual and governmental leadership for a while. I'm getting too old to manage everything myself." She sighed. "I would like you to lead with me."

"What?"

Is she actually saying she wants what God's placed on my heart?

He must have misheard her.

"I've come up with a structure I think you'll approve. Instead of dividing our village in two and hating each other, we work together as the body of Christ. I will be the Judge of Justice, and you will be the Judge of Mercy. Together we will make decisions for Fides as a whole. And we can pass it along to future generations, training our children to lead wisely."

Hannah squeezed his hand twice.

"Really?"

"Do you not want to? I can always offer it to someone else. But you're the one who's proven himself trustworthy."

"No, I do, or yes, I—" Steven laughed. "I would love to take that role. It's an honor."

Esther nodded once and gave a slight smile. "Well then, congratulations. You are the first Judge of Mercy."

CHAPTER 51

MOUNT GRAVE, NOVITAS—DAY 38, YEAR 371

As the sun finished its descent, setting with beautiful shades of blue and purple as a final bow for another day's work, and the embers in the fire began to fade out, Joshua and Namid continued to talk.

"Did you tell Don or the others anything?" Joshua asked.

"Nope, I figured that was something you'd have to explain yourself when we get back to the village."

Joshua sighed. "Yeah, that's not going to be a fun conversation with the council or the village ... actually, now that I think about it, there're a lot of people I probably need to apologize to. I was kind of a jerk while you were unconscious."

"Well, you're doing the right thing in telling the truth and apologizing."

"I know," he said, sighing again, "Well, if the village will have me, I guess I'll continue to be the leader."

"Excuse me, but I believe you mean co-leader," Namid said with pretend outrage. "Don't you go around thinking that you have more power than me. We're equal partners in this."

"Right, co-leader, sorry," Joshua said, laughing as he brushed the hair out of his face.

"Now that we have that out of the way, I do have a question about one thing that just doesn't make sense," Namid said. "If I didn't start climbing the mountain a day after you did, then how did I manage to catch up with you?"

"Really?" Joshua laughed even though it hurt his chest and ribs. "That might be the only thing that did make sense in my mind when I saw you holding my ankle. Not only did I accidentally oversleep on both days, but you've actually gone rock climbing before. You're almost as good as Dedecus. Meanwhile, if you haven't noticed," Joshua gestured at his tunic that had been torn to shreds, "I kinda suck at rock climbing. I'm surprised you didn't catch up to me sooner."

"Okay, fair enough."

"What I don't get," Joshua said, "was how you managed to find me. It's not like I stayed in a straight line up the entire time."

"Don't you know the answer to that? Every few seconds, there'd be a huge rockslide from all your terrible rock climbing and kicking up dirt and rocks. I had to be careful to avoid being crushed under all the rocks you kicked up. Combine that with the trails of blood you left everywhere, and it was pretty easy to find you. When we start heading home tomorrow, I'm staying above you so I don't drown in the big mess you'll make."

"Okay, fair enough. So, um, speaking of heading back ... um ... how would you feel if we didn't go back down right away?"

"Oh, I get it. Little Joshua wants to say he made it all the way to the top," Namid teased.

"Not exactly," Joshua said, knowing she wasn't going to like what he said next. "I know every single reason and logical argument for why this is a really bad idea, but I think God wants me to go after Dedecus."

Namid laughed nervously. "You're joking, right? I know he was our friend, but he did try to kill us the last time we saw him."

"I know, but he also spared us if it's any consolation."

"It's not." Namid was no longer laughing, "He still destroyed our village and killed over five hundred seventy-three of our villagers, including your parents. Plus, even if he did somehow change his mind, the Creativity Stone is literally inside him, and we can't get it out. We wouldn't know what to do with it even if we did get it out, and there's no way Fides would welcome him back with loving arms."

"I know, but I've learned my lesson about trusting God and not going for that cursed stone, but somewhere in Dedecus is the friend we once loved and laughed and played with. And at the very least, we can't keep living in a world where a massive storm could kill us randomly. We need to stop him."

"That doesn't change any of the reasons not to go. There's a difference between showing grace and being stupid. Grace doesn't mean there's no consequences for our actions."

"I know that, but—"

"And why would God tell you to risk your life again going after Dedecus when the village needs you?"

"Why would God allow you to be swept away and nearly die drowning? Why would God take my parents? Why would God allow me to fall and die in the first place, which started this whole chain of events?" He paused and then lowered his voice. "You said it was about taking God's hand and letting him lead. Well, I think he's leading us to go after Dedecus. Even if we don't get our friend back, at the very least, we must stop these storms, or there won't be a Fides Village. And we can only stop them by going after Dedecus."

Namid let out a long sigh. "Well then, it's a good thing I brought lots of food for our trip."

"What do you mean *our trip*? You're going back to the village, and I'll go after Dedecus, You were in a coma for five days. I'm not risking you getting hurt again."

"Joshua, I'm not sure if you can make it to the top of this mountain by yourself, especially considering the shape you're in. You almost died today, plus there's the whole fainting-from-blood-loss thing. The energy in your cells can only take so much. If you're positive God is calling you to go after him—and I promise we'll be praying about that before we leave—then I'm going too, not only to keep you safe and probably save your life again, but because he's my friend too."

Joshua sighed. *She's as stubborn, if not more so than I am.* "All right, fine."

She nodded once. "But you have to promise me something."

"Okay, what is it?"

"Promise to stop trying to be someone you're not. I don't like you because you're some hothead who jumps in front of tornadoes and climbs mountains. I like you because you're strong but humble. You're adorable and awkward but also good and pure. You've grown a lot since being the little boy about to poop himself in terror at jumping across a gap. But stay Joshua. God created you to be Joshua, not Dedecus, not Don, and not your dad. Fides needs Joshua." She placed her hand back in his. "I need Joshua."

Joshua wasn't sure if he wanted to cry or laugh. He'd tried so hard to be the perfect man for Fides and for her. Despite his soreness, he felt freer than he'd ever felt before.

"I promise." He squeezed her hand. "Now, let's do that praying you mentioned, and then get some sleep."

Namid laughed, so they both bowed their heads, and he opened the prayer.

"God, thank you for all your blessings and for healing Namid. Thank you for protecting me as I climbed up Mount Grave. Please give us wisdom about what to do, and please protect us as we're on the mountain tomorrow. Amen."

"Amen," Namid echoed.

They put out the fire and lay down, letting sleep restore their weary bodies for the long day that would be ahead of them no matter which way they went—up or down—Mount Grave.

CHAPTER 52

FIDES VILLAGE, NOVITAS—DAY 38, YEAR 371

As she opened the door further, little Bennie looked up at her with his big, watery, brown eyes and tried to hide his tears. "I'm sorry, I'll go back to bed," he said.

"Don't worry about it, kiddo. What's wrong?" she asked. She walked toward him quietly, trying not to wake any of the other kids.

"I had a dream about my mommy and daddy. We were all together again and having a yummy picnic. We were playing tag together and running through the trees laughing. It was so much fun, but then I woke up," he said as he tried to wipe away his tears.

Adia's heart broke for this sweet, innocent little boy who needed his parents more than anything in the world. She would never understand why God had taken them away and left Bennie and his three siblings, but as long as she was there, she'd do everything she could to protect them and show them love.

She went over to where he sat, careful not to step on his sleeping brother, who, like many of the others, had to sleep on the floor because there was no more room in any of the beds. She picked up Bennie from the rocking chair.

"Well, why don't you come sleep with me," Adia said, completely unprepared for how to help Bennie but trying her best.

Bennie smiled brightly as if it was the most brilliant suggestion he'd ever heard. He gave her a big hug. "Do you know any songs? Mommy used to sing me to sleep whenever I had bad dreams."

She headed back to her room, careful not to trip over any sleeping kids.

"Of course, I can sing to you, kiddo."

"Did your mommy and daddy used to sing you songs whenever you got scared?'

"No ... my mommy and daddy would get mad at me for being scared or sad."

Bennie looked up at her in confusion. "Why? Didn't they love you?"

Adia stroked his hair as she walked back into her room. "They were hurting and couldn't be there for me. But they did love me. It was a broken love, but they loved me the best they could."

She sat him down on her bed and lay down next to him. He snuggled up to her. She was struck with the simple yet profound thought that this little boy loved her. To sweet, little Bennie, how pretty or smart she was didn't matter. To him, it didn't matter how many times she'd messed up. As long as she showed him love, he would snuggle up next to her and love her back. She wished she knew of a song she could sing to him to help him fall back to sleep.

The melody to the song the man had sung to her in the cabin as she fell asleep came back to her, and she smiled.

God, my father, protect me tonight.
Take my fears and throw away my fright.

Warm me with your peace and love.
As I look out at stars shining above.

You are stronger than my fears;
You will wipe away all my tears.

You are so vast and immense,
Creator of the whole universe,
And yet you see me here down here.
From your love, I will never disappear.

I pray that as I drift into dreams.
I will always stay in your peace.

Bennie drifted off to sleep curled up next to her in bed. Adia stared at the ceiling and breathed a prayer of thanks to God for getting her through the day. She still missed Lincoln with every breath, but God had put a passion and an impossible dream inside her heart. This was something she could never have done in her own strength, but with God, all she had to do was make it one day at a time and let him take care of the rest.

God, my father, protect me tonight.
Take my fears and throw away my fright.
Warm me with your peace and love
As I look out at stars shining above.

CHAPTER 53

MOUNT GRAVE, NOVITAS—DAY 39, YEAR 371

Joshua followed Namid up the rest of Mount Grave, glad she had eventually agreed to go with him after Dedecus.

Namid was an expert rock climber, moving up the rocks as gracefully as she danced, while he was comparatively clunky and awkward with his movements.

"So, what's the plan when we get to the top?"

Namid glanced down at him. "You're asking me, Mr. 'Hey, I'm gonna climb a mountain even though I can't climb and not bring any food or supplies to find a man who just killed my parents and probably will kill me too'?"

Joshua decided to keep quiet after that. Figuring that planning out what he'd say to Dedecus to get him to heal Namid wasn't what she meant by making a plan.

Despite the soreness still throbbing throughout his body, his climb became much easier now that all he had to do was copy what Namid did. She had a knack for finding the perfect hand and footholds, while he always seemed to choose ones that fell off and sent him painfully tumbling back down the mountain. While she was graceful and barely disturbed the rocks and soil around her, he still caused mini avalanches with every step he took. No matter how hard he tried to copy her, he couldn't figure out how she did it.

"We have no idea what to expect when we reach the top," she said. "Who knows what mood Dedecus is in, especially with the Creativity Stone influencing him."

"So, we're just going to reach the top without a plan?" Joshua didn't care much for spontaneity. The irony wasn't lost on him as he reached for another handhold, pulling himself higher up Mount Grave.

"All we can do is be there for him. Maybe we can remind him who he is and show him what he's doing is wrong. I guess that's what creativity gets you."

"Creativity itself isn't bad," Joshua said through panted breaths. "God's the Creator and made us in his image to use our imaginations and create—it's when we try to become God ourselves that things get messy."

"Well, that's an understatement."

They climbed until, at last, they reached the top, and a view of the world surrounded them on all sides. The air was thin up there and made it hard to breathe, but Joshua could barely think about that. He stood and did a little victory dance, wiggling his shoulders and arms back and forth.

Namid laughed. "Wow, you should become a dancer with those fancy moves."

He grinned and blushed. "We did it! I actually made it to the top, and Dedecus said I'd never conquer my fears."

"Speaking of Dedecus," Namid said. "Where is he?"

Joshua looked all around, searching for his friend.

While the view was absolutely breathtaking from on the mountain, Dedecus was nowhere to be found. The only thing on the summit of the Mount Grave was an ugly, shriveled-up Earth tree.

"As impressive as it is that this tree could survive up here, it's not Dedecus," Namid said.

"I was so sure he'd be here," Joshua said through his panting breaths.

He stared at the tree. Something was wrong with it. All trees on Novitas were palms. They only had a limited number of seeds for Earth trees. Why would someone waste one on a mountaintop few people could climb?

A loud noise came from ahead of them, and they looked up to see the shriveled-up tree shaking and growing into a massive tree that took up much of the space on the mountaintop. The trunk alone had reached twenty feet high. The branches shot out into the sky like black, gnarled claws reaching for a victim.

"What in the—"

"Look out!" Namid shoved Joshua out of the way as a branch shot out toward them.

Joshua fell to the ground, trying hard not to scream as pain shot through him from nearly everywhere on his body.

Namid didn't have a chance to escape. It groped around her, enveloped her, and lifted her off the ground.

"Agghh!"

The branch squeezed tightly around her waist and chest.

"Namid!" Joshua got up and grabbed at the thick branch, but as hard as he pulled, he couldn't budge it.

The tree rose from the ground, its roots working as tentacles moving it toward them and sending rocks cascading down the mountain.

"What's going on?" Joshua shouted over the loud rumbling coming from the tree and the ground.

"Dedecus must have made it!" Namid thrashed wildly, trying to escape the branch that continued to wrap around her body in a spiral. It had covered her chest and most of her legs.

"What do I do?" Joshua looked around frantically for guidance but found none.

The tree squeezed Namid, and she began to give out. Then it moved toward Joshua and shot out another branch to capture him too.

"God, I really need your help right now!" he called out.

Joshua pushed his hair out of his eyes as a strange mix of adrenaline and peace swirled through his veins.

It wouldn't make sense to barrel toward the tree; he would only get caught as well. He needed to be smart to find the best course.

He grabbed a large stone and heaved it at the branch reaching out at him. The stone smacked the branch to the ground and pinned it under its weight.

Roots shot out from the ground, grabbing at his feet. He ran toward Namid's pack of supplies, only walking on places where large stones lay that the roots couldn't grow through.

Reaching the backpack, he tore through it, searching for a creative solution, but all he could find was food, water, and bandages. Wait, and one more item—Namid's cross necklace.

Namid had always said it was sharp. He looked over at Namid. She had passed out from lack of oxygen. The branch was wrapping its way around her neck.

Not again!

Staring down at the necklace in his hands, he realized he didn't have any other options.

A root grabbed his ankles, and he used the edge of the cross as a knife, slashing through the bark. Another branch came toward him. He grabbed it, using his newly acquired rock-climbing skills to plant his feet on the bark and launch himself over the field of roots trying to snare him.

He landed with a smack on the protruding branch holding Namid, knocking the wind out of himself, but he fought to maintain his grip.

Glancing at Namid's limp body, he focused all of his will on holding onto the branch. The rough bark cutting into his skin and the burning sensation from the healing became almost overwhelming.

Using the cross, he hacked at the thick branch. It shook in complaint but couldn't stop him. He made it about three-fourths of the way through when the cross broke into pieces. Tossing it to the side, he pushed himself up and brought his elbow down on the spot he'd been cutting. The impact cleaved the two halves apart and sent Namid crashing to the ground.

The tree let out what Joshua assumed was the equivalent of a scream, and the branch he clung to thrashed wildly in the air, sending him flying.

He landed near the edge of the mountain, creating a mini avalanche of rocks down the side. Before he could fall, he grabbed hold of one of the tree's roots trying to trap him. Then, he heaved himself back up and let go of the root before it could wrap itself around him.

Namid lay unconscious in the dead arms of the branch he cut off. He could see that she was breathing, but he didn't have time to check on her. The tree ignored her and came toward him near the edge of the mountain.

Four branches grew toward him, and he searched for some kind of weapon. He needed a plan. He grabbed the pack of supplies and chucked it at the branches as he dodged out of the way to steal himself some time.

How had Namid made a fire last night?

Then he realized much of the rocks were silica stones. His father had taught him how to make a fire by striking them together.

"Thanks, Dad." He grabbed two stones and smacked them together. Sparks rained down on the roots reaching for him.

The roots recoiled.

Joshua continued to make sparks until one of the roots caught on fire, and the tree retreated, and the root disappeared into the ground. The enormous trunk bent away from him.

He ran around to the other side of the tree and forced it to back up toward the edge of the cliff.

"There are two things I've learned on this stinkin' mountain." Joshua pushed the hair out of his eyes and grinned at the tree now cowering from the fire he'd created. The trunk and branches leaned over the side. "One, you have to be very careful where you put your weight because the rocks are very loose. And two, fear kills."

He shot toward the tree and struck the trunk with two edges of the silica stones. The trunk sizzled, and the tree withdrew, sending it further away from the safety of the mountaintop.

As the rocks below the tree gave out and crumbled down Mount Grave, the burning tree slid down with it.

Joshua stumbled backward as he gasped for breath.

"I guess Dedecus didn't want anyone following him." He looked back to see Namid pushing herself up into a sitting position and ran over to her. "Are you okay?"

"I'm fine. You've got some nasty cuts, though."

Joshua sat down and let the energy in him burn away his wounds.

"I only got to see the end of the fight, but you were awesome. I had no idea you had that in you."

"Me neither."

Namid stood. Her clothing was torn, and her arms were red from the rough bark. She walked over to study something on the ground. "How did this survive the fight? And for that matter, what is it?"

Joshua pushed himself up and went over to get a better look at what she was talking about.

DOWNFALL

A layer of dust and gravel surrounded a perfect circle. Inside, the area was smooth and clean, like something had blown everything from that area.

"It kind of looks as if Dedecus used that teleportation thing he did where he hit the ground with his hand," Joshua said. "Then the wind started to swirl around him, and he disappeared and transported somewhere else."

"I think you're right, but how does that help us get to him now? He could've transported anywhere." Namid walked around it, keeping her eyes on it.

Was she seeing something he couldn't? "What is it?" Joshua asked.

"Maybe I'm just crazy, but while the other portal sites went back to normal as if nothing had happened, this one seems to have made some sort of permanent impression. I'm not sure how it's possible, but if you look closely, it's almost as if the circular area where the wind had surrounded him is glowing slightly. And the stone inside the glowing circle looks like an entirely different stone from the rest of the mountain."

She was right; the stone inside the circular area was glossier and darker, while the rest of the mountain had a lighter and dustier look. "I know we would've noticed if this happened with any of the other places he teleported to, and this area should've been affected by the battle with the tree thing, but it's almost as if it never happened."

"So, there must be something special about this spot. Maybe it means we can use it to teleport to where he is."

"Do you think we just take a step inside the circle?"

"I guess so, but something tells me he doesn't want company."

"We've come too far to stop now." He prepared himself to go through as the wind on the mountaintop whipped his hair into his face.

"Wait!" She grabbed his arm. "What did I say about tornadoes. You can't just run in."

"We don't know if it'll work with two people. I don't like going into danger either, but I feel like we're committed now. If we go to wherever Dedecus is, then maybe we can rescue him."

"Fine. You go through and wait for me. Then we'll take stock of our surroundings and come up with some sort of course of action. We also need to make sure to mark the spot when we get there so we can get home to the village."

"Sounds like a plan."

He stared at her. Despite the red gashes, sweat, and dirt covering her hair and body, she was incredibly beautiful.

"But just in case something happens, there's something we need to do before you go." He took a step toward her.

Before she could ask what he meant and before his nerves and fear could stop him, he pulled her close and kissed her.

She seemed surprised at first, but her shock quickly turned into passion. She returned his kiss, and they both stood in that moment for as long as they could, enveloped by the love they felt but never thought would happen.

Then the moment was over, and Joshua stepped back.

"God, please help me," Joshua muttered as he turned and faced the circular area.

In his head, he could almost hear orchestral music as he cautiously took a step into the circle and stood in the middle, expecting a huge rush of wind to envelop him.

They stood there for several moments as absolutely nothing happened.

"Well, that was incredibly anticlimactic."

"Maybe you have to hit the ground like he did."

He brushed his hair out of his face, opened up his hand, and smacked the ground with his palm like Dedecus had.

DOWNFALL

The thud echoed in the mountains around them. "Well now—"

A wind grew out of nowhere and circled him, slowly at first but then faster and faster until a complete tunnel had formed around his body.

"Don't worry, Joshua, I'll be right behind you!"

And then, with a flash, he was completely gone.

Namid quickly jumped into the circle and copied his movement. The wind encircled her in a tunnel that made her hair fly in every direction.

"I'm coming, Joshua," she said as the breathtaking mountaintop view of Mount Grave faded away.

EPILOGUE

TRANSCENDENCE, DAY 39

Namid pulled her light brown hair out of her face as the wind from the portal died down.

She gasped as she looked around. Surrounding her was a rich and beautiful garden that rivaled Peaceful Plateau and put the stories of gardens on Earth to shame. The flowers themselves were a mixture of every color imaginable. But instead of looking chaotic, it was stunningly beautiful. Blue vines with silver-colored flowers traversed the ground, and other plants tied everything together like a ribbon.

The sky above her looked painted on.

Joshua stood beside her, equally in awe.

She breathed in, and the strong aroma of the plants assaulted her. The aroma was heavy and evocative. It stirred up memories that made her smile, even though her brain couldn't put a name to the smell or to the memories they conjured up.

The ground was soft, a pillow her tired feet welcomed after the long climb up Mount Grave. She looked over at Joshua and took his hand.

Beside them was a sign that read, *Welcome to Transcendence.*

The adventures of Joshua, Namid, and Dedecus will
continue in

The Creativity Stone—Book 2: *Transcendence*

ABOUT THE AUTHOR

There are so many great stories and worlds out there, but we need more fantastic worlds of escape that also point to truth. Just as Jesus gave us parables or CS Lewis gave us Narnia, we need more stories that deepen our relationship with God while also drawing us into worlds of adventure, excitement, and complex characters. That is Caleb Ward's passion as a Christian fantasy author.

Since childhood Caleb has been "imaginating," a term he self-coined. He would create stories and worlds in his head, but never dreamt he would have the privilege to give life to his characters through writing. And yet God placed people in his life who recognized and called out that passion within him.

Writing is worship to Caleb—it's connecting his imagination as a creator with God's imagination as the creator. And so whenever he writes, he loses himself, becoming the characters, living their lives, experiencing their emotions. He becomes totally enmeshed within the story. His dream is to share that experience with his readers and give them the chance to let the characters touch them and their relationship with God as they have touched Caleb.

Caleb would love to connect with you. He can be found on Facebook at https://www.facebook.com/calebwardauthor, on his website https://www.calebwardauthor.com/, or find his world Novitas on World Anvil here https://www.worldanvil.com/w/novitas-ciward1999④gmailcom

SHARE THIS BOOK WITH A FRIEND.

If you buy a copy for a friend and mark it as "This is a gift" on Amazon, email a screenshot to calebwardauthor@gmail.com and get an exclusive short story to find out what happened to Namid's parents after they left Novitas.

DISCUSSION QUESTIONS

1. Which character did you most identify with—Joshua, Namid, Adia, Dedecus, Don, Steven, etc.? How do you deal with the struggles these characters face?

2. How did each character have to overcome and grow when they faced challenges?

3. Do you think it was right for the New Day Separatists to leave earth?

4. How can you apply what Adia learned in the cabin to your own life?

5. How can you apply what Steven learned in the cabin to your own life?

6. Do you truly believe that God is always in control and knows what's best in your own life?

7. Is creative power bad? We're all made to be creative, where does it cross a line?

8. Do you ever feel like Joshua in the beginning of the novel, wanting to do more, but for one reason or another, you feel stuck?

9. What is one thing the judges of justice were right about? What's something the judges of mercy were right about?

10. What is the balance between mercy and judgment?

Made in the USA
Coppell, TX
23 January 2022

72202606R00184